Sarah greeted me at the kitchen door. "Most of the crew and the actors are still over at the lighthouse," she explained. "I don't think there'll be a rehearsal this afternoon."

I glanced at my phone. "It's after two. We had lunch, I got food for dinner, and Pete's still holding on to everyone down there?"

She shrugged. "I texted him once, but he just answered, 'Busy. Lunch ordered. Ethan on way.' Of course, I knew he was busy. And—'lunch ordered?' Maybe people were beginning to complain. At least it's a beautiful day. Maybe they're waiting for everyone to be questioned before they let anyone leave. And Hank is there, so if the producer can't get away, no one else really has much to do. There's no director at the moment."

"I guess," I said, glancing around the Lawrence kitchen, which was full of coolers of water and large carafes of coffee and tea, all pretty much untouched today. "I told Ruth we'd pick her up at about five o'clock at Aurora. She sounded tired and stressed. I promised her it wouldn't be a late night." Then what Sarah had said connected. "Pete said Ethan was on his way?"

"I know. It made me wonder, too."

Ethan Trask was a state homicide detective. He was only called in when a death was ruled a homicide, or when that outcome was likely. Marv's death had certainly looked accidental. What did Pete know, or suspect, that I didn't?

Books by Lea Wait

TWISTED THREADS

THREADS OF EVIDENCE

THREAD AND GONE

DANGLING BY A THREAD

TIGHTENING THE THREADS

THREAD THE HALLS

THREAD HERRINGS

THREAD ON ARRIVAL

THREAD AND BURIED

Published by Kensington Publishing Corporation

THREAD and BURIED

Lea Wait

KENSINGTON BOOKS
KENSINGTON PUBLISHING CORP.
www.kensingtonbooks.com

KENSINGTON BOOKS are published by

Kensington Publishing Corp.
119 West 40th Street
New York, NY 10018

All Kensington titles, imprints, and distributed lines are available at special quantity discounts for bulk purchases for sales promotion, premiums, fund-raising, educational, or institutional use.

Special book excerpts or customized printings can also be created to fit specific needs. For details, write or phone the office of the Kensington Sales Manager: Attn.: Sales Department. Kensington Publishing Corp., 119 West 40th Street, New York, NY 10018. Phone: 1-800-221-2647.

Kensington and the K logo Reg. U.S. Pat. & TM Off.

First Printing: December 2019
ISBN-13: 978-1-4967-1675-0
ISBN-10: 1-4967-1675-2

eISBN-13: 978-1-4967-1676-7 (eBook)
eISBN-10: 1-4967-1676-0 (eBook)

10 9 8 7 6 5 4 3 2 1

Printed in the United States of America

ACKNOWLEDGMENTS

With great thanks to my editor, John Scognamiglio, and my agent, John Talbot, both of whom encouraged me to keep writing even under difficult circumstances.

To my many friends and readers, who cheered me on and told me they were waiting for the next book in this series.

To my daughters, Caroline Childs, Ali Hall, Becky Wynne, and Liz McNeal, all of whom took time from their lives, families, and jobs to help out. To JD and Barbara Neeson, the best neighbors possible, and, especially, to JD, who drove me to appointments and explained the importance of blower fans on boat engines.

To my friends and family who stayed in touch: Nancy Cantwell, Linda Morra Imas, Susan Price, Diane Veith, Joan Jacobus, Anne-Marie Nolin, Bob Adler, Richard Thomas, Karen Thomas, and so many others. To my fellow Maine Crime Writers, who called, brought food, drove me to conferences, wrote encouraging notes, and listened to me vent, especially Brenda Buchanan, Kathy Lynn Emerson, Barbara Ross, Bruce Coffin, Dick Cass, and Kate Flora.

And to all the librarians and booksellers who've read my books and told people about them, the readers who've written reviews, and the fans who keep in touch. Without all of you it wouldn't have been possible for me to have a second career doing what I love.

With all thanks, joy, and no regrets,
Lea Wait

Chapter 1

Still as through Life's meandering path I stray
Lord be the sweet Companion of my way.
My kind Conducter, to the Blest abode
Of Light, of Life, of happiness and God.

—Sampler titled "An Emblem of Innocence,"
stitched in silk on linen by Eliza Mallonce
in 1825. Eliza's sampler does not include
an alphabet, but is intricately embroidered
with a border of strawberries on two sides,
and flowers, birds, and trees on both the top
and bottom.

From *Harbor Hopes*
by Ruth Hopkins

July 4, 1963, a small town on the coast of Maine

The red, white, and blue scarf tied around Amy's
ponytail blew behind her as late afternoon sea breezes
cooled the air. She ignored the boats in the harbor,
the tourists snapping pictures of the lighthouse, and

her red apron, stained with the salt water she'd been steaming lobsters in, and turned inland, toward the pergola on the town green, where Caleb had said he'd meet her.

Caleb. She smiled, just thinking of him. Fate and heritage had brought them together. When she was in kindergarten he'd defended her from first-grade bullies. In junior high he'd carried her books home from school and they'd done homework together on the pine kitchen table while her mother made molasses cookies for them.

When her mother was sick he'd brought flowers to her hospital room, and held Amy as she cried. He and his family had sat behind hers at the funeral.

When she was sixteen he'd asked her to wear his class ring. She hadn't taken it off since then, and had encouraged him to stay in high school even when she knew the life he'd planned as a lobsterman didn't require graduation.

She turned the corner and waved. He was standing, tall and slim, his crew cut as short as ever, waiting for her, just as he'd said he'd be. He'd never failed her.

Amy waved back, and glanced at her watch. She couldn't stay long, and neither could he. The Sea Fare, where she worked, expected her back from her break in half an hour, and Caleb would be heading out to Second Sister Island to help his father set up tonight's fireworks.

She started to run as he held out his arms. They both smelled of lobsters and the sea, and, as their lips met, they knew they were always meant to be together.

"Meet me after the fireworks tonight?" Caleb murmured in her ear. "Down at the wharf?"

Amy nodded. Caleb's Sea Witch, *the inboard lobster boat his grandfather had left him last year, and that he was so proud of, was docked near his father's lobster boat. "I'll be there. But not for long."*

Caleb sighed. "Your dad?"

"He told me he wanted me in by ten thirty tonight."

Caleb broke away and moved to the other side of the pergola. "He won't always be able to control you, Amy. You're not a child anymore. You're seventeen. I have a lobster boat; I can make a living for both of us. And I'm not disappearing."

"I know," she said. "But it's easier if I just tell him I'm going to watch the fireworks with Carol and Joan and Marty."

"He really hates me, doesn't he?"

Amy didn't say anything. They both knew the answer to that question. "We'll find a way, Caleb. We will."

He put his arms around her again. "Yes. We will."

Thousands of vacationers head for the coast of Maine every July looking for lighthouses, beaches, lobster rolls, and cooler temperatures than in their home states. But for those of us who live in Maine full-time, temperatures in the eighties seem hot, and summer isn't a time for relaxing. It's a time to run restaurants and tourist attractions, sell the art and crafts we created during winter months, and convince visitors that Maine is, indeed, "the way life should be."

That's the goal of the police, state troopers, Marine Patrol officers, and Coast Guard, too. "The way life should be" should not include murders. And if it does, then solving them as quickly as possible is critical, not only for the victims, but also for Maine's reputation.

Somehow in the fifteen months I've been back in Maine I've gotten involved in helping the police do just that.

I'm Angie Curtis. I grew up here in Haven Harbor, but took a ten-year hiatus working for a private investigator in Arizona, which is why I have some of the skills the police are looking for, although you probably wouldn't guess it if you met me. I'm twenty-eight, I live with my black cat, Trixi, I have ordinary straight brown hair that I pin up in summer. And, oh yes. I have a Glock. Which I know how to use.

But what most people in town know about me is that I run Mainely Needlepoint, a business started by my grandmother. I make sure gift shops, galleries, and decorators have all the needlepointed pillows of eider ducks and lighthouses and harbor scenes they can sell, update our Web site, meet with customers who want custom work, and keep track of the schedules of all the needlepointers who have other jobs.

Nothing to do with crime.

Which is fine by me.

I've also been seeing Patrick West. He's an artist, and runs a gallery in town. And, yes, what most people know about him is that his mother is movie star Skye West.

This summer Patrick and I'd hoped to spend time together, exploring Maine and each other. Patrick even hired a student from the Maine College of Art to "gallery-sit" so he'd have more time in July and August for his own painting and for me.

We didn't schedule time for any activities other than art and needlepoint and romantic evenings.

That fantasy crumbled when Patrick's mother announced that her friend, producer Hank Stoddard, had found enough investors so he could make a movie here this summer. *Harbor Heartbreak* would be directed by Marv Mason, and written by Thomas and Marie O'Day, who'd spent last Christmas with Skye here in the Harbor and fallen in love with the idea of making a movie based on a book written by my friend and fellow needlepointer Ruth Hopkins. Ruth has supported herself for years by writing, and many of her stories are based here in the Harbor. Not many people in town even knew she's an author, since she writes under different names. Or, they didn't know before now.

Of course, Patrick's involved in the film. Skye also recruited me and another fellow needlepointer (and antique dealer) Sarah Byrne, to help lighting and set designer Flannery Sullivan create two sets, one for scenes set in the early 1960s and one for contemporary scenes.

They'd hired a number of locals, and were paying a lot more than minimum wage seasonal jobs paid here, so that was good. "It'll be a summer to remember," Gram kept reminding me.

But so far I kept remembering what I'd hoped this summer would be: time for Patrick and me to spend more hours together.

Looked now as though we'd have to wait for fall.

Here it was, already the third week of July, *Harbor Heartbreak* was set to begin filming in a week, and Patrick and I had hardly seen each other in the past couple of weeks.

Chapter 2

The familiar work-basket should be a loved article of household furniture, and mother or sister should be associated with it, not as hurrying, driven, tired and overstrained sewers, but as enthusiasts, finding it a relief to sew, simply because by sewing social chat can be indulged in, and a time to think would be secured, if talking is not agreeable.

—*The Hearthstone; or, Life at Home: A Household Manual* by Laura C. Holloway. Philadelphia: L. P. Miller & Co., 1888.

Sarah and I had spent all morning visiting souvenir shops and galleries, picking out details to add to the decors we were working on. Shopping wasn't my favorite activity, although downtown Haven Harbor was lined with souvenir shops, art galleries, and antique shops. Plenty of places to investigate. Sidewalks were crowded with tourists wearing "Haven Harbor" T-shirts, shorts, and sea glass earrings. But now Sarah and I were both sweaty and exhausted.

We'd finished our shopping, and piled our bags full of props and decorative Maine accessories in Sarah's van.

Although it was almost time to pick up a couch upholstered in needlepoint that a friend of Gram's was loaning
the movie company, right now we were taking a break,
looking out at the harbor, and hoping for a cool breeze.

Haven Harbor was as busy as I'd ever seen it on a hot
July day. The air smelled of salt and steamed lobsters. The
dark blue water was full of working lobster boats, larger
boats offering tours of the area to tourists, small sailboats
used by the Haven Harbor Country Club in their sailing
classes for summer residents, and skiffs ferrying visitors
to and from visiting yachts to the town dock.

"I don't remember a summer as busy as this one,"
Sarah said, smiling, as she looked from the harbor to the
shore, her white hair streaked with pink and blue shining
bright in the hot sunlight. "I agreed to help with the movie
sets because the money was good, and I like Skye. Sales
at my shop are usually steady in July and August, but
Sandy, that nice girl from Bowdoin I hired to shop-sit for
me, has been busier than I ever was. I go home at night
and have to add items to the shop inventory, and then do
hours of accounting. By the end of the summer I'm going
to need a very long nap."

"But you'll also have a bank account that should see
you through the winter," I reminded her.

"'Summer—we all have seen—/A few of us—believed—/
A few—the more aspiring/Unquestionably loved—/But
Summer does not care—/She goes her spacious way/As
eligible as the moon/To our Temerity,'" Sarah quoted. She
had an Emily Dickinson quotation for every occasion.

Sarah'd learned the antique business (and needlepoint-
ing) from her grandmother when she was growing up in
Australia. A set of strange circumstances had brought her
to the coast of Maine, where she'd decided to settle. I'd
learned a lot about history and antiques from her, and she

and I had become close friends. I was even beginning to like Emily Dickinson.

I nodded. "You're right. I'd hoped it would be a quiet summer. Instead, we're all working harder than ever."

"But, as you pointed out, making more money," Sarah reminded me as we rounded the corner from the waterfront and stopped at the stand selling locally made ice cream. "One small black raspberry chip sugar cone," she ordered.

"Small mocha chip for me," I added as the teenager serving the growing line of customers nodded. I didn't recognize her. She was probably from out of town, here for the summer. Haven Harbor offered dozens of summer jobs for young people who'd work for minimum wage. I'd steamed lobsters at the restaurant on the wharf when I'd been in high school. The smell and the heat had been hard to bear, but the money was decent, and customers sometimes even tipped me. I watched as this teenager reached deep into the bins and scooped out ice cream for our cones. Her shoulders and wrist would ache tonight. But she smiled as Sarah paid for both of us and added a dollar to the "Money for College" jar on the counter.

"Thanks," I said, taking a lick. "This is the first day in a while I've been free to walk around a bit. Even if most of the walking was shopping for the movie."

Sarah nodded. "When we agreed to work with Flannery Sullivan I thought it would be fun. And I guess it has been. But it's taken a lot more time than I'd imagined."

"He's not easy to please," I agreed. "And I'd hoped to spend time with Patrick this summer."

"You went out on Skye's new boat once," Sarah reminded me as we headed up the street toward her van, parked behind her shop.

"True. Once. In late June. We cruised around for a couple of hours on the *North Skye*, but that's all."

"I figured you'd at least spend the night. It sleeps eight, doesn't it?"

"It does. Skye's letting some of the young men working on the crew who couldn't find places to stay here in town sleep on it. Sounds glamorous, but they'll have pretty tight quarters."

"She's filled her own house, too."

"Basically with the same people she had here at Christmastime. Thomas and Marie O'Day, who're finalizing the script. Marv Mason, the director, Hank Stoddard, the producer, our favorite set designer, Flannery Sullivan, actor Jon Whyte, and, of course, Talia Lincoln."

I made a face that Sarah ignored. She knew how I felt that the cast of *Harbor Heartbreak* included one of Patrick's old girlfriends. Especially one who was tall, blond, gorgeous, and was staying in his mother's home, just down the driveway from the carriage house where he lived.

Sarah glanced at her phone. "We have about half an hour before we have to pick up that Victorian couch."

I finished my cone and nodded. "Patrick's going to meet us there. He borrowed one of the trucks the crew's using and said he'd try to hijack someone else to help hoist and carry. Oak is heavy. I'm curious to see that couch. Gram did the needlepoint after I left for Arizona. It took her almost a year. After that she started Mainely Needlepoint, and turned down projects that large. We make more money doing smaller projects."

"I wouldn't know how to begin to design and needlepoint upholstery for more than the seat of a straight chair," Sarah agreed. "It's great that the family your gram did the work for is willing to lend it to be in the movie."

"It'll be the center of the contemporary living room set," I agreed. "The nineteen-sixties set won't be as elegant."

"I've never worked on a movie before," said Sarah as

we headed for her van. "But I love that we're creating both sets in the same house. Plus, it makes life a lot simpler for us."

Ted Lawrence, an artist who was a relative of Sarah's, had died last fall. Marv Mason had heard about his empty multi-roomed estate and rented it for the duration. The living room was going to be the contemporary set and the studio and gallery the 1960s set. Walking down the long hall at the estate felt like walking between decades. Or would, when Sarah and I finished the rooms.

For now, Flannery was leaving us alone and focusing on the outside scenes to be shot at the town dock and lighthouse.

We turned on Sarah's GPS and headed out of town. We'd only seen pictures of the couch, but Flannery Sullivan had fallen in love with it. "I want both living rooms to be realistic; exactly what would be in a Maine living room," he'd declared. "That's why I hired you both. Skye assures me you'll be able to handle the details."

Sarah and I'd exchanged glances. Patrick's mother had often found ways to hire Sarah and me and other Haven Harbor residents when she'd needed something done. At first it felt awkward, but then we'd decided saying no would insult Skye, and, after all, we could all use the money. Since Patrick and I had been a couple it was even more uncomfortable, although neither he nor Skye understood that. They both thought of money as something handy to have, because it could get things done, not as something that for many people outlined what they could do with their lives.

Until I was ten I'd lived with my single mom, who waitressed and drank most of her earnings, and my grandmother, who kept our household running. After Mama disappeared when I was ten, it was just Gram and me. For us, money wasn't to hire people to help: it was to pay for food and fuel.

I was just beginning to get used to Patrick's way of thinking, even though I knew not everyone thought of finances the way he did.

We passed two stands where families were selling the small wild blueberries that ripened this time of year. Setting up an awning or a tailgate by the side of the road was a way to make a few extra dollars in late July, and even young children could help with the picking. Wreaths at Christmastime; blueberries in summer. Every penny counted.

"Here it is," said Sarah, who'd been paying attention to where we were going while my mind was wandering. "Barn Swallow Lane." She turned right, off the main street onto a narrow curving road. When I was a child roads in Haven Harbor had names, but not numbers. Most private roads, basically long unpaved driveways with homes along the way and, often, dead ends, didn't have names. And no buildings had numbers. When 911 service was put in, Haven Harbor had been forced to change its long-standing "we all know where Warren Smith lives" policy. Those living on unnamed roads were given the opportunity to name their own street, and numbers were assigned by the town. We passed a half dozen houses, some set near the road and some farther back in the woods, before reaching number ten. Not surprisingly, it was a large nineteenth-century house with a barn. Two hundred years ago it had probably been the center of a farm, before the land connected to it had been broken up and sold for new homes.

And, I smiled to myself, most likely the barn then was home to barn swallows. Barn swallows brought good luck.

Sarah parked her van near the barn as Patrick pulled up in the truck he'd borrowed.

I headed to the truck, which he'd parked near the front door. I hadn't seen him in a couple of days, and I suspected we both could use hugs.

I'd almost reached the driver's door when I realized Patrick wasn't alone. He'd said he was going to hijack one of the other men on the set, and Leo Blackwell, a young man who'd moved to Haven Harbor a few months ago and was living with Dave Percy, one of the Mainely Needle-pointers, was with him. But Patrick and Leo weren't alone. Talia Lincoln was also with them.

As she opened the passenger's door and stepped down from the high truck she smiled, and tugged at her brief pink shorts. People from away wore shorts; I certainly knew that. But I'd never seen any as short as Talia's. I tried not to stare. Her underwear was also pink.

Sarah caught up with me and whispered, "Maybe she borrowed something from the nineteen-sixties costume rack."

"She's not in the nineteen-sixties scenes," I answered, feeling as though my feet were stuck to the ground. "She's the contemporary ingenue."

"What an old-fashioned house!" Talia said, as she came around the truck, ignoring Sarah and me, and talking to Patrick. "It's even older than your mother's!"

"Mom's house is late Victorian," Patrick answered, glancing at the house in front of us. "This one's a Colonial."

My family home, where I'd grown up and which I now owned, had been built in 1807. Talia would probably have deemed it ancient, although in Haven Harbor it wasn't unusual.

"You know so much," Talia oozed, taking Patrick's arm. "I love this part of the country. I've never seen so many old houses before!"

He looked at me and moved away from Talia. "Angie, why don't you let Mrs. Whitman know we're here. Leo, come with me. We'll open the back of the truck and put down the ramp."

"Fine," I said, and Sarah and I headed for the door of the house.

Before we'd rung the bell it was opened by a middle-aged woman wearing faded jeans and a yellow T-shirt, her graying hair pulled back in a ponytail. "You must be here to borrow the couch," she said, smiling at us. "Follow me, and I'll show you."

The couch was just as the picture had shown—a Victorian sofa, most likely stuffed with horsehair, upholstered with delicate needlepointed lilacs and a pair of swallows.

"I've always loved it," said Mrs. Whitman. "It's not the most comfortable piece of furniture in the house, but the embroidery is so beautiful. Your grandmother did it, didn't she, Angie?"

"She did," I agreed, looking at the couch carefully. "But this is the first time I've seen it."

"My mother commissioned it," Mrs. Whitman explained. "It will be fun to see it in a movie. A Skye West movie!"

"It's perfect for the room we're designing," I agreed.

"But you will be careful with it, won't you? I hardly sit on it because I don't want the needlepoint damaged."

"We'll be careful," I promised, crossing my fingers.

Patrick and Leo had followed us into the house, with Talia behind them.

"This is Patrick West, Skye's son," I introduced them, "and Leo Blackwell, and Talia Lincoln. Patrick owns the art gallery downtown."

"Of course. I'd heard Skye West's son had taken that over after Ted Lawrence died," said Mrs. Whitman. "I'll have to stop in and take a look one of these days."

Talia pouted a bit. Maybe because I didn't point out that she was one of the major actresses in the movie.

"The gallery is open year-round," said Patrick, walking over to the couch. "With four of us I don't think this will be too difficult to lift. Would it be all right if we moved the small table and the lavender flowered chair to get them out of the way?"

Mrs. Whitman nodded. "No problem. I thought of moving things before you got here, but then realized I'd rather you decide what needed to be done."

Patrick nodded. "Leo, help me with the table and chair."

The two of them carefully moved both pieces of furniture to in front of the fireplace.

"Sarah and Angie, could you each take a corner of the couch?" he asked. "Leo and I'll take the front end; that should be a little heavier to get down the front stairs and up into the truck."

"No problem," said Sarah, moving past Talia, who was clearly in the way.

"Talia, why don't you go ahead of us," Patrick said, pointedly asking her to move. "You can open the front door when we get there."

The four of us each took hold of a side of the couch and a leg and began moving toward the front door. It didn't take long to get the couch out of the house and onto the truck, and covered with padding to protect it.

Patrick had paperwork for Mrs. Whitman to sign saying the production company had borrowed her sofa, and it would be returned by September 30 at the latest. I knew the production company planned to finish filming in Haven Harbor by late August. I assumed the extra time was in case of a delay.

As Patrick closed up the truck he winked at me. "Leo and I'll take the sofa over to the Lawrence house so you can decorate around it. See you at my birthday party tomorrow night?"

I smiled back. "Assuming we finish the set before then."

"You shouldn't have a problem," Patrick said. "And Hank Stoddard and Marv Mason will have fits if you don't. They've told Flannery they want sets in place so location rehearsals can start early next week."

"Is everyone staying with Skye coming to your party?" I asked, thinking of Talia as well as the producer and director.

"Yes," Patrick said, looking at me. "We couldn't very well have a lobster bake and not include Mom's houseguests. But Sarah and Dave and Leo and Ruth and your gram, our local friends, are coming, too."

So Talia would be at the gathering. I could hardly wait.

Chapter 3

Though heaven afflict I'll not repine
Each heart felt Comfort still is mine.
Comfort that shall over death Prevail
And Journey with me through the vale.

—Sampler stitched by Ruhammah Larimer
in Library, Allegheny County, Pennsylvania,
in 1832, picturing two houses close together,
trees on each side, a bird on the roof of one
house, and a latticework border.

Sarah and I got back into her van. "Patrick and Leo are going to the Lawrence house. Sounds like we should follow them. After we get the couch in place we can arrange the pictures and ornaments we got downtown today."

"Good," Sarah said as she started the van. "The sooner we get the contemporary set done, the sooner we can work a little more on the nineteen-sixties one. I don't think that one is quite right yet. It's a lot easier to do an upscale room belonging to a family with some money than a cottage where a father and daughter are struggling to get by."

"A lot of people in Maine live in small houses," I said,

hoping Flannery would have turned on the fans in the Lawrence house.

Both Sarah and I had grown up with our grandmothers, and despite the large captain's house I called home and the business Sarah's grandmother in Australia had run, neither of us had had much money. Not like Patrick, who'd grown up in California with a single parent—a single parent who was a movie star. "You're going to Patrick's birthday party tomorrow, right?" I asked.

"Wouldn't miss it," Sarah confirmed, turning onto the main road.

Ted Lawrence's house wasn't in downtown Haven Harbor. His father had designed the large home, set at the end of a peninsula on a hill overlooking the ocean and the small beach he'd created between rock formations. The estate proved that some artists made money. It was private, so the scenes set there would be easier to control than those set in Haven Harbor itself and at the Haven Harbor Lighthouse. How would they manage to film the scenes downtown and at the lighthouse when they needed so much equipment? I promised myself to get to at least one of the locations when they were filming to see how they did it.

This afternoon the long private drive to the Lawrence estate was lined with trucks and cars. Sarah parked as close to the house as she could and we walked the rest of the way. The major actors in the 1960s scenes were rehearsing on the lawn and, although we were too far away to hear the dialogue, both Sarah and I stopped to watch. It was fun to be a part of a movie, much as I complained about the time it took.

Director Marv Mason had found Cos Curran, who'd just graduated from Haven Harbor High. She was now playing Amy, the teenager in love with Caleb, a young lobsterman her father didn't approve of. Caleb was played by Linc Fitch, the son of a local Realtor. Ironically, Cos and Linc had been dating for a few months. I didn't know how close their relationship was, but in the scenes I'd seen them rehearsing they looked very much in love. Marv had promised Cos and Linc he'd finish filming their scenes early enough so they'd be able to get to college by the time classes started next month.

"What are you giving Patrick for his birthday?" Sarah asked.

Her question brought me back to today. "I don't know," I admitted. "He can buy anything he really wants, and I've already given him a needlepointed pillow based on one of his paintings. What are you giving him?"

Sarah shrugged slightly. "Nothing big. But I'm not dating him. In one of the box lots I bought at an auction in the spring I found a souvenir bowl from the nineteen thirties that pictures the Hollywood Hills. It doesn't go with the other antiques in my store, and I thought it might make Patrick smile."

"Sounds as though you've solved the problem," I agreed. "He may laugh, but he and the others from California should enjoy seeing it. I wish I had something as perfect as that."

"You'll think of something," said Sarah. "I wonder what the other Mainely Needlepointers will bring? I think all of them were invited."

"Captain Ob and Anna aren't coming. They have a big charter fishing party tomorrow that's been booked since spring. But I'm sure Ruth will be there; she's at Aurora most of the time now, anyway. She and the O'Days have set up the solarium as a writers' room. And Patrick mentioned Dave, and that would include Leo, since he's helping out with sets and lighting."

"Leo's having the time of his life," Sarah agreed. "Last week he told me the only thing that would be better would be if he had a role in the movie, and I suspect Marv may slip him into one of the crowd scenes. Leo's been working really hard this summer."

"And Gram and Reverend Tom were invited, too. After all, her couch will be in the movie."

"We may be seeing more of everyone starting in a couple of days, when rehearsals go into high gear. So far it looks as though they're basically reading lines and working on blocking. Once the sets are finished, I assume they'll start tightening the action."

We'd reached the kitchen entrance to the Lawrence house. I wondered for a moment how Sarah felt about all the time we were spending here after what happened last fall. But there wasn't time to wonder for long.

Patrick and Leo were already there, in the contemporary living room set, which had been the Lawrences' real living room.

"We weren't sure where you wanted the couch," Patrick called. "By the window? Or the long wall?"

Flannery Sullivan, a big man with an orange beard and a beer belly, hesitated. "In front of the window." He glanced over at Sarah and me. "Drapes. We'll need drapes so the lighting will be right."

Sarah pulled out a pad and started writing.

"No, Forget it. Put the couch against the wall." He turned to Sarah. "We'll still need the drapes, though. Maybe curtains instead. They'll filter the light a bit."

Sarah glanced at me in frustration and wrote another note as Patrick and Leo moved the couch against the wall.

"We'll put the oil painting of the surf above the couch," I suggested. "And the prints of seabirds on either side of it."

Sarah nodded. "The two armchairs can be in front of the windows."

"Anything else you ladies need moved?" Patrick asked. "If not, I'm trading the truck in for my own car and taking

Leo down to the lighthouse where they're figuring out camera angles and need a gofer. Then I'm heading back to Aurora to see if Mom needs any help with the party. She was rehearsing with Talia all morning on the opening scene, but I think they're finished now."

"We'll be okay," I said. "Thanks for your help with the couch. I think Sarah and I can manage the rest, assuming Flannery agrees."

Patrick bent down and kissed my forehead lightly. Not the kind of kiss we usually shared, but we weren't exactly in a private place. I missed the intimacy that had developed between us in the past several months, but the show must go on. "See you tomorrow, then." He turned toward Leo, who was focused on two men setting up lights. "Com'on Leo. I'll get you down to the lighthouse. Dave will pick you up when you're through there, right?"

"Sure." Leo nodded as he and Patrick headed out toward Patrick's BMW parked in the driveway.

"Okay," I said, turning to Sarah. "What about arranging the old books we borrowed from your shop in the bookcase over in the corner?" The room was contemporary, but we'd decided to mix old books and new, so they looked as though they were actually read. Sarah had told me some antiquarian book dealers sold old leather-bound books by the foot. Who bought them? Decorators and movie production companies looking to create an image. Not just for a movie: for a home. I didn't read a lot, but I couldn't imagine buying books as though they were wallpaper.

Sarah nodded. "The books are in the boxes beneath the windows. Why don't we bring in some of the stuff we got today first? Some of those things can go in the bookcase, too. Then we'll hang the paintings and prints."

The room was beginning to look like a real living room, assuming a real living room only had three walls.

Originally Flannery had told us "two walls," but then decided he could maneuver cameras and lights so three walls would work. Sarah and I had already hung a nineteenth-century "sailor's valentine," a shadow box filled with carefully arranged seashells collected by a sailor on a long voyage and glued together to form a picture, probably intended as a gift for a mother or sweetheart.

As a contrast, our 1960s living room included a worn, slipcovered couch and a selection of beach stones and shells on a windowsill. Probably no one watching the movie would notice, but we liked the idea of contrasting but similar details.

Sarah and I headed back to her van to collect the bags we'd filled this morning.

Cos and Linc were still rehearsing on the lawn overlooking the beach.

Translating a book into a movie wasn't easy, and I suspected Ruth had some strong feelings about changes that were being made to her dialogue and story line.

Her arthritis had made it harder for her to write during the past year. I just hoped she wouldn't wear herself out. I looked forward to seeing her at Patrick's party.

Almost everyone I knew was working on this movie. It would be fun to see it in a theater, although that would be at least a year from now.

"Let's go down the hill a little and see if we can overhear what they're saying," I suggested to Sarah. "I'd love to know more about the plot."

"I'm not sure Marv would approve," Sarah said hesitantly. "Directors can be sensitive about voyeurs."

"Just for a few minutes," I pushed. "Then we'll get the stuff we bought this morning from your van."

I started down the hill beyond the gallery on the right side of the house. From the outside it looked like a barn.

The real barn, on the other end of the house, was now being used as storage for props and costumes. Sarah followed me, cautiously.

I stopped as soon as I could hear anything. Cos, as Amy, was running into Linc's arms and kissing him. Marv made them do it several times, but clearly they didn't seem to mind. I wondered what it would be like to rehearse and play a scene like that with someone you didn't like.

"Well, that looks like a movie scene," I said quietly to Sarah.

She tapped me on the shoulder. "Look over there." She pointed toward another part of the hill we were standing on. Below us producer Hank Stoddard was watching the scene, too. I hadn't seen him around any of the locations or sets. But maybe once the actors were being put through their paces he'd be around more. After all, it was his money (and that of his friends) that was making *Harbor Heartbreak* possible.

Cos/Amy had just run a few steps again as Linc/Caleb was holding out his arms.

Where were they? Some romantic location, no doubt. Not on the sloping lawn leading from the Anderson home to the sea.

"Meet me after the fireworks tonight?" Linc/Caleb was saying. "Down at the wharf. I'll be on the *Sea Witch.*"

That must be his lobster boat.

Cos/Amy turned away a bit but then agreed. "I'll be there, Caleb. But I can't stay long."

"Your dad really hates me, doesn't he? He doesn't think I'm good enough for you, just because I lobster. He wants you to be with someone who'll go to college and end up wearing a suit to work every day. But I'm my own person, and right now I'm making more money than anyone I know who's talking about college, or working for someone else."

Amy went closer to Caleb, and put her hands out to him. "We'll find a way, Caleb. We will."

He put his arms around her. "Yes. We will."

"Stop!" Marv shouted. He went up to the two teenagers and started pointing, and heading them in different directions. Sarah and I were too far away to hear what he was saying, but clearly he wanted changes in what they'd been doing. We turned and went back up the hill.

"Well, that gives us a hint of what at least the early sixties story will be," said Sarah. "Sort of Romeo and Juliet. Teenagers in love, with a father who disapproves."

"And we know it won't end well for them," I added. "Or the movie wouldn't be called *Harbor Heartbreak*."

Chapter 4

How Blest the maid whom
Circling Years Improve
Her God the Object of her warmest Love
Whose Useful Hours Successive as they slide,
The book the needle and the pen divide.

—Stitched in fine linsey-woolsey by Lydia
Burrill in Salem, Massachusetts, circa 1795.

I spent the first part of that evening checking the Mainely
Needlepoint Web site (no new orders) and trying to think
of something I could give Patrick for his birthday. By the
time I'd finished a load of laundry, assured no-longer-a-
kitten Trixi I still loved her even if I was away from home
a lot, and promised to steal a piece of lobster from
Patrick's party to bring home to her tomorrow night, I was
ready for bed.

I almost didn't answer my phone when it rang, but I
couldn't refuse a call from Gram.

"Everything all right?" I asked.

"Fine here. Just hadn't heard from you in a few days
and thought I'd check in before the party tomorrow night,"
said Gram.

"I'm sorry. Between Mainely Needlepoint work and helping out with the movie set, I've hardly had a chance to keep in touch with anyone but Sarah. And that's because I'm working with her."

"I understand. Tom and I are fine, too. I'm looking forward to the lobster bake at Aurora tomorrow evening. Unfortunately, Tom can't come. Choir rehearsal followed by an outreach committee meeting at the church. Work before pleasure."

"Being married to a reverend isn't just a Sunday job," I teased a bit.

"Not at all. And I'm sure he'd like me to attend more of the meetings he's involved with. But I do my best to keep both of us calm and save time to spend together. It's hard to believe we've been married only a little more than a year. I don't think I've ever been happier, Angie. Not to say I didn't love the years we had together. . . ."

I smiled. "Gram, you deserve all the happiness you can get. And so does Tom."

"How is Patrick coping with his mother's work encroaching on the life he's been trying to make for himself here?"

I sighed. "Thanks for reminding me. He loves his mom, of course, but he wasn't thrilled when he found out what she and her friends had planned. One reason he moved here was because she'd said Haven Harbor was to be their private place; one where she could be herself, and not a Hollywood star. And he could be an artist, not just Skye West's son. But you know our dear local chamber of commerce was so excited by the idea of a movie being made here that they arranged for the cast and crew to have pretty much whatever they wanted in town, so there wasn't much Patrick or anyone else could say. Skye always said she wanted her Maine life to be separate from her work, but this summer it doesn't look that way."

"The chamber folks are convinced the movie will bring more tourists to the area. And tourists bring money," Gram reminded me. "Have you seen any of the scenes yet, or are you still carting furniture and props around?"

"Yes—and yes. I haven't seen much, but I'm really curious. You know *Harbor Heartbreak* is based on one of Ruth's books, and she got her plot ideas from actual events here in the Harbor."

"She did, indeed. But isn't this one of her early books? The ones she wrote in the early seventies? Before she focused on erotica."

"Right. And the film won't be following her book exactly. They're adding a lot, because there are two time periods in the film, and only one in the book. I did get a peek at one of the nineteen-sixties scenes today. Cos Curran and Linc Fitch were rehearsing on the lawn at Ted Anderson's, and Sarah and I listened in."

"I love that the director—Marv Mason, right?—has given jobs to so many young people in town. How were Cos and Linc doing?"

"They looked fine to me, although Marv was clearly giving them directions. We couldn't hear him, but we could hear the scene. Cos's character and Linc's are in love. She's seventeen, he's a young lobsterman, and her dad doesn't approve of their relationship."

Gram hesitated. "What happens then?"

"I have no idea. Maybe I'll hear more tomorrow. Or maybe not. Skye and Talia are going to rehearse a scene in the contemporary part of the movie, on the set Sarah and I arranged. And I can't believe I haven't mentioned it, but this afternoon we picked up the couch you needlepointed. It's gorgeous! And it looks wonderful on the set. I can't believe you spent a whole year on one project."

"At this point, neither can I. But that was after you left for

Arizona, the house was quiet, and I needed something to keep me amused. And, after all, it was one of the stepping-stones that led me to creating Mainely Needlepoint."

"For which I'm very grateful. I think most of the needle-pointers will be at Aurora tomorrow night, since Patrick has become friends with them. Ruth and Sarah and you and I will be there, of course. Leo's working on the film, and he and Dave are coming, too. Captain Ob and Anna are the only two who had other commitments. And Reverend Tom, of course."

"Well, he isn't exactly a Mainely Needlepointer," Gram laughed. "But he is part of the crowd, for certain. In any case, I'll see you there tomorrow night."

Trixi jumped into my lap and curled up as I put down my phone. "You're a good girl," I said, scratching between her ears. "But now that I'm wide awake again I'm going to take a warm bath, despite the weather, and then go to bed. You can sleep on the other pillow if you want to, but I'm not quite ready to go to sleep yet."

Trixi purred. Sometimes I wondered whether she understood English. She moved over and plopped down on the pillow next to the one I usually slept on.

What did people do if they had more than one cat and only one extra pillow?

I wasn't going to worry about that tonight.

Chapter 5

*May smiling health attend the Babe
and happiness the Mother.*

—Stitching on a layette pincushion,
probably from about 1900.

"All quiet on the set!" bellowed Marv Mason.

Sarah and I'd finished the contemporary living room set and Marv said we could watch the first run-through this morning to check for any problems. I suspected he also wanted us available should he want set changes or new props.

"This is the opening scene, so we have to capture the audience's attention and not distract them," he'd admonished the actors. He'd removed several of the prints we'd hung, and reorganized some of the books. I wasn't sure why he'd done either of those things, but, after all, he was the director. The boss, who reported only to the producer, Hank Stoddard. Hank had been in the background at the rehearsal Sarah and I had watched yesterday, but I suspected he spent most of his time at Aurora on the telephone talking to investors and setting up his next project.

Sarah and I stood in the Anderson house hallway between the kitchen and the living room, in back of the cameras and lights. No one was filming today, but Marv wanted everything to look as though they were.

Every day I learned more about how complicated it was to make a movie. It definitely involved a lot of yelling by the director. And they hadn't even turned on the cameras.

This first scene in the contemporary section of *Harbor Heartbreak* was an intimate meeting between a grandmother (Skye West, playing Amy as an old woman) and her mid-twenties granddaughter, Emily, played by Talia Lincoln.

Since it wasn't a dress rehearsal, both women were dressed comfortably. Skye had pinned up her long hair with a hairpiece of some sort, probably to keep cooler. Her natural hair color was gray, with streaks of white, and the hairpiece was all white. A little strange, but no doubt comfortable. Talia's natural hair was long and blond, and she was wearing intentionally torn jeans that covered more of her legs than had the shorts she'd worn yesterday. Both women were sitting on the couch Gram had needlepointed. Papers I assumed were their scripts were on the low coffee table in front of the couch.

"Teacups!" Marv yelled. "They should each have a flowered teacup!"

The set was quiet. He'd had no reason to shout, unless he was trying to intimidate those of us nearby. Sarah dodged between two lighting technicians and handed Skye and Talia each one of the teacups we'd borrowed from her antiques shop and left on a side table. Neither actress looked as though she knew exactly what to do with the cups, but they held them as though the empty cups were full of tea. Skye looked a bit amused. Talia's hand holding her cup was shaking. Luckily for her, Marv hadn't asked for liquid to be in the cups. That would probably be part of a later rehearsal.

"Okay! You both did fine in our read-through yesterday. Just relax and remember who you are." He pointed at Talia. "From the top."

"It's simple. I love Richard, Gramma. I want to be with him. And he works at a law firm in New York. That's why I have to sell the business here and move."

"That business supported me, and your mother, and now you. You've done a fine job growing it from a small diner to a serious restaurant with excellent reviews. You're going to give that up for someone you've hardly seen since high school?"

"Richard and I've been in touch for almost a year now. High school was a long time ago."

"Your mother was still alive then, and you were working the grill. I remember your burning yourself one afternoon you were so distracted by Richard."

"That was years ago, Gramma. I'm not a teenager anymore."

"You said you were in love with him then, too, but he left you to go off to college, and then to New York. He didn't even visit. He thought he was too important for Haven Harbor. He didn't stay in touch with his family or friends, or value his roots. Roots are important, Emily. Don't let your infatuation with an old beau separate you from what's important."

"Richard's a busy man. And, yes, we were out of touch for most of the past twelve years. But we've been talking and texting for almost a year now. He hasn't come to Maine, it's true, but I've seen him in New York. I didn't tell you, because I knew you wouldn't approve. This time he loves me. I know he does. And I love him, too. We want to be together. To get married. We can't do that if I'm running a restaurant on the coast of Maine and he's working long hours in New York."

Skye was silent. She "sipped" out of her cup, and then put it down on the table. "Love isn't enough, Emily. You should know that by now. You're not a teenager. And you don't know everything about Richard. Maybe you've been in touch on the computer and you've seen him a few times, but that isn't the same as seeing someone every day. Living with him. You'll be giving up what's kept you focused and successful and supported you for the past ten years. If your marriage doesn't work, you won't have anything to come back to."

"Gramma, I'm not you. I'm not in love with a poor lobsterman. Richard loves me, and we could have a wonderful life together."

"Cut!" Marv said. "Okay; not bad. But I need to see more distress, Skye. You love Emily, but you don't want her to make the same mistake you made. You know Richard and his family, but you don't want to tell all his secrets. You want Emily to make her own decisions, but you want them to be the right ones. And, Talia, remember you've lived in the same town all your life. You have a successful business, but you don't have love. You're almost thirty, and there's a part of you that's feeling desperate. Maybe Richard is your only chance for love, and even having a family someday. You love your grandmother, but you think she wants you to stay in Haven Harbor to be there for her. You don't see that she doesn't want you to be hurt."

Talia nodded. "I guess. But aren't I blinded by love?"

"Sure, sure," said Marv. "But you're also a businesswoman. You've taken care of yourself and the people who work for you. You love Haven Harbor. There's a part of you that doesn't want to leave." He made a note. "I'll get the O'Days and Ruth to make that more evident in the script."

One of the lighting guys went up to him and said something I couldn't hear.

"Okay. We'll take this scene over, but we'll move to the other set. The lighting team has a problem with the spots." He turned to the man who'd spoken with him. "I told you to watch out for the windows! We can't wait around for perfect sunlight when we start filming."

Sarah touched my arm. "Doesn't look as though they need us right now." She glanced at her phone. "Patrick's party's at six, right?"

"Right. I'd like to go home and change," I said. "Nothing fancy. But clean."

"Sounds good to me. I want to check with the girl who's sitting in my store, too. She's sent me a couple of texts today with questions about English porcelain. I need to give her a brief seminar on china markings."

"Then I'll see you at Aurora in a couple of hours?"

"Six o'clock. They'd better have lots of lobsters! I think I could eat more than one tonight."

I grinned. "If Skye and Patrick are involved, you know they'll have plenty. I'm going to focus on the champagne, I think."

"Not driving home tonight?" She smiled at me and winked lasciviously as we headed out the back door in the kitchen toward her van.

"I hope not," I said. "Patrick deserves company on his birthday. And I could use some, too."

Chapter 6

Semper Fidelis.

—This embroidery was stitched for the American
souvenir trade in Japan about 1890. It pictures
elaborately intertwined American flags and the
Marine Corps symbol of an eagle on a globe,
above a laurel wreath and space for a small oval
photograph to be inserted. Americans had been
trading with the Japanese since 1853, and the
Japanese souvenir trade was a profitable one.

July evenings in Maine are still light at six in the evening.
We wouldn't see a sunset over the harbor until almost
eight thirty.

Two security guards were posted outside the gate to
Aurora. One of them had a list of invited guests that he
checked off as people arrived.

When Skye was in town she hired a security company
to make sure she had no unexpected guests or photogra-
phers. It was a nuisance, but after a year even I was used
to it. When Patrick was here alone the guards disappeared.

I wasn't surprised to see the large circular drive in front

of Aurora lined with cars and trucks. Sarah's van was already there, as well as Dave's car, and Gram's, and about a dozen vehicles I didn't recognize. Some of Skye's guests had rented cars, and I assumed some belonged to the caterers.

The caterers had set up their tent on the hill leading from the large house down to the harbor. Last summer Skye'd hired the same Camden caterer to do a lobster bake, and they'd done a great job. Catering parties in the summer months were bread and butter for many Maine restaurants.

I drove until I was close to Patrick's carriage house, where his home and studio were. If I spent the night there, I didn't want my car to be close to his mom's house. Patrick and I deserved some privacy.

I smiled to myself as I remembered a similar party here at Aurora last year. Before that occasion I'd spent hours figuring out what to wear, and had been nervous and self-conscious about how to act at a lobster bake where other guests were major Hollywood figures I hadn't met.

Tonight I was relaxed. Right now the temperature was still in the eighties, and I'd put on a pair of relatively new jeans and a tank top, and tied the sleeves of a navy sweatshirt around my waist. As soon as the sun went down so would the temperature, and I wanted to be prepared. I also had no doubt eating lobster would be messy, and nothing I had on would stain horribly.

I glanced around at the other guests.

Even from a distance it was easy to separate the locals from those from away. Most of the Haven Harbor folks, from teenagers like Cos and Linc and Leo to older people like Ruth Hopkins, wore jeans of some sort with plain T-shirts or sweatshirts. Ruth was sitting next to her pink wheeling walker, a glass in her hand. She was wearing a cardigan over her shoulders instead of a sweatshirt, her jeans weren't designer ones, and she was talking to Gram. Linc Fitch's jeans had a few holes in them. He was circling the group, taking pictures of everyone.

Skye's guests from out of state were more dressed up. Talia was wearing a short bright-patterned sundress with sandals whose high heels were sinking into the lawn. Marie O'Day was wearing a long skirt. Flannery Sullivan, Thomas O'Day, Marv Mason, and Hank Stoddard were all wearing slacks and golf shirts. Maybe it was a California uniform.

Skye, who waved at me from where she was consulting with the caterers, was also wearing slacks. Hers were white, and she'd topped them with a silk tank top and a long-sleeved jacket that looked Asian.

I didn't see Patrick, but he was probably wearing jeans (we'd converted him to Haven Harbor styles) and currently running an errand for his mother. A table a short distance from the drinks and appetizers was covered with wrapped birthday gifts. I added my small package, hoping I hadn't made a major mistake in what I was giving Patrick. He might like it, because I'd given it to him, but it wouldn't be in the same league as some of those other boxes.

My friend Dave Percy, Mainely Needlepointer, Haven Harbor High School biology teacher, and now Leo's guardian, was standing alone. He looked as though he could use some company, so I headed in his direction.

"Angie! I'm glad to see someone I know," he said with relief. "Leo's thrilled to be working on the movie and meeting so many important people." He gestured down the hill a bit where Leo was talking to Jon Whyte, the young actor who played Richard, Talia's love interest in the contemporary section of the film. Linc was taking pictures of them. "Everyone has been so welcoming to him. I was a little worried about what he and I would do this summer, since he'd only been in Haven Harbor a few months, but I haven't even had a chance to take him out on the water and teach him to row. Leo's dream was always to be an actor, and this summer he's getting a taste of what that really involves."

"I'm glad," I said. "I hope he can settle down by the time high school opens in September."

"I'm with you on that," Dave agreed. "When all this started I told him he'd have to continue doing his chores; that finishing high school was a must. So far—" Dave held up crossed fingers. "Can I get you a drink?"

"Champagne, please," I agreed.

A year ago I would have hesitated. Now I knew that to the Wests champagne at a party was the same as ginger ale or cola would be to the rest of us. Most people were holding flutes, although, based on the glasses they were holding, Marv and Flannery and a few of the other men were sipping whiskey.

Cos Curran was talking to Marv Mason over near the house. She'd fixed her hair in a more elegant arrangement than the ponytail she wore in *Harbor Heartbreak*. Marv's eyes weren't on her hair, though. They were definitely on her tight jeans and tank top, and he'd just handed her a glass of champagne. I watched Cos move a half step backward as he stayed close to her, and touched his glass to hers. A toast to his new protégée?

Linc circled them with his camera. She was his girl, and clearly he was keeping an eye on her. As I looked around I saw several other people using their cell phones to take pictures. Talia's phone was also focused on Marv and Cos. Then she moved back, trying to get a wide shot of the people in front of Skye's large Victorian house.

Dave was back with my glass, which I raised to him. "I wonder if Pete's coming tonight," I said, looking around. Sarah was talking with Ruth and Gram. Pete, our local

Haven Harbor cop, had been dating Sarah for several months now, and I suspected Patrick would have invited him. "Look over there," I said, gesturing toward Cos and Marv. Cos had moved down the hill, but Marv had followed her every step. "I wonder if Marv remembers Cos isn't of legal drinking age. Or if Pete would do anything about it."

Dave laughed. "I warned Leo about that. I think he and Linc and Cos are the only guests under twenty-one tonight. Other young men are working crew, but they weren't invited to the party, and I don't think any of those staying on Skye's yacht are here, either. Basically"—he glanced around—"it looks like Patrick's friends, which is as it should be, and Skye's houseguests."

"I agree," I said, nodding.

"I told Leo if I caught him drinking anything but water or soda his days working with sound and lighting would be over. So far I've kept an eye on him, and he seems to be behaving. I can't speak for Cos, however. I'm not responsible for her. But she's definitely drinking that champagne."

"Leo's still with Jon Whyte," I pointed out. "Jon's probably in his late twenties. Maybe he's amused by Leo's enthusiasm." I looked closer. "Leo's glass looks like soda."

"I hope so. Leo's certainly talked a lot about Jon. And Talia, of course." Dave glanced at Talia, who was now chatting with Thomas and Marie. Maybe they were discussing the script. Or maybe not. "I can't blame him about Talia. She's something," Dave said, shaking his head. "After seeing her all summer, I'm afraid Leo's going to be disappointed with girls at Haven Harbor High."

"Did you know Patrick used to date Talia?" I asked.

"No! When was that?" Dave asked curiously.

"I don't know exactly. When they were younger. But I guess it went on for some time." I wished I could accept

Talia the way she was and not feel the pangs of jealousy
that kept popping up whenever I saw her.

"How old is Patrick, anyway?" Dave asked.

"Thirty-three today," I told him.

"A little old to have a birthday party this large. Or
maybe it's a Hollywood thing. Any excuse for a party. At
least there aren't balloons. Wonder if there'll be a cake
with candles to blow out?"

"If Skye wants a cake, or Patrick does, one will be
here," I assured him. I'd felt self-conscious at the surprise
birthday party Gram had given me in April, and I was only
twenty-eight.

Dave and I sipped our champagne and played voyeurs.
"Cos and Marv seem to be getting pretty friendly," he
pointed out.

I looked over at where they were standing, even farther
down the hill from the rest of the guests than they had
been before. Marv had put his arm around Cos, who was
leaning slightly away from him. "He must be at least thirty
years older than she is," I pointed out. "She should leave
him and come over here."

"He's the director, right?" Dave said. "In this crowd he
has a lot of power. And she's just eighteen, Angie. Probably she feels indebted to him for the role she has and
doesn't want to be rude."

"Linc may disagree," I said as we watched both Talia
and Linc join Cos and Marv. Linc took Cos's hand and
pulled her away, up the hill toward where food was beginning to appear. Talia kept smiling and laughing. And
blocking Marv from following the young couple. Maybe
she was looking for some of the attention Cos had been
getting.

"Good for Linc," said Dave.

"And where's my lady been all evening?" Patrick's voice
startled me as I turned toward him. "Dave, you're my

friend, but it's my birthday. You can't monopolize the prettiest woman here."

"Pouting?" I said, as Patrick refilled my champagne glass and then Dave's with the bottle he was holding.

"Absolutely. It's my birthday; I should be able to do as I want to," he answered, tossing his now-empty champagne bottle into a nearby recycling bin. "The caterers are going to begin serving very soon. Would you two consider joining me at my table?"

I looked over at the tables and realized the major figures in the film were already finding places to sit. Skye and Talia and Marv were sitting together. Marv reached out and pulled Cos toward them, and Linc followed, filling the table. Ruth was at another table, sitting between Gram and Sarah. I didn't see Pete anywhere. "Is Pete coming tonight?" I asked Patrick.

"No. I invited him, but he had to work," said Patrick. "Crowds in July, you know, and he's also overseeing the security guys we hired to protect our equipment at some of the downtown locations and the lighthouse. It would be too much of a pain to set everything up every day. Marv's planning to do some background filming at the lighthouse tomorrow if the weather holds."

"We've been lucky. The weather's been beautiful, if a bit too warm for my taste," I agreed.

Patrick headed Dave and me over to a table where Jon and Flannery Sullivan were sitting.

Dave looked around. "Has anyone seen Leo?"

Jon answered, "He went inside to use the bathroom. He should be back in a few minutes."

"Good. I just wanted to make sure he had someone to sit with," said Dave. He reached out his hand to shake Jon's. "I'm Leo's guardian, Dave Percy."

"Happy to meet you," said Jon. "Leo seems like a good

kid. Works hard, and is excited about everything. Reminds me of how I was at his age."

I was seated between Patrick and Dave, which was fine with me. Patrick was paying more attention to the caterers than to the rest of us.

"Those two bartenders are supposed to keep our glasses filled," he said. "Maybe I should go and remind them."

I glanced around the table. "No one seems desperate for more champagne. And we should have some clam broth soon, right?" Generously filled cups of haddock chowder were already at our places, and people were starting to dig in.

Lobster bakes include steamed clams as well as lobsters, and the clams usually come with mugs of broth (to swirl the clams in to ensure they don't have any sand or mud on them, and then to sip from after any detritus has sunk to the bottom of the mug). At the moment waitresses were giving each of us small cups of butter, to dip both the clams (after the broth) and lobster meat in.

Baskets of warm blueberry muffins and large bowls to collect empty lobster and clam shells were in the middle of each table. Jon was the only one at our table who didn't take a muffin. Maybe he was one of the Hollywood actors who were on perpetual diets. I almost took two in response. They were delicious.

"What about the lobsters and clams?" Dave asked, dipping a bit of his muffin in the butter planned for the seafood.

"They should be coming soon," Patrick assured him, keeping an eye out for the waiters. "Usually they're also served with a steamed potato, but Mom noticed that at the lobster bake last year most people didn't eat their potatoes, so this year she told the caterer to eliminate that part of the menu."

"All we're going to eat is seafood?" Jon asked. "That's

no problem for me, but what if someone is allergic to shellfish? Or doesn't like seafood?"

"The caterers also have grilled chicken in reserve, if that should happen," said Patrick. "Most people vacationing in Maine want lobsters and clams." Two servers came to our table, picking up the now-empty chowder cups and putting platters of lobster and steamed clams in front of each of us. Most guests had taken out their cell phones and were snapping pictures of the platters, I assumed for posting on Instagram or Facebook.

"Jon and Flannery, if you don't know how to eat the lobster or clams, you have three experts at the table. Angie grew up in Haven Harbor, Dave's been here—how many years, Dave?" Patrick asked.

"About five years," Dave answered.

"And I'm the newcomer, but after a little over a year, I can handle a lobster pretty well." Patrick winked. "These all should be soft shells—new shells, some people call them—but everyone also has lobster shears and nutcrackers and picks in case you need them."

We each also had our own pile of napkins and wet wipes to clean up with.

No one said much as we all got down to the serious business of taking the clam and lobster meat out of their shells, tossing the shells into the communal bowl on the table, and then dunking the seafood into the clam broth and melted butter before savoring it.

"Why is it that lobster in Maine is so much better than lobster in other places? I've paid a fortune in New York restaurants for lobster that wasn't close to as good as this one," Jon said, breaking off his lobster's tail.

"Simple," said Patrick. "These lobsters were in the water early this morning and were kept in salt water until they were steamed. The fresher the better. Even shipping live lobsters carefully means they'll lose some of that sweet taste."

No one else had any questions, and we all continued digging in.

When I'd lived in Arizona someone who'd heard I'd grown up in Maine asked if we ate lobsters every day. Of course, we didn't. Some lobstermen and their families didn't eat them at all except when prices were so low they couldn't afford not to.

Even if you'd grown up along the coast of Maine and lived here full-time, lobsters were special. Some visitors preferred lobster mixed with macaroni and cheese. A lot of people savored lobster bisque. I liked lobster BLTs myself. And, of course, lobster could be mixed with other seafoods in pasta dishes or in a stew, or served in a classic lobster roll. If you were in Maine, there were endless ways to eat lobster.

As I worked my way through the body of my lobster, savoring the bits of meat behind the legs, I admitted to myself that, despite all those other alternatives, this was the perfect way to eat a lobster: sitting outside, looking at the harbor below, and dipping the meat into a cup of butter.

Right now the clams and lobster and champagne (our glasses had been refilled, although most people were focusing on the seafood, not the champagne) were perfect. Not to even mention the guy sitting next to me.

"When do you think you'll have another birthday?" I whispered to him as he used his pick to get the last piece of meat out of one of his lobster's claws. "This is delicious."

"You may have to wait a while for another birthday," he answered. "But I suspect we could find some other lobsters around town if we wanted them."

I reached up and kissed his cheek, and then rubbed off the spot of butter I'd left there.

Across the table, Jon looked at us with amusement. Tonight I didn't care.

After the lobsters had disappeared the caterers served vanilla ice cream with a raspberry and cognac sauce. Rich and delicious. There was no birthday cake with candles. But Skye did lead everyone in singing "Happy Birthday" to an embarrassed Patrick while dessert was being served.

"Are you going to open your gifts now?" I asked him after the singing had stopped and everyone except Talia and Cos was concentrating on the homemade ice cream and raspberry sauce. Talia and Cos must have skipped their desserts. They'd left their table and seemed to be having a serious conversation over near the house. Maybe Cos was getting some acting advice?

Patrick shook his head. "No. Mom and I decided I wouldn't open the gifts when everyone was here. I'll open them later, privately," he said. "And thank people tomorrow. I'm a bit embarrassed that anyone brought gifts. Whatever they brought may be very different, and probably not everyone here brought something, so we didn't want to draw attention to them." He bent down close to my ear. "Maybe you can help me open them later, after the guests have gone home, or gone back to their rooms at Aurora."

"I think that could be arranged," I agreed.

The sun was going down, a sea breeze had come up, and although some guests stayed for an after-dinner drink, or another refill of champagne or something stronger after dessert had been finished, Marv Mason reminded everyone that work at the lighthouse would start shortly after dawn the next day. He was the first I noticed leaving the party. After that people started coming up to Patrick to wish him a happy birthday, thanking Skye for her hospitality and heading for their cars or trucks or their rooms at Aurora.

The caterers made swift work of cleaning up. As soon as all the guests had left, Patrick pulled a wagon from the gardening shed and we put all his gifts in it and headed for his carriage house. Patrick also tucked two bottles of chilled champagne in the wagon. I hoped he didn't think I could drink any more tonight, but they probably weren't for now. Patrick usually kept a bottle or two of champagne in his refrigerator. He was always prepared to celebrate.

Settled back in his living room Patrick opened his gifts, being careful to write down what everyone had given him so he could thank them tomorrow, either in person or by phone.

He'd been given several books on famous artists in New England, a recipe book, a book on Maine history, two cashmere sweaters, and one flannel shirt in blaze orange which he thought might be a joke. Patrick wasn't a hunter, although I reminded him that anyone walking near woods during hunting season should wear blaze orange. Ruth had somehow found time to bake him a box of cookies, and Gram had frozen two quarts of her lobster bisque that she knew Patrick loved. His mother had given him a check—he didn't tell me how large it was—and Sarah had framed a Winslow Homer wood engraving from the Gloucester series for him, as well as giving him the Hollywood Hills bowl.

He saved my little box for last. First he shook it, smiling. "It rattles," he announced. "Jewelry?"

I smiled and shook my head. "Just open it. Then I'll explain."

He opened it carefully, revealing two small rounded sea stones—one totally white, and one totally black. He look at me, confused. "Stones?"

"From Pocket Cove Beach," I explained. "There's an old Maine saying that if you hold one black stone and one white stone in your hand, close your eyes, and make a wish, then your wish will come true."

He carefully put the stones back in the box. "I'm going to save these for a special occasion," he promised, reaching down to kiss me. "Right now I don't need to wish for anything. I have everything I want right here."

Chapter 7

The occupations of drawing, music, or reading should be suspended on the entrance of morning visitors. If a lady, however, is engaged with light needlework, and none other is appropriate in the drawing-room, it may not be, under some circumstances, inconsistent with good breeding to quietly continue it during conversation, particularly if the visit be protracted, or the visitors be gentlemen.

—"In Receiving Morning Calls," *The Book of Household Management* by Isabella Beeton, 1861.

Patrick had set his alarm to wake us before dawn. I groaned and rolled over. But I had to go home, change, and feed Trixi, and Patrick had promised to drive several of his mother's guests down to the lighthouse so they could see the setting before any filming or recording took place. Haven Harbor Light seemed to be the place to be this morning.

It was another gorgeous Maine day. The production crew had been lucky so far. No matter where you were filming, weather couldn't be counted on, and sequential scenes needed to match, so matching clouds and light were essential. A lot could be done by computer editing, I'd been told, but still, weather seemed very important, especially to Marv and Flannery.

Yesterday Flannery had been back and forth between the Anderson house, where Sarah and I'd been, and the lighthouse, where the lighting and sound crews were working. I was curious to see what they'd arranged, and where they planned to film. I'd heard at least two scenes would be shot there, one in the earlier time period and one in the later. I didn't know who would be in either, although I could guess. But today was a day for recording background shots and cutaways, and recording surf and seagulls.

I wished I understood more about the whole process, but every day I learned something just by watching. That's why I wanted to be at the lighthouse this morning.

Ruth was still working on the script with Thomas and Marie. Not even the actors had full scripts, or knew how the movie would end.

That sounded pretty disorganized to me, but when I'd mentioned it to Patrick he'd shrugged and said it happened with a lot of films. One day at a time. "And I predict there will be a happy ending," he added.

He handed me a cup of coffee "to go, even if I don't want you to," and we shared a quick kiss before I headed my car for home. It had been a wonderful night, but we'd stayed up pretty late. At the time it had seemed perfect, but this morning I would have appreciated a few more hours of sleep.

At home, Trixi didn't hesitate to inform me that she needed to be fed. I reminded her that I'd fed her before I left the night before, but she didn't seem to care about my explanation. I filled her bowls with water, dry food, wet food, and, yes, a small piece of lobster as a treat. Then I headed for the shower. I suspected I still smelled of lobster myself.

I gave myself a little extra time; after all, I didn't think I'd be asked to do anything at the lighthouse. Sarah's and my work so far had been on interior sets. And the sun was still low.

I layered a T-shirt with a flannel shirt and jeans, and sneakers, since I'd be climbing over rocks even if I were just watching.

Tourists often climbed down these rocks to take pictures of the dramatic surf, and when I was growing up I'd had my favorite spots on the ledges to sit and think, or dream, or just be alone. Despite the rocks and ridges below the lighthouse having been fatal to several eighteenth- and nineteenth-century clipper ships, I loved the high layers of rocks that overlooked the sea. They'd been there centuries before I'd seen them, and would be memories for people centuries after I'd died. I loved the idea that places like this could span lifetimes, and take you back, or forward, into the lives of others.

As I pulled my car over to the side of the road at the foot of the cliffs I shivered as I remembered last year, when I'd sought out one of my special spots and found a body there. Some memories should be repressed.

But I was also realistic. Not all deaths near this point had been in earlier centuries. The lighthouse had been built to warn ships away from the rocks, but it wasn't only ships that had met their ends here. Unfortunately, despite warning signs, visitors to the Haven Harbor Lighthouse and its surroundings sometimes climbed down too close to incoming waves, and were washed to sea. If that happened even the strongest swimmers would be dashed against the rocks. That had probably been true when the Abenakis were the only humans who lived in this area, and it was true today.

Nature was stronger than humans, at so many times, in so many ways. When I was a teenager I'd once come down to the lighthouse right after a hurricane and seen giant waves rising above all the rocks, and crashing down on the lighthouse itself. I hadn't needed anyone to tell me the dangers of staying nearby.

This morning the ocean was at mid-tide and the rocks were already dotted with people and equipment. I hoped they were planning to film at low tide. The breakers weren't as dramatic then, and the rocks would still be damp and slippery from the tide that had just gone out, but, overall, it would be safer, for people and for the expensive equipment they'd brought. I didn't know much about cinematography or editing, but I assumed they could insert cuts of high surf or breakers later, when no one was in danger.

The technical crew and a group of actors were there in full force. Skye, Cos, Linc, Talia, and Jon were standing near the lighthouse, where a table had been set with coffee and doughnuts.

Several spotlights were already focused on the ledges, maybe to balance the rays of the sun, and a mic boom was in place. I assumed the mic was to record background sounds of the sea. I was pretty sure most films today used wireless microphones to record dialogue.

Leo and two other young members of the crew were trying to get another boom set up below the first one, closer to where the tide was hitting the rocks. They seemed to be having trouble. Leo certainly didn't have experience with either crashing surf or mics. I hoped the men with him, who I'd heard were from Portland, did.

Marv Mason must have been watching them, too. He headed in their direction, holding a paper cup of coffee, and lurching a bit as he climbed down the ledges. He wasn't wearing slip-proof shoes, or even sneakers. Not smart. Talia followed close behind him, taking pictures of the surf.

Marv was the director, the boss. He knew what he wanted out of today's work. Maybe he'd decided the boom and mic should be moved. Maybe he was intrigued by the challenges of filming on rocks near rough ocean. Maybe he was here in case any questions came up or decisions had to be made about what was recorded for the film. But why was Talia following him so closely? Another person that close to the equipment would just be in the way.

Then I saw Linc and Cos heading in their direction, too. At least they'd both grown up in Haven Harbor. They'd know the ledges, and which rocks wobbled, and which were safe to stand on. Maybe they were going to tell the others. I hoped so.

I couldn't hear what Marv was saying to the technicians setting up the boom as he headed in their direction. He slipped on the rocks twice, barely avoiding falls.

The crew started moving the equipment to another ledge, farther west. The boom was tipsy; the heavy top wobbled from side to side as the three men tried to adjust its legs. None of the men looked happy. Leo glanced at Marv, who was getting closer to them, clearly gesturing that they weren't doing what he wanted them to do. One of the men pointed to Flannery Sullivan, who was officially in charge of lighting, sound, and sets for this low-budget film. Leo hesitated, caught between two sets of directions. His hesitation threw the other men off balance and the tripod holding the boom wavered in the wind.

"Watch what you're doing!" Marv yelled loud enough so I could hear him from where I was standing, on ledges high above the others.

I hoped the legs of the tripod had rubber feet; the rocks they were trying to balance on were still dark. That meant they were wet and slippery from having been covered at high tide a couple of hours ago.

The light breezes we'd been feeling changed to gusts. Marv shouted something that was lost in the winds. The changing winds were making moving the boom or balancing it even more difficult. It wavered in the air above the men.

Cos and Linc had joined Talia, not far from Hank or the equipment. Maybe they'd warn Marv and the others about the dangers of getting too close to the water.

Why did they need the boom to be where it was in the first place? Making a movie was complicated; it involved so many moving parts. And people.

I watched in fascination, hoping someone in that group knew what they were doing.

Then, just as the three actors reached the equipment the whole contraption—metal legs and mic and boom—teetered and, as another gust of wind blew around the end of the peninsula, fell, almost gracefully, across several ledges, its end close to the water.

Leo quickly let go of his section of the tripod, and dodged to get out of the way. The other two men maneuvering the contraption did the same.

Someone above me, by the lighthouse, screamed. Then I saw why.

Without thinking, I reached for the gold angel on the necklace Mama had given me for my first communion. It was for luck, and I wore it most of the time.

Right now, Marv Mason was the one who needed luck.

Marv was no longer standing on the rocks. He hadn't been able to dodge out of the way, as the younger men had done. The falling boom had knocked him into the sea and his head and flailing arms were beneath the heavy waves crashing down on him.

Beyond him, beyond the breakers, a raft of eider ducks,

mothers and babies, swam peacefully, ignoring what was happening on the ledges and beneath the waters.

All over the cliffs surrounding the lighthouse everyone who had a cell phone was dialing 911. I didn't move. I knew what would happen. Someone at the Emergency Center in Haven Harbor would reach the Coast Guard and call the local police, like Pete, and the Marine Patrol (the "clam cops" as other police in Maine called them), whose job was checking waters closer to land than the Coast Guard, although the two organizations worked together in an emergency. Whoever was closest came to the rescue. If you included the islands, Maine had almost 3,500 miles of coastline, so the chances of having a rescue boat close by were slim to none.

I'd lived in Haven Harbor too long not to know two things. First, it would take minutes, possibly many minutes, for any rescue mission to begin. And, second, no one would be able to save Marv. The surf had already battered his body against the cliffs. No one could swim under those circumstances. The mission would be a recovery mission at best.

I began climbing up the rocks to the lighthouse. A woman I'd never seen was standing alone by the base of the light, sobbing.

Chapter 8

As this fair sampler shall continue still
The guide and model of my future skill
May Christ the great exemplar of mankind
Direct my ways and regulate my mind.

—Priscilla Dutch made this sampler, which
included several alphabets and a family record,
when she was eleven years old, in 1808, the
same year her mother died. Priscilla lived near
Ipswich, Massachusetts. In 1844 she married
widower Ebenezer Putnam and became the
mother to his thirteen children from an earlier
marriage.

From *Harbor Hopes*

Amy sat, slumped on the old green couch her par-
ents had bought at a yard sale when they were first
married. Now she was seventeen. She'd grown up
sitting on that couch.
"You're still a child," her father said, standing

over her, close enough so she could smell the oil and gasoline he'd been using today at Beaman's Shipbuilding, where he worked. "If your mother were still alive she'd tell you a girl your age is in no position to disobey her father."

"Well, Mother isn't here. And she liked Caleb. Remember how he came to the hospital and sat with me by her bed all those days? She told me I was lucky to have a friend like him."

"Ha! Caleb was in high school then. You weren't talking about ruining your life by marrying him. Your mother may have thought he was a nice kid, but that doesn't give you permission to stay out beyond curfew and make plans I don't approve."

"I was only ten minutes late! And it's summer. There's no school. I'll be on time for my job tomorrow."

"You'd better be. That money will help pay for your college, or trade school. I can't afford to pay for the education you'll need to support yourself." Mr. Wilde collapsed onto the faded overstuffed armchair opposite Amy. "The world is changing. Just because you're a girl doesn't mean you won't have to make a living. It's time you focused on your future."

"Caleb just inherited his grandfather's lobster boat. He'll make a living for both of us. And I'll get a job somewhere in town. Neither you nor Mother went to school after high school, and you did all right. You apprenticed at the boatyard, and Mother worked at the bakery after I was old enough to go to school."

"Your mother didn't need to work when you were little. I made enough for the three of us. I had a steady job, with benefits. Lobstering's dangerous, and undependable, and doesn't come with benefits.

Caleb's lucky to have a boat that big when he's just twenty, I agree. But it's forty years old, and will be needing a new engine soon, and that will run him big bucks. A good season's earnings. If you're going to be so stubborn and determined to marry early, you should at least look around for some young man who has a steadier future. Maybe someone like Marty—what's his name? Your friend Carol's brother. Everyone has to have a car or truck, and he's a good mechanic."

Amy wrinkled her nose. "Marty's a bore and smells of the automobile shop where he works or his dad's delicatessen. Caleb and I love each other, Dad. Didn't you and Mother love each other? Don't you remember what that's like?"

Her father leaned forward and raised his voice. "I loved your mother, and I miss her every day. Don't think I don't know what it's like to love someone. And I know what it's like to lose someone."

"I miss her, too," said Amy, her eyes filling.

"I know you do, honey. I didn't mean to imply you didn't. It's been wicked hard for both of us since the cancer got her. But that's why I want your future to be a solid one. I don't want you to spend your life in poverty, or worried about the next season, or being sorry you made a decision too early."

"I'll be all right, Dad. And I'll make a living without going to college or some trade school. I'm going to be a writer. You don't need a degree to be a writer."

Hank Stoddard had reached Leo and the two other men who'd been handling the stand holding the telescoping arm of the boom mic. He pushed Talia aside as he reached for the fallen equipment. Flannery joined the group.

Clearly they were all arguing, gesturing toward the water, while they tried to gather up the pieces of the equipment that had knocked Marv off the rocks.

Cos, Linc, and Talia were focused on the sea breaking over the spot where Marv had disappeared.

One of the technical support men pointed at Leo. Was he blaming Leo? The men kept glancing over their shoulders at the water, but there'd been no sign of Marv after the first seconds.

I shivered, imagining what was happening under the surf.

Cos, Linc, and Talia gravitated toward a ledge above those with the equipment, about halfway from the lighthouse to the churning sea. Perhaps they hoped Hank, the man producing this movie, would know what to do.

The director being knocked off the cliffs wasn't in the script.

No one was screaming anymore. The only sound was that of the breakers hitting the rocks and the occasional cry of a gull. The woman standing by the lighthouse had sunk to her knees, and was sobbing quietly. I was the only one who seemed to have noticed her. If she'd been from Haven Harbor I'd have recognized her. It was a small enough town so few people remained anonymous for long. But whoever she was, she was clearly in distress, and being ignored. How long had she been there?

Her crushed dress looked expensive and her disheveled hair was probably gray under her color treatments. Her three-inch heels were precarious at best on the ledges. She looked isolated and alone and mascara was running down her plump cheeks.

I couldn't help Marv. Maybe I could do something for her.

Who was she? How had she gotten here? The production company's security guards weren't letting anyone not connected to the movie into any of the areas where they were working.

"Can I help you?" I asked as I reached her. I asked again, "I'm Angie Curtis."

She turned to me, as though it was an effort for her to leave wherever her mind had been. She looked at me as though I were crazy. Then she shook her head. "Marv's gone," she managed to gasp.

"Yes," I said. So she knew who Marv was, and had seen him fall. I decided to be blunt. "These rocks are dangerous, especially when they're slippery, and the strong currents pull people under."

She pulled herself up and stood. Then she reached into her purse, dug out a pile of tissues, and began mopping her face. Her mascara blurred more, mixing with her foundation. "Maybe someone will find him. Save him."

"I grew up here in Haven Harbor. I know the waters. Where are you from?"

For the first time she looked at me as though she saw me. She got up from the ground and stood, still looking at the sea below us. "I'm June Mason. I grew up in Nebraska. Now I live in California."

"Mason?"

"I'm Marv's wife." She started crying again.

I put my arm around her and guided her to one of the granite benches the Haven Harbor Chamber of Commerce had set out so tourists visiting the lighthouse could sit and admire the breaking waves and view of the sea safely, without climbing on the rocks.

She went with me, but her eyes remained focused on the spot where Marv had disappeared.

In the background we could hear sirens. Police and fire and ambulance, I guessed. They wouldn't be able to do much. They wouldn't even be able to get their equipment close to the lighthouse, much less the rocks below it. All the film-related cars and trucks had filled the small parking lot below the lighthouse and lined the street leading up to it.

A few minutes later Sergeant Pete Lambert appeared, slightly out of breath from running up the hill from the parking lot. I was the first person he recognized. "Angie! What happened?"

"A gust of wind hit the tripod holding the boom mic. It fell, and knocked Marv Mason off the rocks into the water."

"Mason. He's the director, right?"

"Right." Before Pete could say anything else, I added, "This is his wife, June."

That information registered. Pete turned to June and said, "Sorry for your loss, Mrs. Mason. I'm with the local police here in Haven Harbor. We'll do our best to find your husband."

He cut himself short. He'd almost said "your husband's body."

Pete turned to me. "Any sign of him after he hit the water?"

I shook my head. "He went under right away and didn't come up."

"The nearest Coast Guard vessel is down the coast a few miles. But the Marine Patrol should be here any minute."

Firemen and EMT men and women were scrambling up the hill after Pete. This was not the first time they'd been called to a scene like this. They knew the drill. They also knew there probably wasn't much they could do.

They looked at the actors who'd gathered on the other side of the lighthouse and the men on the rocks trying to rescue the equipment. Pete gestured to several of the firemen. "A couple of you, get down there. See if you can get that contraption off the rocks before it knocks anyone else into the water," he directed.

They were all Haven Harbor men and women. They headed down the familiar ledges, and, to the clear relief of the men who were grabbing dented and possibly broken equipment, took over the equipment rescue operation. If they couldn't save Marv, at least they could save the equipment.

Pete had moved away from me and June to watch the operation. Unless there was a miracle and Marv emerged from the sea, there was nothing else he could do. Finding Marv's body would be up to the Marine Patrol. Sometimes bodies weren't found.

Pete came back to where I was standing.

"Who are all these people?" Pete asked me quietly. "Anyone else hurt? And what exactly happened?"

"No one else is hurt that I know of," I answered. "The guys down there"—I pointed toward where the sound equipment had been—"were the ones working with the boom when a gust of wind blew it down and it hit Marv. The people over by the lighthouse are actors. Some of them were nearby when the boom fell. Things were just getting started today. Not everyone who's usually on a set is here."

Where was Patrick, I wondered. He didn't have a formal role on the set, but he was usually close by and ready to help out, or run errands. Sarah wasn't here, either. I didn't remember whether she was coming today or not. I'd come out of curiosity: I'd never seen a movie filmed.

"You saw what happened?"

"I told you. They were trying to move the boom. A gust of wind blew it out of control and knocked Marv into the waves."

"Where was he standing?"

"On that streak of limestone leading toward the water," I said, pointing at a jagged ridge whose sides had been worn down by thousands of years of tides.

"In other words, too close to the water."

"Yes. But he didn't expect that boom to come crashing down," I said. "If it hadn't fallen he'd probably have been all right."

"And if President Lincoln hadn't gone to Ford's Theatre that night he wouldn't have been shot," Pete said grimly. "I've seen too many people over the years who've fallen off these ledges, or were washed away by a wave they didn't expect."

I agreed. "Most of the people here today don't know how dangerous it can be close to the waves, especially when the rocks are damp. And they are. You can see." The tide was going out, leaving rocks dark with sea water, tide pools hidden in crevices and indentations in the rocks, and treacherously slippery wet rockweed covering many of the rocks.

Pete nodded. Unfortunately, deaths in the waters surrounding the point were not unusual. Every two or three years someone who felt too confident about his or her footing climbed down near the surf, often with a camera in their hands, and didn't make it back. I'd even seen men fishing, casting their lines within feet of the tide and not paying attention to large waves coming toward them.

I went back to June Mason, who was still crying. "Can I get you anything? Maybe some water, or coffee?"

I'd just remembered the large cooler and container someone had lugged up to the lighthouse for those working on the set.

"Thank you, no," June sobbed. "I just want my husband."

Nothing I could say would bring him back.

"I flew all night to get here. Flew, and then took a bus and rented a car. This place is at the end of the world."

She'd gotten little sleep and arrived just in time to see her husband die. Definitely a nightmare scenario.

"Do you know any of the other people in the production company? Someone you might want to be with?" I asked. "Talk to?" I wanted to help, but I couldn't imagine anything I could do or say that would make a difference.

"I don't know any of those people well," she answered. "I don't usually come to movie sets."

"Why did you decide to come to this one?" I asked out of curiosity.

She fished in her purse, pulled out her cell phone, and turned it so I could see the picture she was showing me.

I recognized it immediately. It was a close-up of Marv Mason cozying up to Cos Curran, his hand on her back. It had been taken last night, at Patrick's birthday party, probably just before Linc had taken Cos's hand and led her away, leaving Marv to talk with Talia.

Linc had been taking pictures, I remembered. But, then, others had been, too. Cell phones had been everywhere. I didn't remember who was taking pictures of Marv or Cos. All I remembered was that when the platters of lobsters had been brought out, cell phone cameras were everywhere.

How had June gotten that picture? Had someone posted it on Instagram or Facebook? No wife would have appreciated the scene, or the leering expression on Hank's face. Or the words I just noticed under the photo: *Be smart. Get to Maine ASAP.*

"That was taken at a party last night. A party at Skye West's home," I said. "Who sent it to you?"

"I don't know," she said. "It was sent from an anonymous account. But I did as it suggested. I threw some clothes in a bag and got on a plane. I expected to confront Marv. It wouldn't have been the first time he'd had eyes for a young actress." She looked at me. "I assume that's who that young woman is? A young actress?"

"Yes. Cos Curran. She lives here in Haven Harbor. It's the first time she's ever acted," I said quietly. "Marv hired a number of local people to work both in front of and behind the cameras."

June watched as a Marine Patrol boat appeared by the point and idled its engine while the men on board leaned over the side, looking for Marv's body. "Marv told me he was staying with Skye West."

"Yes," I answered. "Along with Hank Stoddard and Flannery Sullivan and the O'Days, Talia Lincoln, and Jon Whyte."

Pete had directed the firemen and cinema men to put the equipment they'd just rescued next to the lighthouse.

"Leave everything here," he said. "No one touch it. And no one leave. I'll need statements from all of you."

"We're in the middle of trying to make a movie here," Hank explained, not quietly. "This is our equipment. We need to see if we can fix it, and then get on with our work. There's been a tragedy here today, but we still have to work."

The Marine Patrol boat was circling the area where Marv had disappeared beneath the waves, and where the currents might have taken him.

"I agree," said Pete. "A death is a tragedy. But until Marv Mason's death is officially ruled an accident, I need to know every detail about what happened. That means that for now I'm declaring this whole area a crime scene."

Leo looked scared. His past experiences with police had not all been positive. The other men just looked surprised.

"Of course it was an accident," said Hank. "We all know that. And they"—he gestured toward the Marine Patrol boat—"haven't even found his body. How could this be a crime scene?"

"Mason didn't just fall off the ledges," Pete explained. "He slipped, and he was knocked off."

Hank and Flannery looked at each other in disbelief. "Knocked off by equipment hit by wind," Hank said loudly. "Blame the wind if you want to. Go, arrest it. No one else was involved."

"That's what I have to verify," said Pete. "So just hang on and calm down. I heard there was coffee somewhere up here. I'll take statements as quickly as I can. I'll need to talk to everyone who was here when Mason was knocked into the water. And to you guys who went down to help with the equipment," he added to the firemen who'd been down on the rocks. He turned to Marv's wife. "And I'm sorry, but I'll need to talk to you, too, Mrs. Mason. You were here when it happened."

June Mason started sobbing again.

Pete moved slightly away and was already on his phone to his office. "Get the crime scene guys up to the light-house, stat. Have them bring a lot of tape. We have a large area to mark off."

"Maybe I'll have some of that coffee you mentioned," June said, tears still falling, as she walked slowly back to the bench where we'd been sitting. "Black."

I went and poured her a cup.

"Angie, did I hear you say Marv Mason was one of those staying out at Aurora, Skye West's house?" Pete asked.

I nodded.

"Then I'll need to have his room searched, too. Is Skye here?"

I pointed to the group of actors, some of whom were getting coffee.

"Fine," he said. "I'll need to speak with all of them."

I pulled him aside a bit. "Pete, why all the drama? It was an accident."

"And I'll need a statement from you, too, Angie," he

answered quietly. "I'm sorry. Under normal circumstances I wouldn't go through all this. But we've got a dead Hollywood director on our hands and some famous witnesses. The media will make a big deal of this. I don't want any questions as to how we handled it. I agree, right now it looks like an accident." He glanced at the men who'd been working with the boom. "A stupid accident caused by people who didn't know how to deal with these ledges. But I want to know for certain what happened to Marv Mason, and why."

Beyond him the Marine Patrol boat had stopped circling. Its engines were on neutral, and the officers were lowering a small skiff into the rough waters.

They must have seen Marv's body.

Chapter 9

On the breast of her gown, in fine red cloth,
surrounded with an elaborate embroidery
and fantastic flourishes of gold thread,
appeared the letter A.

—Nathaniel Hawthorne (1804–1864), Chapter II,
The Scarlet Letter.

Everyone on the shore watched with morbid interest as Hank's body was hooked and dragged into the skiff.

"What will they do with him?" June asked quietly. "I want to see him."

"The Marine Patrol will take his body down to the Haven Harbor Town Wharf," Pete explained. "Then he'll be taken to the medical examiner's office in Augusta for an official ruling on cause of death."

"Why is that necessary?" she asked. "We all saw. That boom hit him and knocked him into the water. He drowned."

"We won't know that for sure until we hear from the medical examiner," Pete said.

June sank down on the granite bench.

"Why don't I start by questioning you?" he said. "Then

you'll be free to go to wherever you're staying and get something to eat, and rest."

She nodded, and looked at me. "Can Angie stay with me while you're asking questions? I'm alone. I have no friends here." She reached into her purse, pulled out a small bottle, and swallowed a couple of pills with a sip of her coffee.

I would have thought the director's wife would know a few of the Hollywood people on the set. But maybe she thought of them as business associates of her husband, not her friends.

Pete looked at her questioningly. "Are you all right?"

"Of course not. My husband just died. Those pills were to help me relax and deal with your questions, and anything else I'm expected to do here when all I want to do is be alone and mourn."

I sat next to her and patted her arm gently. "It's all right. Pete's questions won't take long. Will they, Pete?" I looked up at him.

"I'll do my best to keep this as painless as possible," he answered. "Mrs. Mason. Your first name is June?"

She nodded.

"And your address?"

She gave him a street address in Beverly Hills.

"And your cell phone number."

"It's private," she protested.

"Not from the police," he said.

She gave it to him.

"And when did you come to Haven Harbor?"

"Pete, she just got here. She's been traveling all night," I answered for her. "She's exhausted and probably in shock." She did look very pale. "Maybe I should take her to the emergency room."

"I'm fine, dear. That won't be necessary. Let Sergeant Lambert get on with his questions.

"I assume you flew into the Portland Jetport," he said. "Did you rent a car there?"

"I did."

"Could you give me the license plate number and description of the car?"

She pulled some papers from her purse, probably the rental agreement, and gave him the information he'd asked for.

"And you drove this car to the lighthouse this morning?"

"I certainly didn't walk! The car is parked on the street, down the hill," June said, gesturing. "Is all this really necessary?"

"I'm afraid so," said Pete. "And when did you get here, to the lighthouse?"

She glanced at her phone. "I didn't clock myself in. I'd say about nine fifteen."

It was now an hour after that.

"And who was here when you got here?"

"My husband was down on those rocks." She pointed at a place close to where he'd been when he'd been knocked off the ledge. "He was talking to some young men, I assume about the equipment they were setting up. I don't think he saw me."

"Anyone else here?"

"This young woman was standing on the rocks below here. She was by herself. I don't know why she was here. And several people were standing on rocks close to the other side of the lighthouse. I think I recognized Skye West, and maybe Talia Lincoln. I didn't know anyone else."

He nodded. "Then what happened?"

"Hank Stoddard was yelling at my husband and the

men he was with. I couldn't hear what he said. That surf is really noisy. Does it ever quiet down here?"

"Not really, Mrs. Mason," Pete said, smiling. "You didn't mention Hank Stoddard before."

"Oh. Well, he was there, with Flannery Sullivan, higher up on the rocks."

She hadn't mentioned Flannery before, either. Pete was making notes.

"So you knew and recognized both those men."

"They work with my husband sometimes. They're not close friends. They're business acquaintances."

"And what happened then?"

"The men with Marv and the equipment seemed to be trying to move it. I think the young man in the red T-shirt wasn't sure what to do—he was looking toward the other men and seemed to be following what they said to do."

The young man in the red shirt was Leo. And June was right. He didn't know anything about lighting or sound so far as I knew. He was just filling in where he was needed.

"So they were all trying to move the equipment from where to where?" asked Pete.

"From on top of that ledge"—she pointed—"over to the next one, closer to the water. I don't know for sure. But that's the way it looked."

"Your husband was the director of this film, right?"

She nodded.

"Do you normally go to the place where a film is being made, and onto the set?"

June hesitated. "Not often. Sometimes. I'd never been to Maine and I wanted to see it. Marv was enjoying his time here. He thought Maine was beautiful. And Skye West has been a friend of his for a long time. I think he decided to direct this film primarily because she was going to be in it."

"She was his friend? Was she yours, too?"

"I knew her, of course. But I didn't work with her, the way he did."

I wondered for a moment about her use of the word "work." But, after all, life was different in Hollywood. Although based on what she'd told me earlier, she'd come here because of a picture she'd received on e-mail. She'd been concerned that her husband was with Cos, who was probably forty years younger than Skye. I didn't stop to do the math, but although it made sense that Skye and Marv could have been a couple at some time, if he had a preference for younger women, Skye wouldn't be on his list now.

"Hank yelled something at them all. I think he wanted them to move the equipment somewhere else. It all happened so fast." June shook her head. "Then a gust of wind hit the boom, and knocked everything down. The men tried to keep it up, but the tripod fell. Marv reached for it, to steady it, I guess. Instead he slipped on the rocks and fell into the water." She'd started to cry again. "I think his arm came up once, but then, he was gone."

"Thank you for your patience, Mrs. Mason. If we have any more questions, I'll be in touch with you. And I'll let you know as soon as you can have your husband's body." He handed her his card and closed his notebook. "Angie, since you're here, why don't I talk with you next."

June had already started walking down the path to the parking lot, and then the street. The others waiting to be questioned were clustered around the table that held the coffee, if there was any left, and several boxes of Dunkin' Donuts.

"So, when did you get here, and why?" Pete asked. "I thought you and Sarah were just working on the inside sets. She's over at Ted Lawrence's this morning."

I felt as though the principal had caught me playing hooky. He and Sarah were dating, so of course he'd know where she was and what she was doing. "Right. Sarah and

I are doing the interior sets. But I was curious about the production, so I came over here this morning to watch. I'm going to Ted's as soon as I've answered your questions."

"I think I can skip the basics about name, address, and phone number," he said wryly. "So when did you get here?"

"About eight o'clock," I said. "Maybe a little later."

"And who was here then, and what were they doing?"

"Everyone who's here now was here then, except for Marv's wife. The three young men were putting up the equipment on the rocks, and the actors and Marv, Flannery, and Hank were up by the lighthouse, drinking coffee and eating doughnuts."

"So no one was with the three guys putting up the equipment?"

"No. Not until right before everything started to go wrong. Then it was what June told you," I confirmed. "Cos, Linc, and Talia Lincoln were down near the equipment, too. Talia was taking pictures."

"I thought their job was acting, not technical setups," he questioned.

I shrugged. "True. They didn't stay there long. I thought Cos and Linc had gone down to warn the technicians about how the rocks were slippery. Then Marv fell, and all three actors went back up toward the lighthouse."

"Rocks are slippery, for sure. Treacherous and fatal," Pete agreed. "To be official, that's Linc Fitch, right? And Cos Curran."

I nodded. "Right. Linc plays opposite Cos in the nineteen-sixties part of the movie, and they're an off-camera item too these days. They were together at Skye's birthday party for Patrick last night."

"Sorry I couldn't get there," Pete acknowledged. "But with all these extra people in town, along with the usual summer visitors, our force is stretched pretty thin."

"Do you really think Marv's fall was anything other than an accident?" I asked. "It certainly looked as though he reached for the boom and it knocked him over."

"That's probably what happened," Pete agreed. "But in case anything else was involved, I don't want people thinking I gave the visiting celebrities a pass. A death during a production isn't the kind of publicity Haven Harbor needs."

I looked out at where the Marine Patrol had been. They'd raised the skiff, attached it to the side of the boat, and it and Marv Mason's body had gone around the point toward the harbor. "I wonder if his death will mean the movie funding drops, or if the movie is cancelled."

"Interesting point," Pete acknowledged. "If someone dies unexpectedly we look for someone who might benefit from the death. Certainly the movie losing funding wouldn't be a benefit to anyone. Of course, the movie might be insured. I don't know anything about that sort of thing."

"I don't either," I said. I could imagine scenarios when someone wanted to stop a production to punish one of those involved, or free them up for another gig.

But chances were Marv's death was accidental. No one would benefit financially from his death except maybe his poor wife.

"So you have nothing more to add?" Pete asked.

"I don't think so," I said. "But if I hear any talk or gossip I'll let you know."

"I'll bet you will," Pete said, grinning. "You always do seem to be around when there's an unusual death in town."

I shrugged. "Sometimes I can talk to people who won't talk to the police. Or put pieces of a puzzle together that don't fit neatly."

"Indeed," Pete said. "And in this case, I know you're tight with Patrick and Skye. But don't get involved with whatever is happening here. These aren't our people, Angie. They're from away. They see things differently."

"They're not filming a detective story," I teased, as we headed together to where I would take the path down to the road and Pete would go to question the others.

"Let's make sure they're not," he agreed seriously.

Chapter 10

They who are moderate in their expectations
Meet with few disappointments.
The eager and presumptuous are continually
disappointed—
Virtue and good behavior are naturally
productive of good fortune.

—Silk and linen sampler stitched by Mabella
Jane Dobson of Chesterfield (Derbyshire, England)
dated June 14, 1833. Mabella included birds, deer,
and flowers within her border of vines.

As I walked toward my car I called Sarah. Had she heard about Marv?

Of course she had. Everyone had cell phones, and word of his accident had gone out within seconds of his fall.

"I've got the living room set up at Ted's. We were waiting for Talia and Skye to come and rehearse that opening scene again," she said. "I'm not sure what's going to happen now."

"Would they rehearse without a director? And Talia and Skye have to stay here until Pete questions them," I told her. "I'm just leaving now. So far he's only talked with Marv's wife and me."

"Marv's wife?" asked Sarah. "I haven't heard anything about her. Isn't she on the West Coast, or wherever they live?"

"She was," I agreed. "But she was at the lighthouse this morning. She saw what happened to Marv. She said she'd flown in overnight."

"Why?" Sarah asked. "Hank and the rest of the production people are working long hours. I wouldn't think they'd have time to entertain relatives. Not even wives."

"I don't know, Sarah. So many things are happening. Pete's just making sure everything is done right, so no one will question that Marv had an accident. I suspect his wife and the actors won't be high on Pete's interview list, so that shouldn't take long. Meet me at the Harbor Haunts Café for a quick early lunch?"

She hesitated a moment and then agreed. "I'll let people here know where I'll be. If I'm needed they can reach me easily enough. Everything's pretty much set up."

"See you downtown in a few minutes," I said, climbing into my car. Right now I didn't feel like dealing with any of the movie types. I kept thinking of June Mason. Where had she gone?

Maybe I should have suggested she come home with me. I had two extra bedrooms. Most places to stay in town were full, between July vacationers and people connected with *Harbor Heartbreak.*

I shuddered. What a horrible situation.

The Harbor Haunts Café was open all year round, but in the winter it was simple to stop in. You could always find an empty table. In July, the place was crowded. But it was still late morning, before most people were thinking about lunch. I found Sarah and me a table near the windows, with a view of summer crowds filling the

Haven Harbor streets, and ordered a glass of pinot noir. It was early for a drink, but Marv Mason was dead. Nothing to celebrate, but at least to acknowledge.

I'd finished half my glass before Sarah joined me.

"Everyone's talking about Marv. I don't think much will be done today," she said, calling the waitress over and ordering a glass of wine for herself. "What was it like at the lighthouse? You saw it all."

"I did. But there wasn't much to see. It all happened so fast. Marv went down on the ledges, I assume to advise the technicians how to adjust the boom. Leo was one of those trying to set it up. I was nervous as Marv headed down to where the equipment was. He was unsteady. He wasn't even wearing the right shoes for climbing on the rocks. The wind picked up and knocked the boom toward him, and he fell."

"Horrible," said Sarah. "I hardly knew him. I just saw him wandering around the sets at the Anderson house and last night at Patrick's party. But what an awful way to die."

I nodded. "Pete is treating it as a possible homicide," I added.

"Why? It certainly sounds like an accident." Sarah took a sip of her wine and picked up the menu.

"I think so, too. I think he's being overly cautious because of who Marv is—was—and the other Hollywood types who were there."

"Probably," Sarah agreed. "He won't say anything official until he gets the postmortem from the medical examiner's office in Augusta. I assume that's where they took Marv?"

"That was the plan. The Marine Patrol picked up his body, and were headed for the town wharf the last time I saw them."

We both looked down toward the harbor.

"We should order," said Sarah. "I know not much will

probably happen today. Marv had wanted to run through the opening scene again with Talia and Skye. I don't think that will happen now."

"They were all at the lighthouse," I pointed out, picking up a menu. "Pete was going to question everyone before releasing them."

"Patrick dropped them off there this morning," said Sarah. "When I headed here he was planning to go back to the light to bring anyone who needed a ride either to Aurora or to the Lawrences' house."

Yesterday Marv was going to ask for script revisions. Who knew what would happen now?

"I wonder how long it will take for Pete to get the medical examiner's report," I said. "Marv's wife was anxious about that."

"I still can't figure why she's in Maine."

"Remember last night, when lots of people were taking pictures? Someone sent June a picture of Marv and Cos with a note that she ought to come to Haven Harbor. She told me she'd come immediately."

Sarah frowned. "Marv's a pain. He pinched me twice, and I'm no ingenue. But his wife dropped everything and got on a plane? That reaction sounds a bit extreme."

I shrugged. "That's what she said. Maybe she and Marv have had problems before."

"Well, I hope Cos doesn't have any problems with him. She's so young, and excited about this opportunity to act in a movie."

"Cos will probably be okay," I assured both of us. "She coped with her boss at the bookstore who was harassing her this spring. And she has Linc looking out for her, too, of course."

The waitress had come back to our table. "I'll have the crab cakes," Sarah said.

"And a bowl of clam chowder for me," I added, handing my menu back to the waitress and turning back to Sarah. "I'd like to see the opening scene again. We know a little about the nineteen-sixties setting and story, but I don't know much about the contemporary one. Have you heard anything?"

"Not really. Some parts of the film are supposed to parallel each other. And I overheard Skye telling Talia the script was being delayed because Ruth wrote the first part, but Thomas and Marie were writing the second part, and Ruth wasn't happy about how they were handling it, so they weren't ready to start filming. Or even to have serious rehearsals."

I nodded. "I had a feeling that might be true. A few days ago Patrick said things were a bit tense in the writers' room. You sat with Ruth last night, right? Did she say anything?"

"Not much. Just that she'd written fiction, and Marie kept asking her 'what really happened?' It was driving her a bit crazy, I think. Your gram was sympathetic. She knows more than we do about the history of the story, but she kept saying it didn't matter. No one would remember."

"Ruth looked tired last night," I said. "Maybe all those hours she's spending in the writers' room are a bit much for her."

"The room we called the solarium, right?" Sarah said. "She did look tired. Maybe you and I should take her out for dinner one day."

"Or, better, take dinner to her house. I suspect she's tired of being out in the world with a lot of people. She once told me she liked being a writer because she could hide out in silence when she needed to."

"Which definitely isn't happening now," Sarah agreed, as our lunches were put in front of us. "How's Patrick doing? He's another one who prefers small gatherings to mob scenes, and he's been in the middle of all this since his mother came back to town. I assume you got to spend a bit of quality time with him last night, after the party."

"True enough," I said quietly, smiling. "But we didn't talk about the production. Why don't I call Ruth after lunch and see if she'd like company for dinner at her house tonight? I could get something boxed up."

"Excellent plan," said Sarah. "I assume she'll be at Aurora this afternoon, unless someone decides to do a run-through despite everything else and they need the writers."

"It usually takes at least twenty-four to forty-eight hours for the medical examiner to come up with a report for the police. So I assume the production will go on in the meantime."

"Without a director?"

Sarah shrugged. "I guess they could read lines to each other. If they have approved lines to read. In any case, I think I should get back to the Andersons' and see if any of the cast showed up there."

"I'll meet you there in half an hour," I agreed. "In the meantime I'll see if Ruth is free tonight."

"Agreed," Sarah, said, nodding and gesturing for their checks. "I hope Ruth agrees. It will be good to get her away from everyone at Aurora. They'll just be talking about Hank's death and wondering who will be the new director. Changes to the script won't be their top priority."

Chapter 11

And they made coats of fine linen of woven work for Aaron, and for his sons, and a mitre of fine linen and goodly bonnets of fine linen and linen breeches of fine twisted linen, and a girdle of fine twined linen and blue, and purple, and scarlet, of needlework, as the Lord commanded Moses.

—Exodus 39: 27–29, *The Holy Bible*, Authorized King James version.

From *Harbor Hopes*

"Marty's going to be disappointed you can't come to the movies with us tonight," Carol said. "I think he has a bit of a crush on you, Amy!"

"He's crazy, then," said Joan, shaking her head. "Amy's taken, for sure. Right, Amy? I mean, I know your dad complains, but you've been with Caleb since you were about five."

"True enough," Amy said, laughing.

"Why can't you come?" asked Carol.

"Caleb's painting the inside of his boat, and I promised to bring him sandwiches and help out. Besides, The Parent Trap *isn't exactly his kind of movie."*

"It's a little young for all of us," Joan agreed. "But they're showing it for free in the high school auditorium, so why not? There's not much to do in Haven Harbor in the summer."

"I'll bet you'll buy popcorn," said Carol. "The pep squad will be selling it."

"What's better than popcorn at a movie," Joan agreed. "And it's supporting the school, too."

"How'd you talk Marty into going with you?" Amy asked out of curiosity.

"You mean, how did I talk him into changing his mind and joining us when he found out you weren't coming too?" said Carol. "I'd already gotten him to agree to take all of us. He has a car, after all. That's something even Caleb doesn't have."

"No. But Caleb has a boat," said Amy. "A truck is next on his list."

"Not an engagement ring?" Carol teased.

"We don't need a ring to show the world how we feel," said Amy. "And we're not going to have a big wedding. Just a few friends and family."

"Family? You mean, your dad will come?"

"I mean he'll be invited," said Amy. "And it won't be until after I graduate next spring."

"A June wedding? How romantic!" said Joan.

"Maybe by then Dad will understand, and change his mind about Caleb," Amy said. "That's what we're hoping. Caleb's family is fine with it all. They've said we can convert part of their barn this winter and make a little apartment there."

"You really sound serious," said Joan.

*"Wicked serious, for sure. So you tell Marty he'll
have to find another girl to have a crush on. I'm
taken," Amy said, and laughed again.*

"Ruth? Angie. Sarah and I wondered if we could pick
you up at Aurora this afternoon, take you home, and have
dinner for you at your house."

Ruth hesitated, and her voice was soft. "That's kind of
you both. I'm dreadfully tired, though. This whole production is a strain. I'm afraid I wouldn't be very good
company."

"We just want you to see other people than Thomas
and Marie," I assured her. "And we promise not to stay
long. Is there anything I can get for you at the store besides dinner?"

"No. I'm all right. I've been eating at Aurora all week.
My pantry is fine. If you're sure about tonight, why don't
you and Sarah pick me up a little after five o'clock? If
we're not finished working by then, I'll just say I'm an old
lady and need to go home and rest." She paused. "Which
will be the truth."

"We'll see you then," I promised.

Luckily, the best deli in Haven Harbor was near the
patisserie, and I was able to pick up a quart of shrimp
bisque and three baguettes, plus three éclairs (my personal
favorites). On a hot night that would be simple, easy to
eat, and the only preparation would be heating the bisque.
I put everything in the cooler I leave in my car for such oc-
casions and headed to the Anderson estate to see if Sarah
or Flannery needed any help with the afternoon's rehearsals, or even if there were going to be any.

Sarah greeted me at the kitchen door. "Most of the crew
and the actors are still over at the lighthouse," she explained.
"I don't think there'll be a rehearsal this afternoon."

I glanced at my phone. "It's after two. We had lunch, I

got food for dinner, and Pete's still holding on to everyone down there?"

She shrugged. "I texted him once, but he just answered, 'Busy. Lunch ordered. Ethan on way.' Of course, I knew he was busy. And—'lunch ordered'? Maybe people were beginning to complain. At least it's a beautiful day. Maybe they're waiting for everyone to be questioned before they let anyone leave. And Hank is there, so if the producer can't get away, no one else really has much to do. There's no director at the moment."

"I guess," I said, glancing around the Lawrence kitchen, which was full of coolers of water and large carafes of coffee and tea, all pretty much untouched today. "I told Ruth we'd pick her up at about five o'clock at Aurora. She sounded tired and stressed. I promised her it wouldn't be a late night." Then what Sarah had said connected. "Pete said Ethan was on his way?"

"I know. It made me wonder, too."

Ethan Trask was a state homicide detective. He was only called in when a death was ruled a homicide, or when that outcome was likely. Marv's death had certainly looked accidental. What did Pete know, or suspect, that I didn't?

My phone buzzed. "Hi, Gram. Sorry we hardly got a chance to talk last night at the party," I said. "Sarah and I are taking some food over to Ruth's tonight. We thought she might need some time off from the Hollywood types."

"Lots of tension on the set?"

"More than you might think. This morning Marv Mason fell off the ledges at the lighthouse."

"Oh, no! He's the director, right?"

"Right."

"Too many accidents happen down there," said Gram. "I know it's a beautiful spot and people like to climb on the rocks, but I've often wondered why someone doesn't put up a fence, or some other barrier, to keep people from getting too close to the ocean. That must be very upsetting to everyone working on the movie."

"It is. Was," I said. "Even his wife was there at the time. She saw everything."

"His wife? What was she doing there? Was she at the party last night?"

"She'd just flown in from the coast. She wasn't at Patrick's birthday party."

"At least I assume Ruth wasn't there at the lighthouse."

"She was at Aurora with Marie and Thomas, working on the script."

"My Tom will be stuck at the church until late tonight. Would you mind if I joined you and Sarah and Ruth? I know I saw her last night, but there were so many other people around we hardly had a chance to chat. And I've been a little concerned about this script she's working on, and how it's affecting her."

"You'd be welcome to join us. I'm going to pick Ruth up at five. I think I have enough bisque, but I only bought baguettes and éclairs for three."

"I'll bring some bread and dessert to supplement that, then, if you don't mind my barging in."

"You're always welcome, Gram," I put in. "See you later."

Sarah smiled. "I'm assuming your gram is joining us for dinner."

"She is," I said. "You heard; I told her about Marv. But she also said she's been concerned about the script. Why would Gram be concerned about the script?"

"I have no idea. But I suspect we'll find out tonight," Sarah said. "Since we seem to have a little extra time, I think I'll do some errands. Do you mind getting Ruth yourself? I'll meet you all at her house a little past five."

"Sounds good to me," I said. "And, honestly, I think I'll go home, check in with Trixi, collect any e-mails we've had for Mainely Needlepoint, and maybe even take a nap. Between the heat and all we've been doing, I could use some time off, too."

Chapter 12

Attend ye Fair to Wisdom's voice
And happiness shall crown your Choice
See virtue and her Sacred charms
Will prove a shield against death's alarms.

—Hannah Davis of Roxbury, Massachusetts,
age fifteen, included a full scene of houses
along a riverbank, men fishing, and a wide
border of flowers in her sampler, dated 1805.

I got to Aurora a few minutes before five. Pete must have
released everyone who'd been at the lighthouse. The driveway was full of cars and security was in full force. One
television truck was parked outside the gate. Not surprisingly with so many people using cell phones, the media
knew about Marv.

I knocked on the door, and, to my surprise, Patrick answered. "Angie! What are you doing here?" He ran his
hand through his hair the way he did when he was frazzled.

"I'm here to pick up Ruth," I explained. "What's happening? I know about Marv. I was at the lighthouse this morning."

"Right. The world seems to know about Marv now.
Everyone's phones have been ringing, and one reporter

even climbed over the wall and knocked on the door. When I heard your knock I was hoping it wasn't him again."

"Not to worry. Just me," I said. "I heard Pete called in Ethan. Have they gotten the postmortem yet?"

"Not yet. I don't think they were able to get Hank's body to Augusta to the medical examiner until early afternoon. But everyone's upset, of course."

"They all knew Marv well," I sympathized.

"Actually, no. Most of them didn't know him well. Mom did, of course, and Hank, but not all of the others. What they're upset about is wondering whether the filming will go on."

"It's hardly started," I said. "Haven't they just been doing background shots?"

"Exactly. And no one seems to know what the contracts say about if the director dies during the production." He sighed. "Sorry, come on in. I'm glad you came for Ruth. At least one person can get away from the craziness here." He pointed down the hall to the solarium, just past the kitchen. "She's with Thomas and Marie. So far they've managed to stay away from everyone who's calling their agents and *Entertainment Tonight.*"

Thomas and Marie might have been away from the others, but they looked worn and frazzled, too. Ruth looked pale and tired. "Good, Angie. You're here." She stood carefully, holding onto the glass-topped table. "Would you help me get myself and my walker to your car?"

"Of course," I said, as she leaned on her pink wheeling walker.

"Thomas, Marie, I'm going home for the night. I'll be back in the morning unless you call to say that won't be necessary."

Marie nodded. "We've had a series of long days. I think Thomas and I will take the night off, too. Maybe by tomorrow we'll know more about how the movie will be affected by Marv's death."

"And rule out this murder possibility that's got everyone on edge," Thomas agreed. "How the police could imagine Marv was murdered when a dozen people saw him knocked off a ledge is beyond me."

"But clearly not beyond the local police," Marie added. "That sergeant was even here this afternoon to talk with us, and we were miles away when it all happened."

"Deus ex machina," said Thomas, shrugging. "I don't know what's happening. Sorry we don't have a place to escape to. Enjoy your evening, Ruth."

"I plan to," she answered. "And I plan to make it an early evening."

I put my arm around her and guided her toward the door. She seemed weaker than usual, and unsteady. "My car isn't far."

"Good. I just want to get away from this place," she said. "It's been a rough week, but this afternoon was especially difficult. People in and out, tears, yelling, Hank telling us to ignore everything and get back to work. He and Marv haven't been happy with anything we've written. I keep wondering why I agreed to do this."

I held on to both Ruth and her walker. "Money, as I recall," I reminded her. "The same reason all of us are involved in this movie."

"Ah, yes, of course," she agreed.

Patrick came to open the front door for us, helped Ruth down the granite step to the circular drive, and went and opened my car door for her.

"Thank you, Patrick," I said quietly. "Why don't you call me later? Ruth needs an early evening, and that doesn't sound bad to me, either, so I'll probably be home by nine o'clock or so."

He nodded. "I'll see how chaotic it gets here. I keep

hoping all will simmer down after everyone's had a drink or two. Right now that's a work in progress."

We'd gotten Ruth and her walker settled when she said, "Oh, Angie! I'm sorry. But I was so anxious to get out of there I left my purse back in the solarium. Would you mind going to get it for me? My medications are in there. I don't need my arthritis to get any worse than it already is."

"No problem. I'll be right back," I said. "You relax."

Patrick had already gone back in the house.

I went through the kitchen, but stopped when I heard Marie's voice. What harm was a little eavesdropping, especially when everyone seemed so uptight.

"Thomas, I'll admit I'm conflicted. Do we follow the script exactly, as Ruth wants? After all, she wrote the first draft. But Marv said he needed more to work with in those nineteen-sixties scenes, especially since he's chosen to cast both Amy and Caleb with local kids. The brief scenes we have now don't show how in love Amy and Caleb are, or how long they've loved each other, or how supportive Caleb was when Amy's mother died. Those details are in Ruth's original manuscript, but not in our script. And unless we use a voice-over, which no one wants, all those details will be lost, and the audience may not be pulled into the story the way they should be. We need more of Marty's role in all this, too. He's hardly mentioned, and he's Caleb's rival, at least in his own eyes. And what about those changes Talia's been suggesting?"

Thomas sighed. "You're right. I wish we'd been able to get all this worked out before we came to Maine. Haven Harbor's a wonderful little town—not that we've seen much of it—but Marv only had permission from the chamber of commerce to film downtown for a couple of days. A couple of days there, a couple at the lighthouse. And one of those days was pretty well lost today. The rest of the film we'll either have to fake, or film at the Anderson house."

"At least there's a beach there, and a small wharf. Plus the outside, and the barn, and the rooms inside."

"Flannery's over there now, checking out other possible locations on the property."

"Good. If he's doing that he won't be bothering us. Despite all the glass and the view of the harbor, I'm getting claustrophobia in this little room. Especially with Ruth debating everything we try to do."

"You're right. We have enough people bothering us with Hank and the actors staying here. At least the two kids live in town. They seem oblivious to all the script issues, and that's just as well."

Marie got up and went to look out the large window overlooking the back field. I moved farther toward the kitchen wall, hoping she wouldn't notice me.

"Talia's being a pain, too. Wants more lines, as always, and as far as I can tell, she hasn't talked to Marv about her concerns. She comes to me directly. She's even got ideas about changes to the script in the sections she's not in. She thinks she can write better than we can. Any vibes from her or Patrick yet? If I'd been Skye I'd have suggested she stay down at the Wild Rose Inn with some of the others."

Thomas shrugged. "I doubt Skye even thought about it Talia and Patrick broke up, when? Two years ago? I don't think they've been in touch since then."

"A lot has happened in that two years. Including his involvement with that local girl, Angie."

"Who Flannery hired, along with her friend, Sarah, to help with the inside locations. Make sure they looked authentic."

"I suspect that was Skye's idea," Marie suggested. "Keep Angie busy and away from both Patrick and Talia."

"Whatever. What we have to do is make that scene work," Thomas said, picking up the pages on the table.

"Maybe we need to include a scene with Amy's father earlier in the script."

"He could be talking with Marty," Marie said, joining him back at the table. "That way we could get in more information about that conflict. Although now, with Marv gone, maybe we don't have to make as many changes."

Neither of them said anything for a moment or two, so I took advantage of the situation to enter the room. "Ruth forgot her purse," I said, hoping my cheeks weren't too red from what I'd overheard. I picked up the purse and fled.

Could Skye really have invented jobs for Sarah and me just to keep us away from Talia and Patrick? I hadn't sensed any problem with Patrick, and although I wasn't thrilled with Talia, I'd never seen her do anything I could really object to. I was probably jealous, I admitted to myself, and I needed to get over that.

In the meantime, I understood why Ruth was upset. It sounded as though there were serious script conflicts.

I couldn't wait to hear her side of the story.

Chapter 13

*He would have left quite lost . . . if, every little while,
he had not been conscious of a gentle twitch at the
silken cord. Then he knew that the tender-hearted
Ariadne was still holding the other end . . . and giving
him just as much of her sympathy as if she were close
by his side.*

—"The Minotaur" in *Tanglewood Tales* by Nathaniel
Hawthorne (1804–1864), published in 1853.

Gram and Sarah arrived at Ruth's home at almost the
same moment as Ruth and I. Sarah helped Ruth, who
looked even more exhausted now that she was able to
escape the tensions of that solarium at Aurora, while
Gram opened the house door and I carried in the food I'd
bought.

Gram had made a tomato and basil salad to go with the
bisque, and bought lemon sorbet for dessert, so we had
plenty of food. I heated the bisque while she set Ruth's
table and Sarah poured small glasses of wine for each of
us. Ruth didn't usually drink much, but tonight she didn't
object. Within fifteen minutes dinner was on the table.

"So, what is it like to be a Hollywood screenwriter?" Gram asked, only half joking.

"Between us," Ruth said, "I'm not sure I should have gotten into all this. Not just because my story's being changed. I expected that. But because my agent insisted I also be a 'consultant,' so I'd be paid more. But that means I'm being asked questions I'm not comfortable answering about the town, and the people in it."

"Like what?" Sarah asked, sipping her wine while her bisque cooled a bit.

"Thomas and Marie have the idea that Haven Harbor is a sort of Peyton Place. You know, a small New England town where everyone has secrets and is good at burying them."

"'Secrets is a daily word/Yet does not exist—/Muffled—it remits surmise—/Murmured—it has ceased—/Dungeoned in the Human Breast/Doubtless secrets lie,'" Sarah said quietly, quoting Emily.

"They keep wanting to add more sex and more violence. I don't mind watching a movie like that, or reading a book. But I wrote *Harbor Hopes* before I learned I could make more money writing erotica. Sex isn't a part of that story. There's love, of course, and a death. Caleb, the character Linc plays, drowns."

"But his death isn't accidental, right?" I asked. "Wasn't his lobster boat sabotaged?"

"It may have been," Ruth said, turning to me. She paused and took a bite of her baguette before she said, "I always believed it was, so the character of Amy does, too."

"So the story is based on something that really happened here in Haven Harbor," Sarah said. "I didn't know that." She glanced at me. "Although I suspected it might be."

Ruth sighed. "The core of my original story was set here in town. Some people in Haven Harbor will know that. But it all took place so long ago not many people still alive would remember it, although they might have heard rumors, or versions of the story. I don't know what they'll think when they see how this all turns out on the screen."

"It's just the nineteen-sixties part of the movie that's based on your book, right?" I said. "The contemporary story, based on descendants of the original characters, is all fictional."

"Right. And that's the part with the happy ending. But now I'm involved with it all. Of course, theoretically the whole movie is fictional," she said seriously. "I wrote a story. Not a history of the town. But the original story was one of the first I wrote, so I borrowed from what I knew."

Ruth had said she'd written the story in her pre-erotica day, and so far I hadn't seen any rehearsals that hinted at more sex than a few kisses. Certainly, no sex scenes. On the other hand, what had Ruth borrowed from what she knew?

"I went back and read your original book," Gram said. "Of course, it takes place before I was born."

"My young grandmother," I put in, as we all laughed. Gram was over sixty, but Ruth was fifteen years older.

"I do remember hearing stories, though," Gram said seriously.

Ruth paled and sipped her wine. "I'm hoping not many people in Haven Harbor have as good a memory as you do, Charlotte."

"You can't leave us like that," Sarah said. "What really happened?"

Ruth hesitated. "The basic story? A teenaged girl loved a young lobsterman her father didn't approve of, and the young man died when his lobster boat sank."

"That's a pretty short story," I put in. "The movie script must be adding to that."

"Oh, yes. For sure," Ruth said grimly. "In the movie the boy had a full-sized lobster boat, and he wasn't much older than the girl. Like in the movie, the girl's mother had died when she was twelve, and her father raised her. He wanted her to have a future that didn't depend on making a living from the sea. His own father had been drowned at sea, and he was a shipbuilder who believed his family would be safer on land. He wanted his daughter to marry someone who also had a land-based business. He was hoping she'd end up with a young man in his twenties who was the older brother of one of her friends, and who had a crush on Amy. His father owned a delicatessen in town down near where your shop is now, Sarah."

"But Amy, or whoever she really was, didn't want him. Or that life," I said.

"Right. Amy was in love. She only wanted Caleb."

"I don't remember the other young man being in the script," said Sarah. "I've been listening in to rehearsals when I can. But maybe I just haven't heard that part of the story."

"It's hardly mentioned in the script as it is," said Ruth. "That's one of the things we've debated. I wanted it clear that Amy had two choices, even though she has no doubt which one she prefers. The script focuses on the conflict between Amy and her father, and the love story with Caleb."

Gram looked at Ruth. "How does that make you feel?"

"As though we're just hearing part of the story. And that the ending will be much simpler than it really was."

"Okay. Now you have to tell us," I said. "I know the film is called *Harbor Heartbreak*, so it probably doesn't have a happy ending. What happens?"

"In the movie," Ruth said carefully, between bites of her baguette, "Caleb's boat sinks, and he drowns. Amy blames her father for his death."

"His boat just sinks?" asked Sarah.

Gram looked at Ruth. "And no questions are asked?"

"Amy asks questions, but no one listens to her."

"What kind of questions?" I asked.

Ruth hesitated. "In my original story Caleb is pulling traps beyond the Three Sisters Islands, too far out for anyone to get to him, when his boat explodes. Amy's sure someone sabotaged it."

"Exploded?" I almost gasped. "Like, with a bomb?"

"Not a bomb," Ruth assured me. "A fuel vapor explosion. Before you turn on an engine the blower should be turned on. It blows flammable gasoline vapors away. Once that's done, the engine can be turned on." She paused. "Most people assumed Caleb had forgotten to turn on the blower. A few people, including Amy, wondered if the blower had been tampered with. Maybe the fan's blades had been broken. The blower would have sounded normal, so no one would have noticed it, but it wouldn't have removed the flammable vapors."

"Wouldn't that have set the boat on fire as soon as the engine was turned on?" I asked.

"Not necessarily. Sometimes it takes time for the vapors to build up."

"Didn't they look for evidence in the boat? If the blower had been broken, I'd think the police would be able to say the explosion was intentional, even if they couldn't say who'd messed with it."

Ruth shook her head. "The boat sank. The body did, too. And in those days people weren't as conscious of evidence as they are today, especially if they thought the explosion was the result of an accident."

"So was it an accident or murder?" I wondered. "Sounds like Marv's death."

"A little," Ruth agreed.

"And none of that is in the movie?" asked Sarah.

"No. Not in the way it really was. In the book, Amy was sure her father had damaged Caleb's boat, to keep her from marrying him. She leaves home, at first staying with friends, and then, a couple of years later, she marries. She never spoke to her father again."

"How awful," said Sarah. "That Amy believed such a thing."

"But if it was true," I put in, "if her father really damaged Caleb's boat intentionally, then no wonder she felt that way."

"Without those overtones, the story is just a thwarted romance," said Gram. "Not nearly as interesting."

"Thomas and Marie didn't want to get into all those other details. They said that would be opening up the whole question of what really happened. It would become a mystery, and they wanted a romance."

"Does she marry the guy whose family owns the deli?" asked Sarah. "I remember the contemporary scene where Skye is talking to Emily, Amy's granddaughter, about a restaurant she's been running."

"That's the connection they wanted to make," said Ruth, putting her spoon down. "I'm sorry, but I get upset every time I think about it. It was wonderful of you all to bring me home, and have supper for me, but I think I'd like to go to bed now. These days are exhausting, and thinking about all this is difficult."

"Of course," Gram said immediately. "Would you like some help getting ready for bed, Ruth?"

"No, thank you. I can manage, now that I have the stair lift to get me to the second floor."

"Then we'll just stay and clean up. We'll leave the left-over food for you to have tomorrow or the next day," I suggested. "You get your rest. I'm sorry if we've tired you."

"It's not you who've tired me. My friends could never do that. It's all the pressure from this movie. I'll just be glad when it's over."

Ruth got up and I walked with her to the stair lift, while Sarah and Gram cleared the table.

"Thank you again for this time," she said. "It was good to vent a little and share what's been happening."

"Maybe we shouldn't have asked you so many questions," I admitted.

"No. It's good for me to talk about difficult things," Ruth said. "You're a dear, and so are Sarah and your grandmother. Just remember: the story in the movie isn't what really happened. Amy was right to never forgive her father."

Chapter 14

On God for all events depend
You cannot want when God's your friend
The Ant against Cold winter wisely hoard
 Provision which The Summer's wealth afford
Reading a Silent Lesson . . .
Nothing is
More unmannerly nor rude
Than that vile temper of ingratitude.

—Stitched by Mary Shields in 1827. Mary's
sampler includes two alphabets, two dogs,
and several geometric borders in wool
and silk on linen.

From *Harbor Hopes*

Caleb hugged Amy as they stood on the town
wharf. The sun was dawning, coloring the water
pale pink. "Wish I could go out with you," said Amy.
"You'll be with me, in my heart," said Caleb,
smiling and giving her a quick kiss. "And in my
stomach." He pointed at the small cooler full of cola

and sandwiches she'd prepared for him. "Thank your father again for coming down to look at my engine yesterday."

"I was kind of amazed he did that," Amy said, nodding. "He hasn't exactly been cheering for us recently. But he'd mentioned a couple of times that you should check the engine, since the boat was so old. I told him you didn't have the money just now, but if he'd like to take a look at it . . ."

"And so he did. And said everything was okay, but worn, and that I should be saving for a new engine. By next summer I'll definitely need one."

"Which you already suspected," Amy agreed. "But, still. He does know engines. He works on them at the boatyard."

"Thank him again, when you see him," said Caleb, stepping on board. "I'm going to start with my traps on the other side of Second Sister Island. No one else works that area this time of day." He started the blower fan and waved as the engine started, and his boat headed out of Haven Harbor and between two of the Three Sisters Islands.

Twenty minutes later Caleb had finished one can of cola, and finished pulling in three traps. An average morning. He'd caught a total of two keepers, lobsters that met Maine lobstering regulations. Not too large and not too small, and no females with eggs.

He'd just opened another can of cola when he smelled smoke. Seconds later he heard a small explosion in the engine. Then the hatch blew off, and the boat exploded in flames.

Caleb jumped into the water, but there were no other lobstermen nearby to help, and, like so many other Maine fishermen, he wasn't a strong swimmer.

The currents were powerful and cold. By the time the smoke alerted another lobster boat across the bay that someone was in trouble, both he and his boat had disappeared.

It didn't take long to clean up after dinner, and it had been a long day. Ruth wasn't the only one glad to get home.

My mind kept going in different directions.

I kept thinking of Marv being swept off the rocks, and Ruth, frustrated by the way her story was being interpreted. Where was Marv's wife? When would Pete hear officially that Marv's death was accidental, so the police could step back and let the movie production proceed?

I suspected I wasn't the only one with too many questions on her mind, and that a lot of drinks were being consumed at Aurora tonight.

Trixi was grateful for her dinner and my company, even though I headed upstairs earlier than usual. I decided to take a cool shower. It had been a hot day on top of everything else, and the fan in my bedroom window only offered slight relief. Trixi curled up near the breeze, and promptly fell asleep. She'd lived with me for a year now, and I was still amazed at how much company one small animal could be. I wondered if she thought the same about me, or if she thought of me as her just due: provider of food and water and an occasional snuggle.

When my cell buzzed at about nine o'clock I realized I'd forgotten Patrick was going to call. Usually when he'd spent the evening at Skye's house he called a lot later than nine.

"So how is everyone at Aurora dealing with Marv's death?"

"Not well," he answered. "He was a good friend of Mom's, so she's feeling guilty that it was her buying a Maine home that started everything that led to his death.

The others, especially Hank, seem most concerned because they've lost their director. Everyone is worried the movie will be cancelled and they'll be out of jobs."

Understandable.

"And wondering why Pete and Ethan put a hold on everything connected with the film until they hear from the medical examiner. Marv's death was clearly an accident, but in the meantime the crime scene people were here, looking at everything in his room."

"Did they take anything?"

"His laptop, I think, and some medications. They didn't exactly advertise what they were doing, but Pete and Ethan know me, so they both spoke to me at different times."

"So Ethan's definitely involved now."

"Until they get those results. Pete and Ethan are pretty much convinced that the cause of death will be officially determined tomorrow, and that it was an accident. Then at least everyone here can get back to a semblance of order, and plan what will happen next. And all the texts and calls from the media should slow down, if not stop. They're not as fascinated with Marv's death as they are about the possibility of the movie being cancelled."

"It's earlier than I thought you might call."

I could hear Patrick's smile through the phone. "Absolutely right. I grabbed some dinner in the kitchen before the mob descended on the dining room, and then excused myself. Mom understood, and I don't think anyone else cared."

Good. That "anyone else" would have included Talia. I shouldn't be jealous about Talia, but somehow it was hard not to be. After all, she'd been part of Patrick's life for a lot longer than I had, and she knew his world well.

"Did anyone mention Marv's wife?"

"No. Hank asked if she'd been notified, and Pete, who was here at the time, said she'd been at the lighthouse this morning; that she knew. No one asked where she was, or why she'd been at the light. I don't think any of them know her well. They were all more concerned about themselves and the film than about Marv's relatives."

"I can understand that," I agreed, although I was still concerned about June. How would I have felt if I'd seen Patrick slip off the ledges into the water?

"You took Ruth home. How is she coping? Every time I see her she looks more stressed and tired, and she's not young. I hope Hank and the O'Days aren't giving her a lot of trouble. I know Marv wasn't happy with the script as it was written."

"I'm worried about her, too. Ruth's written shelves of books but except for a few comments from her editors or agents over the years, I think she was pretty much left to write the story she wanted to write. Recently she's been self-publishing, so she hasn't even had to please an agent or editor. It's hard for her to see her work criticized or changed."

"Is this story one of those she borrowed from what really happened in Haven Harbor?"

"She talked about that at supper tonight. At least part of it is. But even so, it took place so long ago I wouldn't think anyone would care. Gram seemed to know more about that, but even she said it took place twenty years before she was around."

"No one in town forgets a good story. We know that."

"True," I said. "But right now I think the most important thing is getting the questions about Marv's death answered. Is the schedule for tomorrow still on, or is everyone going to sit around and worry?"

"I left too early to hear that," said Patrick. "I know the lighthouse area is still marked as a possible crime scene, though. Pete said they'd had to get protection for it tonight. Of course, they've been hiring security people for the past couple of weeks to protect the filming sites and equipment, so the only difference will be that those at the lighthouse tonight will officially be law enforcement types."

"If or when you hear anything about tomorrow, would you let me know? Sarah and I were supposed to be at Ted Lawrence's place then and if we don't need to be, I have other things I could do."

"Understood. I'll text you if I hear later tonight. You sound tired."

"I am. In fact, Trixi and I are in bed. I thought I'd check the news and weather on the television and then turn in early. You and I didn't get much sleep last night."

"Which was lovely, I might remind you."

I pulled up the one sheet I covered myself with on hot summer nights. "It was. But it also meant an early morning, and then a lot of excitement. So I'm due a good night's sleep."

"Me too. Plus I didn't want to hang around and hear all the problems Mom and her friends were dealing with tonight."

"Of course, you're a year older today, too," I teased. "You want to keep your strength up."

"For a number of reasons," he laughed.

"Good night. We'll be in touch tomorrow," I said.

"Or whenever we hear the results of Marv's postmortem."

I put my cell on the table next to my bed. The fan was beginning to cool my room, and I decided I didn't even care about the news or weather. I'd find out about those tomorrow. The weather would no doubt be hot, and the only news I cared about concerned Marv.

As I turned off my light I hoped his wife, now his widow, was somewhere quiet, and would be able to sleep tonight, too.

If no one had sent her that picture, she wouldn't even be in Maine. And she wouldn't have seen her husband die.

Who had sent that picture?

Somehow tonight the answer to that question didn't seem as important as it had this morning.

Chapter 15

In thy fair book of life divine
My, god, inscribe my name
There let it fill some humble place
Beneath the slaughter'd Lamb.

—Rebecca Ballinger stitched this sampler in 1830.
She included two alphabets, and two weeping
willow trees containing the initials of her
deceased grandparents, siblings, and two nieces.
Rebecca had been born in Pipe Creek, Maryland,
but her family moved to Jefferson County,
Ohio, in 1819, where she studied embroidery
under Ann Thorn.

I woke earlier than usual the next morning. Trixi must
have, too, as she stroked my cheek, requesting breakfast.
I stretched, scratched behind her left ear the way she liked
it, and then watched as she headed for my bedroom door,
stopping to look back to make sure I was following her.

Breakfast was downstairs.

Last year I'd woken early and gone for walks down by
the harborfront. This summer I'd been so involved with the

movie that I hadn't taken much time for myself, and I'd been sleeping more.

Today I was wide awake. I followed Trixi's lead and filled her dish of canned food while my coffee was brewing. I had no idea what today's schedule would turn out to be, but it was a beautiful July day. While I was sipping my coffee I decided to pull on some clothes and walk down to the waterfront as I used to do, and maybe stop at the patisserie for a breakfast treat. Between Mainely Needlepoint and *Harbor Heartbreak* I hadn't really enjoyed summer in Maine. Maybe it was time.

Temperatures might rise later, but now it was still in the sixties, so I put on jeans and a light sweatshirt. I filled the bird feeders and Trixi established herself at her favorite bird-watching window before I left. Within minutes the feeders were covered with five squawking baby starlings who fought with one another, scared off the other birds, and chased a squirrel away from the seeds.

Trixi looked at the noisy starlings doubtfully and retreated to a chair in the living room.

"Don't worry. Those teenagers will grow up fast, and find other places to eat," I assured her as she glanced at the window one more time and then curled up to take a nap.

My home was on the Haven Harbor Green. Reverend Tom's Congregational Church was at the end of the Green, which was circled by homes similar to mine. Now that Gram and Tom were married they lived in the vicarage next to the church, not far from Ruth's home. I hoped she'd gotten a good night's rest last night.

I headed downtown, toward the harbor, past the patisserie and Patrick's art gallery and Sarah's antiques store. If I'd been sure she was awake I might have stopped at her apartment above the store, but last night she'd been tired, too, so I decided to walk by myself. Down at the waterfront the lobster boats were out. Lobstermen and women would have headed to check their traps by five thirty or so. The town dock was crowded with skiffs and small motor crafts, some of which had been docked overnight. Others were there to be filled with groceries going back to one of the islands. The small parking lot reserved for islanders was half empty, which meant others had been up early, and had come to the mainland to buy groceries, propane, or other supplies.

The lighthouse was at the end of the harbor on a curved peninsula that jutted into the sea. Was it still officially a crime scene? Were police guarding it? The chamber of commerce, which had been so excited about having a film made in Haven Harbor, was probably not thrilled that one of the town's tourist attractions was closed for several days. On the other hand, Marv's death had probably added to publicity for the area that might bring in more tourists. It wouldn't be a big story, though, unless the report from the medical examiner wasn't what we hoped it would be.

"We." I smiled at myself. For at least these purposes, I'd included myself with the Hollywood folks.

I decided to continue walking, not as far as the lighthouse, but to Pocket Cove Beach, the small rocky area where I'd spent hours and days of my childhood. I sat on one of the large rocks near the road and inhaled the smells of salt air and rockweed and listened to the quiet splashing of the water as it came in and covered most of the beach. Only occasionally, in a nor'easter or hurricane, did large waves crash here. The beach was flat, protected from large breakers by the point where the lighthouse stood.

The best time for swimming was half tide. The water would then be warmed by the sun on the beach, and the water would be deep enough to wade in or swim. I'd learned to swim here, Mama watching me closely. I smiled, remembering. Patrick had probably learned to swim at someone's private pool. Here I'd worn old sneakers to protect my feet from the barnacles and broken shells on the rocks, and waded in gradually, knowing I'd be most comfortable once my legs were numb with cold. When most of me was numb, I'd run out and Mama would wrap me in a blanket.

Maine had white sandy beaches, but Pocket Cove Beach wasn't one of them. How far out had the young lobsterman who'd drowned sometime in the 1960s been when his boat exploded? Ruth had said he was beyond the Three Sisters, the islands that protected Haven Harbor from direct exposure to the North Atlantic. He wouldn't have had the communications equipment lobster boats had today.

After a few minutes with my memories and thoughts of the past, I headed back home. Two cinnamon rolls from the patisserie managed to find their way into a bag in my hand along the way.

I didn't even feel guilty. After all, no one but Trixi would see me eating them. And dinner at Ruth's had been twelve hours ago.

My cell buzzed with a text. Had the medical examiner's report come in so early?

But it was Patrick, asking if I'd like to come to Aurora for breakfast.

Knowing what might be served there, I immediately agreed.

I'd have the cinnamon rolls for supper.

Chapter 16

*Lamp Rugs: small square mats made of carpet
scraps and placed under table lamps
in the 1830s and 40s to protect tablecloths
from stains from dripping lamp oil.*

—From *Miss Leslie's Lady's House-book:
A Manual of Domestic Economy, Containing
Approved Directions for Washing, Dress-making,
Millinery, Dyeing, Cleaning,* by Eliza Leslie, 1843.
Miss Leslie emphasized that although less
expensive mats could be made of oilcloth,
"those that were handsomely worked in crewel
or other embroidery" were preferred.

As usual when she had guests, Skye had hired a cook to ensure that all her friends' culinary needs were met. The buffet displayed in her dining room this morning included plenty of fresh fruit cut in small pieces, home fried potatoes, broiled tomatoes, platters of Danish pastries, bagels (with lox and cream cheese), and warm wild blueberry muffins. A chef stood ready to cook eggs as requested. I ordered eggs Benedict with Canadian bacon. Adding a small bowl of cantaloupe, pineapple, and strawberries to my plate, I followed Patrick out to the back terrace, where several of Skye's guests were already seated. The day was beginning to warm up.

"Orange juice? Coffee?" he asked. "And then I'll tell you the news."

"I had coffee at home. Juice sounds good," I agreed. "News sounds even better." He headed to the kitchen. I noticed he'd loaded his plate with scrambled eggs to which he'd added some of the lox that had been with the bagels and two cheese Danish.

Skye waved from a nearby table. She seemed to only be eating fruit. I suspected the other actors and actresses would be similarly limiting their calorie intakes.

"Mind if I sit with you?" Talia Lincoln asked.

I almost looked around to see if she was speaking to anyone else.

"We don't know each other, but you're a friend of Patrick's, and have been working on those beautiful sets," she added as Patrick rejoined me, carrying glasses of juice for both of us.

"Talia, do join us," he said.

"Of course," I added. Talia's plate was, as I expected, full of fruit, although she'd also added a hard-boiled egg.

"Where's the coffee?" she asked.

"In the kitchen, just inside the door," Patrick answered, although he didn't volunteer to get it for her. As she headed to the kitchen he leaned over. "I hope you don't mind Talia's joining us. She's an old friend of mine."

"So I've heard," I said, trying not to sound as dismayed as I felt. "So, what's the news? Any word from Augusta?"

He shook his head. "Nothing from Pete or Ethan. But

guess who the replacement for Marv is going to be? The new director?"

I shook my head. I had no idea, and I didn't know Hollywood directors.

"Mom! Hank asked her last night, and she agreed."

I put my juice glass down. "Really? Skye's going to direct as well as act in *Harbor Heartbreak*?"

"Exactly," Patrick said, nodding. "I think secretly she's always wanted to direct. And clearly she knows this movie as well, or better, than anyone. It hasn't been announced officially, but everyone here knows. Last night everyone congratulated her and said they were eager to get on with the production. But Pete and Ethan asked that we all stay here until they have the medical examiner's report."

I looked around. "I wondered. Usually everyone's out and working by now, but today everyone seems to be relaxed and taking time with their breakfasts."

"Right. The only person I've seen working so far is Marie. She's in the solarium with her laptop open. Thomas probably went to get Ruth; he's been picking her up every morning."

Talia returned with her coffee and reached into the pocket of her jeans, pulling out a small plastic bag of pills.

I must have stared at it. "Are you all right?" I asked.

"I'm fine," she said, smiling with a trace of embarrassment. "These are vitamins and supplements. They're supposed to keep me healthy and young and gorgeous." She made a face. "The only prescriptions I take are birth control pills and occasionally something for stage fright."

"That's common," Patrick assured me. "I'd bet almost everyone in the house today has some sort of anti-anxiety medication to help them sleep, or relax before they're on camera. I know Mom's always had some."

Maine was different from California. "I didn't know. I've never taken anything like that," I said, hoping I didn't sound either naïve or as though I condemned the use of medications. Drugs, I thought to myself. Not pills to cure an illness, or prevent one, but to help people cope with their everyday lives.

Talia was swallowing her vitamins quickly, and I bit into my eggs Benedict, which were perfectly cooked. Of course. As though Skye would have permitted anyone less than a top chef to prepare breakfast for her guests. "So, no rehearsals scheduled yet for today?" I asked Talia. I already knew the answer to my question, but I felt I should say something.

"Hank said we should all stay here until we hear from the police."

"You were at the lighthouse yesterday morning," I said, remembering. "It must have been awful to see Marv fall. Had you worked with him before?"

"Awful, yes. And, yes, I'd worked with him before," Talia said. "Not recently. When I was starting out."

"Then he must have seemed like a mentor," I said.

Talia glanced at Patrick. "Some of us are going to go over lines informally, here," she said, sipping her coffee. She'd eaten her egg and a few pieces of the fruit she'd taken but that was all. "I think Flannery's going to gather the crew at the Anderson house to check equipment and schedules."

If that was true, maybe Flannery would want Sarah and me there, too. I glanced around the room, but Flannery had already left. "Maybe I should be at the Anderson house, then," I said, taking a last bite of my eggs Benedict. "Excuse me for a minute while I check."

Flannery Sullivan was in the corner of the living room, on his telephone. I decided to get another glass of orange juice and headed for the kitchen when Skye stopped me. "Have you talked with Sergeant Lambert?" she asked.

"Not today," I said, surprised. "And congratulations! Patrick just told me you're going to be the new director!"

She nodded. "Thank you! It's exciting. But first we have to get through all this police business. Sergeant Lambert just texted me. He and Ethan Trask are on their way here. He called to make sure no one left the house."

"I haven't heard anything," I assured her. Although if Pete and Ethan were on their way here this early in the day, that didn't sound good.

"Let me know if you do," she said. "I know you and he are friends." She headed over to Flannery and clearly interrupted his call. Maybe she was telling him he couldn't leave right now, and he should cancel his instructions to the crew, none of whom were staying at Aurora.

I watched for a few minutes as they talked, and then Skye went and stood near the front door. Her hands were clenched, and she'd started pacing back and forth.

I didn't blame her. Every time she came to Maine there seemed to be a death. And if Pete and Ethan were both coming to Aurora this morning, then she and I both knew Marv Mason's death hadn't been an accident.

Should I tell Patrick? But, not now. He was with Talia. I couldn't tell him without others overhearing. They'd find out soon enough.

What had the medical examiner found?

I went to the kitchen, poured myself another glass of orange juice, and then added some prosecco to it. Skye always left her bar open, and I suspected I wasn't the only one thinking a mimosa would go well with breakfast today.

I'd returned to the front hall, glass in hand, when Pete and Ethan arrived. They must have called from their car or from the Haven Harbor Police Department to get here so quickly.

Skye talked quietly with them for a few minutes, nodded, and then I followed them to the back terrace where most of her guests were still enjoying a view of the harbor and finishing their breakfasts.

All conversations stopped as soon as Pete and Ethan appeared.

I wondered if they'd already talked with Marv's wife.

I slipped into the chair next to Patrick's and listened with everyone else.

Ethan, the Maine state homicide detective in charge of any questionable deaths in Haven Harbor, looked as serious as I'd ever seen him. Pete, representing the Haven Harbor police, stood slightly to the side. He'd help Ethan, but he wasn't in charge.

"Thank you all for staying here until we understood better what happened to Marv Mason yesterday. Unfortunately, the Maine state medical examiner has ruled his death suspicious."

The terrace was filled with gasps and the sound of chairs scraping the slate flooring as people reacted to the news. This was not what anyone had been expecting.

"I know many of you were at the lighthouse yesterday morning. Most of you saw what happened. Most of you are also staying here at Aurora, where Mr. Mason was staying. Our crime scene people went over his room yesterday, but in light of what the medical examiner found we have a warrant this morning to go through the entire house. I'm asking your cooperation in understanding that for the time being you can't return to the rooms you've been using, and Sergeant Lambert"—he turned toward Pete—"and I will be questioning everyone again to make sure we didn't miss anything when we spoke to you briefly yesterday."

"Why was Marv's death ruled a homicide?" asked Hank. "We saw him fall yesterday. No one pushed him."

"I can't tell you why the medical examiner ruled that way," Ethan said. "I hope we'll be able to clarify everything soon, and confirm either that his death was or was not an accident. At this time all I can say is that more was involved than Marv's slipping off the rocks. I look forward to speaking with each of you this morning, and hope we can resolve this issue as quickly as possible. In the meantime, we'll be taking all of your computers and cell phones and tablets. I don't want any new information getting to the media until we know more."

Skye stood up and turned to the group. "I've told Ethan and Pete they can use the solarium for questioning. If you're not being questioned, you're welcome to run lines out here on the terrace or in the living room. Please don't leave the property, though. Flannery, Pete will talk with you about the members of the crew who were at the lighthouse yesterday, and who he'll also want to question. Feel free to finish your breakfasts. Pete is going to come around to collect your telephones and any other electronic gear you have with you now."

Skye handed Pete a Micmac basket I recognized from a shelf in the living room, and he began making the rounds of the tables.

"I realize you've all been talking with each other for the past twenty-four hours, but I'm asking now that you not discuss what happened to Marv," said Ethan. He turned, said something to Pete, and then spoke to Skye. I couldn't hear what he'd said.

I did hear the knock on the front door, though. I glanced at Patrick, and he nodded, and went to open the door.

He was back a few minutes later with Cos and Linc. Hank got up to talk with them; he'd probably called them earlier, asking them to come over to go over lines. Now he took them aside to tell them what was happening. Cos paled, and Linc looked upset. Two local kids, thinking they were going to work with celebrities, and, instead, now involved with a possible murder. Both of them had been at the lighthouse yesterday, not far from where Marv had fallen. Hank led them into the kitchen where I could hear the chef cleaning up. I had no doubt he'd find something for the newcomers to eat.

"How well did you know Marv Mason?" I asked Talia quietly. She was still nibbling on her fruit plate.

"Worked on a couple of films he directed when I started in the business," she said. "Then I went on to work with other people. Marv liked to encourage young people."

That would explain why I'd seen him so often with Cos. And maybe why unknowns Cos and Linc had been hired to begin with. "What made you decide to work on this film?" I asked.

Talia glanced at Patrick, and then answered, "I hadn't made any movies in a couple of years. My agent said no one would remember me if I didn't take this job. It's not a great role, but it's okay, and I like working with Skye."

"It all seems very disorganized to me," I admitted. "The script isn't finished, and the locations aren't ready. And now, with Marv dead . . . I wondered whether the whole thing would be cancelled."

"Probably not," said Talia. "Unless filming's delayed too much longer. It costs a lot to have all these people and equipment here. A major investment. And there are contracts to honor."

"Does a producer put up money ahead of time?"

"Produce*rs*," Patrick put in, rejoining us. "Hank is just one of those for this film, although he's the major one.

Lawyers will no doubt be on the telephone in the next week, reading over contracts to see who's responsible for what."

Pete had come over to our table. Talia and Patrick and I put our phones in his basket. Pete hesitated. "Angie, could I talk with you for a minute?"

I nodded, excused myself, and followed him to the corner of the terrace. "I've never heard you say a death was 'suspicious,'" I said to him. "Usually it's a clear-cut homicide or an accident."

"True. This is an unusual situation," said Pete in a low voice. "And, as usual, Ethan and I don't know any of these people other than you and Patrick. So would you mind keeping your eyes out for a couple of things?"

"Of course not," I agreed. "What are you looking for?"

"Marv was hit by that equipment yesterday, and slipped. His head hit the ledges, and he drowned. But the post-mortem showed his blood had a very high alcohol content, and he'd also taken a large quantity of an anti-anxiety medication that would, combined with the alcohol, make him very unsteady. The medical examiner was surprised he could even stand, much less walk on those rocks. If he hadn't fallen, he would have died within an hour, or sooner."

"Which would explain one reason he fell," I said. "I noticed he was walking unsteadily. But I assumed his leather shoes had slipped on the wet rocks."

"Exactly. That's what we thought, too. And it was early in the morning. We don't know whether Marv drank a lot the night before, or early that morning, and whether he self-medicated. The amount of drugs he had in his system was a lot more than someone would normally take."

"Have you talked to his wife?" I asked.

"We don't know where she is right now," Pete admitted. "Before she left yesterday morning she told me she was staying at an inn out on Route One, but she never checked in there."

"She'd just arrived in Maine," I pointed out. "Maybe she'd planned to stay there but they were full."

"That's another thing," said Pete. "I know she told you she'd just arrived in Maine. But we checked with the airlines. She'd actually been here for two days."

I frowned. "Why would she have lied?"

"I don't know. We have someone checking all the places she could be staying. And the hospitals. We need to find her. In the meantime, could you find out what you can about Marv's propensity to drink or take drugs? Or anything you might hear that would give someone a motive to add medication to his drink."

"Skye leaves her bar open twenty-four hours a day, in the kitchen," I said. "And I've heard a number of her guests take anti-anxiety medications. They talk about it very casually. Remember Marv's wife taking pills yesterday morning? I assumed that's what they were."

"Whatever you can find out would be helpful," said Pete, glancing over at Ethan, who was clearly waiting for him. "I have a feeling not a lot of these folks are going to be forthcoming, especially since we suspect someone gave Marv those pills, along with the alcohol."

"I'll find out what I can," I promised. "Looks as though I'm here for the day anyway."

I glanced behind Pete. Thomas O'Day had just come in with Ruth. The crowd was gathering.

Chapter 17

Embroidery decks
The canvas round
And yields a pleasing view
So virtue tends
To deck the mind
And form its blissful state.

—Two alphabets and the above verse were
bordered by a vine with triangular leaves
embroidered by twelve-year-old Mary W. Tyler.
No further information is known about Mary.

"Is Pete asking you to do some private investigating?"
Patrick had come up in back of me, and guessed why Pete
had wanted to talk.

"Not exactly," I said, knowing Pete wouldn't want me
to say anything. "But he wanted me to keep my eyes and
ears open."

"As usual, when there's a mysterious death in Haven
Harbor," Patrick said, shaking his head a bit. "But you

have managed to come up with helpful information other times."

Noise came from the front hall. The crime scene investigators had arrived and were heading upstairs. They'd take the computers, of course, and, based on what Pete had said, they'd be looking for medications. I couldn't imagine there'd be any need to check liquor. Skye's bar was complete and in full view of anyone in the house.

"What was Marv like?" I asked Patrick, drawing him away from the others. "I'm curious. I assume he had money, and knew other people with money. That's what directors do, isn't it? Besides the actual directing. They try to find producers who can pull together funding for movies. All I know about Marv personally was that he was married."

"Although his wife hasn't been around here, that I know of," said Patrick. "Mom knew Marv pretty well. He'd directed, or been involved in some way, with quite a few of her films over the years. I don't remember them being social friends, though, and I don't know anything about his wife, or whether he has any children. Nothing personal. Remember, Mom's business was part of our life in California, but it was her job. It didn't have much to do with me, although sometimes I met the people she worked with."

"Like Talia," I couldn't resist saying.

"Talia and I were friends, yes," he said. "But I hadn't seen her or talked to her in a couple of years before she came here this summer. Frankly, I was surprised she did. But from what she said earlier, I guess she needed the job. And maybe Mom talked her into it."

"She didn't seem upset about Marv's death."

"They weren't close friends," Patrick said. "Since they've

been here this summer Marv's spent most of his time either with Hank and the writers, or with Cos and Linc."

"Talia said he liked discovering young actors."

"True. And I'm sure Cos and Linc were impressed that someone as powerful as Marv was paying attention to them. Or at least people on the coast would have felt that way. I don't know if Cos and Linc understood all the relationships within the film community."

"Was Marv a heavy drinker?"

Patrick looked at me. "Doing a little investigating? I didn't notice him drinking any more than anyone else. But we weren't measuring the bottles every morning. He could have been drinking. I know Flannery drinks beer. Mom ordered a couple of extra cases a few days ago. The others? Maybe a glass or two before dinner, and champagne at the party the other night. They've been working long hours. Drinking heavily doesn't go with long hours."

I nodded. Talia and Cos were talking in one corner, and Ruth was with Thomas and Marie. I hoped Ruth had gotten a good night's sleep. "Gram and Sarah and I had dinner with Ruth last night. She's concerned about what's in the script, and what isn't."

"That sounds like Ruth. She's probably wondering what other people in Haven Harbor will think about the final story, and whether they'll think it's true."

"From what I gathered, the nineteen-sixties part of the script is based on a real incident here in the harbor; the contemporary part of the story is totally fictional."

"That makes sense. A young lobsterman drowned years ago, and his sweetheart was brokenhearted."

"Basically, yes. At least that's what's in the script. I have a feeling Gram knows more about it. She said she remembered hearing stories when she was growing up here, years later."

"Ruth has always lived in Haven Harbor, right?"

"Except for some time about nineteen seventy when her husband, who'd lost his leg in Vietnam, was in a veterans' hospital in Texas, and she moved down there to be near him. At least that's what I remember her telling me a while back. She'd started writing while he was overseas, and she kept doing that. She supported them since her husband, Ben, was never able to work after that."

"Ben was from Haven Harbor, too?"

"I think so. I think she would have said if he hadn't been from here," I said.

"Patrick?" Ethan had come up from behind me. "Can we do your interview now?"

"Happy to," he said, and then the two of them headed toward the solarium.

I noticed Linc standing alone, looking uncomfortable. Cos was still talking to Talia.

"How are things going?" I asked Linc.

He shrugged. "I guess all right. We're getting paid to be here, even when not much is going on. The money's good."

"What about school?"

"Marv promised Cos and me we'd be finished in time for classes starting in August. College starts earlier than high school, and we didn't want to miss anything. Cos was especially concerned, since she'll be a freshman and they have to get to campus earlier than upperclassmen."

"You're both here for the money, then. Not because you hope to act professionally someday."

Linc looked at me in disbelief. "For sure! I want to be a meteorologist. Weather fascinates me. And meteorologists have steady jobs. With benefits." He hesitated. "You know my dad. He's a Realtor, and when houses aren't selling he has to do odd jobs for people to get by. When Mom was sick last year he couldn't spend as much time with her as he wanted to, and her medical bills were out of sight. I don't want my life to be like that."

"I was sorry when she died," I said, thinking of how hard Carol Fitch had fought breast cancer. "But she'd be pleased you and your brother are still in school. She wanted you both to go to college."

"I know. And it's been rough, with Dad not having a regular income, and school costing so much. But so far we're okay." He glanced around the room. "This acting gig came out of nowhere, but it's been great. I'm earning more than I would sterning for one of the lobstermen, the way I did last year, and I get to be with Cos, too."

"How did it end up that they hired you?" I asked curiously. "Did you try out?" I didn't remember any local advertisements for young actors or actresses.

"No. Somehow it just happened. Last spring when Marv and Hank were up here scouting locations Marv happened to see Cos at the bookstore where she worked after school and thought she'd be perfect to play Amy. At first she thought it was a joke, but he asked her to read some lines and then he offered her a job. He asked if she knew any young men who'd be interested in acting, too, and she mentioned me." He grinned. "No one even asked me to read anything. They just took Cos and me out for dinner down at the Harbor Haunts, and, presto! Contracts."

"Very nice! I'll bet some of the other young people in town are jealous of the two of you."

"Maybe. But they don't know what we're really doing. It's pretty boring a lot of the time, just sitting, or reading over the same lines. But I'm glad to be here. Plus, I can be with Cos."

"You two are pretty close."

"More than we were before this summer, for sure. And we can talk to each other about the production. No one else we know would understand." He frowned a little, looking over at where Talia and Cos were still talking. "Sometimes we don't understand exactly what's happening, on the sets or between the people we're working with. Talia's spent a lot of time with Cos, talking about the business. Cos said Talia wanted to know more about Haven Harbor, too. But I think a lot of what they talked about was Marv. It should be a lot easier now, with him gone."

"Why would that be?"

Linc shifted his weight from one foot to the other. "I probably shouldn't say anything. But Marv's been a real pain. He's been following Cos around and making a big fuss about her, giving her more lines, and stuff like that."

"I noticed they were getting a bit cozy at Patrick's birthday party the other night."

"Cozy! That's one word for it. Cos just graduated from high school. She hasn't had a lot of experience with men who show too much interest in her. One reason I hang around is to make sure she's okay."

Linc was clearly playing the protective boyfriend. "Marv was showing too much interest in Cos?"

"I thought so. He even told her she should forget college, and become an actress."

"Really." That was interesting. Especially since as far as I knew Cos had shown no interest in an acting career.

"She was flattered, I could tell. After all, he was a pretty important director. He might be able to make things happen for her. Or at least that's what he told her."

"I noticed you were taking pictures at the birthday party."

"Yeah. I've kind of gotten into photography this summer. It's been something to do while we're waiting around. I bought some photo editing software and play with that when I get home at night."

Someone had sent Marv's wife a picture of him with Cos. "Do you ever send copies of your photos to people?"

Linc shook his head. "Can't do that. Not now, anyway. Not the pictures I've been taking here. Hank made sure I understood that. Any pictures taken of the actors, or people on the set, have to be released by the publicity people for the film. Hank said if I got anything really good, after we finish filming I could show what I had to the publicity department in California. But I'd be fired if I showed anything to someone who wasn't under contract for *Harbor Heartbreak*."

"So you haven't shown anyone your pictures, or sent them to anyone? Not even your friends?" With so many people sharing pictures on social media sites, I was surprised Linc wouldn't have been tempted to share some of his.

"No way. I've shown some of my pictures to Cos, but I haven't sent them anywhere, not even to her. I don't want to mess up this job."

"I'll bet you've been tempted to share your stuff sometimes."

"Sure. Taking pictures gives me something to do when everyone else is busy arguing or rearranging lights or whatever. I just do it for me. Maybe when I get back to school I'll see if I can take some pictures for the school newspaper. I haven't been involved in any of the school organizations. I'll see how busy I am, when I get back to campus." He smiled. "Only thirty-four days to go."

"Until school starts? You're counting the days?"

"Sure am. I can hardly wait until this summer is over, and life can get back to normal." He glanced around, as Cos came toward us. "Making a movie is definitely not anything I'd think of as normal."

Chapter 18

When wealth to virtuous hands is given
It blesses like the dews of heav'n
Like heaven it hears the orphan's cries
And wipes the tears from widow's eyes.

—Sarah Kurtz, born in 1795 in Georgetown,
District of Columbia, stitched this sampler when
she was nine years old. She included three block
alphabets and one script alphabet as well as trees,
crowns, flowers, and birds. Sarah married Thomas
Orme in 1816 and they had three children.

"Linc, will you talk with Sergeant Lambert and Detective
Trask now?" said Cos, coming up to Linc and me. She
pushed a strand of brown hair off her face. She looked
pale, and was holding a glass of juice. "I wanted a few
more minutes before I talked with them, so I told them I'd
be interviewed after you."

"No problem," Linc answered. "Is everything all right?"

"Everything's fine," she assured him.

He gave her a fast hug and kissed her cheek.

Linc headed for the solarium, and Cos took a deep drink of her orange juice.

"You and Linc have become good friends," I said. "Last spring when we talked I hadn't realized you had such a close relationship."

"We didn't know each other except to say 'hello' until late last winter," she admitted. "When he was home from college on his winter break he came down to the bookstore, and we ended up going to the Harbor Haunts for cocoa and talking for a couple of hours."

"Sounds like a good beginning," I said. I was ten years older than Cos, and beyond the stage of sharing cocoa with Patrick, but I understood her joy. I couldn't help being happy for her. "Linc says you were the one who helped him get the job on *Harbor Heartbreak*."

"Yes. It all happened so suddenly, and I wasn't sure he'd be interested. But the pay is good, and working together has given us a chance to get to know each other even better."

"He said Marv Mason was spending a lot of time with you," I added. "It must feel strange to have him gone."

Cos hesitated before answering. "Marv paid a lot of attention to me, for sure. At first I was really flattered. It feels good to have someone tell you you're special, you know? After my sister went to jail, a lot of people in town started ignoring me, or talking about me behind my back."

"That must not have been easy," I said, remembering my teen years. My classmates had looked at me and seen my mother, who'd had a bad reputation in town. I'd gotten out of Haven Harbor as soon as I could. "But at least you'll be leaving in about a month, right? For college?"

"Yes. And now I have Linc to talk with. We're at different schools, so I'll miss him this fall, but we'll both be in Maine, and we'll keep in touch, I'm sure. And working here this summer has meant I haven't had to see a lot of the people who looked down at me and my family."

"Marv's paying attention to you must have felt good, too."

"At first it did. Then he got . . . demanding. I thought it was me; that I was somehow acting as though I wanted to have a physical relationship with him. Because I didn't! Luckily, Linc stuck with me." She smiled in the direction Linc had gone to be questioned. "Marv wasn't happy Linc and I were always together. I was dumb enough not to see it at first, but he was always trying to get me alone." She hesitated. "He said he was mentoring me; giving me acting lessons."

"Was that true? Or was he putting pressure on you to do things you didn't want to do?" I asked. There'd been stories on the news in the past couple of years about powerful men in Hollywood who preyed on young actresses. Or actors. Could Marv have been one of those predators?

"He didn't say anything directly. He just kept telling me how wonderful I was and how he could help me have a career acting," said Cos, looking down. "He didn't exactly say how that would work, but I knew I didn't feel comfortable about it. And then Talia arrived, and she told me."

"Told you what?"

"That Marv did that to her, too, when she was starting out, and that he had a reputation for picking out one actress, usually a young one, in each film, and focusing on them. That he could get physical with them, too. Talia said she'd fallen for it all when she was a teenager, but that I shouldn't. That if I had any problems with Marv I should just walk away, or go and talk with her."

"Did that help?"

"A lot. I was pretty angry that I'd started to fall for Marv's routine, but Talia knew how he said nice things, and made you feel special, and sometimes he bought you clothes, or took you places."

"Did Marv do that with you?"

Cos shook her head. "No. But I'm lucky. I'm not alone. I'm living at home, and Linc is with me most of the time. Marv talked about how if I came out to California he'd help me find an apartment, and get a photographer to do a portfolio we could show to agents and other directors. I listened. He made it sound very tempting. But I never agreed. And once I'd talked to Talia I tried even harder to stay away from him. I believed her, not him."

"She's been a good friend to you, then," I said, thinking of how I might have misjudged Talia.

"She's cool. She's helped me focus on the future. *My* future, not the future Marv was talking about. And she's a lot smarter than she acts. She's really into history, and so am I, especially Haven Harbor history. I'll miss her when I finish my scenes and leave the production, although then I can go home and start putting together the things I'll need for my room at college. The school sent me a long list of 'helpful suggestions' for everything from lamps and a bookcase to special-size sheets for my dorm room. I'm really excited about being able to take the money I've earned this summer and go to Portland to choose some of what's on the list. Doing that will get me closer to leaving Haven Harbor, and all the people here who were cruel to me." Cos looked excited for the first time. "Don't you think it'll be fun to have a room of my own, or one with a roommate, to decorate?"

I smiled. "It does sound like fun. I never lived in a dorm, but it sounds like a new world starting for you."

Cos nodded. "I felt pretty stupid, actually, when Talia first took me aside. I should have recognized what Marv was doing. But I'm really glad she talked to me. And now

Marv's dead, and I can forget all about what he was trying to do. I can move on."

"I'm glad Talia befriended you," I said seriously. "Marv couldn't have been happy about that."

"Probably not. But she said she didn't want what happened to her, what he did to her, to happen to me."

"And you were smart enough to listen."

Cos nodded.

I'd been listening so closely to what Cos was saying that I'd almost forgotten to ask. "Cos, did Marv drink a lot?"

"I guess," she said. "But he never seemed drunk. He did want me to drink. He kept getting me drinks from the bar when we were here. He always had a glass in his hand."

"And what about drugs?"

"Drugs?" she asked, looking surprised. "He never tried to give me any drugs."

"Did he take any himself?"

She thought for a minute. "He had a couple of little bottles of pills in his pocket, and sometimes he'd take one. He didn't say what the pills were, and I didn't ask. I figured that was too personal. He was pretty old, in his fifties or so, so I figured the pills were for his heart or something. My dad takes medications for his blood pressure. I figured Marv was doing something like that."

"You're probably right," I agreed with her. "I just wondered."

"Did pills or alcohol have anything to do with his falling off the rocks?"

"I don't know for sure," I answered, not wanting to say anything Pete would question. "But some medications can put people off balance."

"I don't know about pills," Cos said, "but that morning Marv was pretty steamed up about something. He yelled at all of us to stay out of his way, even when we were trying to help. It was really windy down at the lighthouse, and the guys setting up the mic were messing around. Marv kept saying 'time is money!' and then he went down to where the crew was. I figured he was going to yell at them, too. But after that everything happened so fast, and then he was gone." Cos looked at me with wide eyes. "I've heard of people falling off those ledges, but I'd never seen it happen before. It was awful."

"It was," I agreed. "Definitely awful."

Chapter 19

Zealously pursue the course
That leads young minds to God
For faith and love & holy hope
to the blest abode.

—Sylvia Hall was born in Wallingford,
Connecticut, in 1805. She did not date her
cross-stitch sampler, but probably stitched
it between 1810 and 1820.

Linc gestured to Cos that it was her time to be interviewed by the police, and she headed in the direction of the solarium. I wished I still had my phone. I wanted to check in with Gram. And Sarah. But that wasn't going to happen; at least not right away.

Patrick joined me, holding what looked like another mimosa. "Sure you don't want a drink?" he asked. "I have a feeling we're going to be here for a while. Pete asked Flannery to call all the members of his crew who'd been at the lighthouse yesterday and get them over here to be questioned."

Flannery had clearly been given permission to use a phone.

"I don't want a drink right now. I'm trying to focus on everyone here and their relationships to Marv. How did your interview go?"

"Fine. Of course, I wasn't at the lighthouse, so I wasn't a witness to Marv's death. But I've seen him every day since he arrived a couple of weeks ago."

"You've said you didn't know him well."

"Not in the past. But I don't think they're asking questions about the past." He hesitated. "They did ask whether he was drinking a lot, or using drugs."

I headed Patrick over to a quiet corner of the terrace. Most of Skye's guests had gone inside, or were walking around the grounds, and the tables had been cleared, although some people were still holding glasses or mugs. Who knew what they were sipping? But I wanted my brain to remain clear. Besides, it was still morning. I'd had coffee and juice and one mimosa. I was saturated for the moment.

"What did you tell them?"

Patrick shrugged. "That he was a single malt guy. I know, because we ordered a couple of extra bottles a few days ago. I didn't know anything about drugs. People here have been popping pills. You saw Talia taking pills she said were vitamins this morning, and maybe that's what they were. And I wasn't watching Marv every minute. I didn't know what he might or might not have taken. But I told them I hadn't smelled pot, or heard anything about illegal drugs. Since I'm local, anyone looking for a supplier might have thought I'd be able to help them. But no one asked."

That was an interesting way to put it. "Do you know any local drug dealers?" I asked.

"No! How can you even ask me that! I don't do drugs.

But it made sense that Pete and Ethan would ask me about them."

"I guess." It had never occurred to me that someone involved in the movie would be looking for drugs. But I wasn't totally naïve. Some people in Maine, like some people everywhere, used drugs, legal and illegal.

"So, now you know I'm not involved with drugs, how about you? Have you found out anything that will help Pete and Ethan?" Patrick asked.

"I'm not sure. I talked to Cos and Linc. They both agreed Marv had a special interest in Cos, and Cos told me Talia warned her about him. Cos and Talia seem to be friends now. It seems Marv had a reputation for having 'special interests' in the young women he directed."

Patrick sighed. "I knew that. Talia had a problem with him some years ago. But I kept an eye on Cos, and she seemed to be coping pretty well. What did she tell you?"

Sounded like a lot of people were looking out for Cos. I wondered why Patrick hadn't said anything earlier, if he knew Marv's reputation.

"She seemed confused, more than anything," I admitted. "I suspect she's different from a lot of the young women Marv showed an interest in during past films. She doesn't want to be an actress, and both she and Linc are literally counting the days until they can get to college next month. Linc was also staying close to Cos, and she's been living with her family, not on her own, so even if Marv was trying to bribe her with promises of future movie parts, or trying to seduce her, there wasn't much time for that."

"Marv was thirty or forty years older than Cos. I'm surprised she even listened to him."

I shrugged. "He had power, though. He was a famous movie director. Talia told her he'd done the same thing with her when she was starting out."

Patrick grimaced. "I'll admit, I'd heard rumors about him. But I didn't see anything obvious here, and I hoped by now he would have outgrown all that. Not to mention that other Hollywood figures have gotten in a lot of trouble recently for similar behavior."

"If he was killed, and he'd been putting pressure on Cos, it could be a motivation for someone to want him gone. Maybe Cos; maybe even Linc, who's very possessive about her, and who was conscious Marv was following Cos around and showing too much interest in her."

"Maybe," Patrick said. "But I still can't see how either of them could have been responsible for Marv's being hit with a microphone stand and slipping on the ledges near the lighthouse."

"Maybe he'd already had too much to drink. Or had taken some sort of drug. Cos said she thought he took blood pressure medication."

"No one else would have been responsible for his drinking that early in the morning. Or taking medication." Patrick shook his head. "I think Pete and Ethan are acting out of an abundance of caution. But in the meantime they've closed the production for at least today, and that will mess up the filming schedule. *Harbor Heartbreak* is a low-budget film. Mom said they were trying to get it in the can within a month. Now she's all excited about it, since she's going to direct. But that also makes her responsible for getting everything done on time."

"If she can bring the movie in on schedule Cos and Linc will have no problems getting to school next month," I agreed. "That will be a relief to them both."

"Their parts are relatively small," Patrick added. "I don't think that should be a problem. The script is still in question, though. The writers are hunkered down in the corner of the living room and from the little I overheard, I don't think they're happy. They're not sure whether to go ahead with changes Marv asked them to make to the early part of the script, so they're working on the second half."

"In other words, deciding whether Talia's character leaves Haven Harbor and moves to New York to be with the man she loves, or whether she stays here to run her business." I shook my head. "I know the movie's called *Harbor Heartbreak*, but if it's like one of those romance movies some of the television channels show, then all will work out. The young couple will be together in New York, and maybe Talia/Emily will open a restaurant there and it will be a huge success." Patrick lifted his eyebrows and grinned at me.

"Sounds like you've watched a lot of those movies."

"A few," I admitted. "They're relaxing, and there's always a 'happily ever after' ending."

"Unfortunately, we're not living in a movie," he pointed out. He looked back over my shoulder. "I think Pete's looking for you. They must have finished questioning Cos."

I'd been questioned by Pete and Ethan before. Not just yesterday, when Pete talked with me at the lighthouse, but in other cases. Murder cases. This was the first time I could think of when they weren't even sure a death was a murder.

"So," said Pete after I'd joined him and Ethan in the solarium. "We know you're in and out of Aurora and the carriage house here because of your relationship with Patrick. And you were at the lighthouse yesterday. We're hoping you've seen or heard something that will help us."

"I don't know that I have," I answered honestly. "You asked me to find out whether Hank drank a lot. From what I've heard so far, he did drink. But no one's called him an alcoholic, or said he was drunk yesterday. Although he was walking unsteadily down at the lighthouse. I saw that, and others have mentioned it, too."

"His blood levels say he was definitely drunk," said

Ethan. "And that he'd taken an overdose of an anti-anxiety medication that, combined with the alcohol, would be fatal."

"Some people in this house have anti-anxiety meds," I said. "They make it sound as though everyone in the film industry takes them. But I haven't talked to everyone, and no one has mentioned overdoses."

Ethan nodded. "The crime scene folks are going through all the bedrooms, and medications like that are one of the things they're looking for. And we know Skye left her bar open and stocked twenty-four-seven, so anyone, including Marv, could have poured themselves a drink at any time. If Marv drank too much and took too many pills himself, then his death would be accidental. The combination of alcohol and medication would have made him unsteady, and he was on slippery, uneven ledges, and was hit by the equipment when he tried to help by adjusting it."

"But wouldn't someone who took an anti-anxiety medication on a regular basis know not to take it with alcohol?" I asked. "That just makes sense."

"Which is why we're considering the possibility that someone else poured a drink or more for Marv, and dissolved the tablets in it. But if that happened, there would have to be a motive. And he fell during the first part of the morning. Not a time of day he'd be expected to be drunk."

"Although he might have been if he was an alcoholic," I mused. "A couple of people said he drank a lot, but never seemed drunk. That can be typical of someone with a problem." I was thinking back to when I was a child. Mama drank too much, but I never saw her fall, or get too angry, or even have slurred speech. Although I'd listened every night to make sure she'd gotten safely home, and up the stairs to her room.

"Angie, when I talked with you yesterday you were

with June Mason, Marv's wife," said Pete, changing the subject.

"Yes. She was standing by herself next to the light-house, and sobbing. I went to her to see who she was. She didn't look well. You'll remember I took her to one of those granite benches the chamber of commerce set up, so she could sit down. Have you talked to her today?" I asked.

Pete and Ethan looked at each other. "We think she's in Portland, at a hotel there. But we haven't spoken with her yet," said Pete.

"Did she tell you why she'd come to Haven Harbor?"

"She said someone had sent her a photograph of Marv with Cos Curran. A note with the photograph said she should get to Maine."

"Did you see the photo?"

I nodded. "She showed it to me, on her phone. I recognized the scene. It was taken at Patrick's birthday party, the night before. In it Marv and Cos were close together, but nothing more." I hesitated. "Today Cos told me Marv was being more friendly than she wanted. He was trying to convince her not to go to college this fall, but, instead, to let him arrange an acting career for her."

"She didn't mention that to us," Pete said, looking at Ethan. "Angie, were they having an affair?"

"I don't think so. No. She wasn't interested in acting. And her friend Linc was pretty much at her side all the time, keeping an eye on her. He thought she was a bit naïve."

"And was she?" asked Ethan. "Could she have gotten involved with something she couldn't handle?"

"She might have," I admitted. "Until Talia Lincoln took her aside and told her Marv had a reputation for being overly friendly to young actresses. That he'd come on to her when she was a teenager, at the beginning of her career. She warned Cos to stay out of his way. Cos believed her."

"So, who sent the photograph to Marv's wife?"

"I don't know. It was from an anonymous account. She said she didn't know where it came from."

"But you're sure the picture was taken the night before."

"I'm positive. I was watching Cos and Marv about the time the photo was taken."

"Then you saw who took it?"

"No. I know Linc was taking pictures, but I asked him if he'd sent any pictures to anyone, and he denied it. He said he'd signed a contract with the film company saying he wouldn't share any pictures he took on the set, or of people involved with the film company. But a lot of other people were taking pictures with their cell phones. Talia was taking a lot, as I remember, and almost everyone had their phones out at some point during the evening. The picture sent to June Mason could have come from any one of them."

"And what time would that picture have been taken?"

I thought back. "Probably about seven. It was before dinner was served. People were just standing around, sipping champagne or something else, and chatting."

Ethan and Pete exchanged glances. "You see, we have a problem. Despite what she told you yesterday, June Mason didn't get that photograph, which was most likely sent after the party, and had to be from someone who knew her e-mail address, when she was in California. She'd left California the day before and was here in Maine during Patrick's birthday party."

"She wasn't at the party. Not many people were. I would have remembered her," I said.

"That makes sense," Pete agreed. "But why would she be in Maine and not be invited to the party? Skye certainly would have included her, although June wasn't staying here at Aurora. If she'd told her husband she was coming to Maine, wouldn't he have suggested she come here?"

"I guess so," I agreed. "But why would she tell me she'd just arrived?"

"We were hoping you might know the answer to that," said Pete.

I shook my head. "I have no idea. I assumed she'd come to check up on her husband. But to get here before Patrick's party she would have to have left California a day or two earlier."

"Perhaps she'd received other photographs?" Pete suggested.

"It's possible," I agreed. "But if she did, she didn't show them to me. Did you take her cell phone?"

"We didn't. Yesterday morning we thought Marv probably died accidentally. We weren't collecting evidence, just statements."

"And now she's disappeared."

"Not totally. Someone at headquarters called to tell us she was at the Eastland Hotel—or whatever it's called now—in Portland. We hadn't really been worried about where she was because we assumed she'd contact us, if for no other reason than to claim her husband's body. But now we'd really like to speak with her. Can you remember anything else she might have said or done while you were talking to her?"

I thought back, trying to picture everything that had happened. "One thing. She took a couple of pills while I was there. She said they were to steady her nerves."

"So she might have had anti-anxiety medications."

"Probably."

"You said earlier that several people here had that sort of medication. Who in particular?" Pete was taking notes.

"Patrick told me that. You should ask him. But he said

his mother sometimes took them, and Talia told me she had meds to ward off stage fright."

"Okay. And, for the record, do you have any anti-anxiety pills?" asked Pete.

"No!" I said. "I don't take any medications. Vitamins, sometimes, but that's all."

"And you'll keep your eyes and ears open for anything that might help in the investigation, right?"

"I will. I know everyone's concerned. The film's schedule is tight. They lost yesterday, and now they're losing today, to the investigation. If anyone is upset about that, then they might need one of those pills," I added. "Especially if your crime scene people have taken them from the bedrooms. I assume they're addictive?"

"They can be, depending on the dose," said Ethan. "But it's a common medication. One of the most prescribed in the country. And that doesn't count pills that haven't been prescribed."

I stood up. "I'll keep my eyes open. And if there's anything else you want me to look for, let me know."

"We will, Angie. Believe me, we want this case tied up one way or another as soon as possible," said Ethan. "It's strange that every time Skye West visits Haven Harbor someone seems to die."

I shivered slightly. "It's a coincidence, I'm sure. Just a coincidence."

I just hoped it was.

Chapter 20

*It may be much, or it may be little, but handwork of
some kind must embellish every gown which has any
pretension to smartness, the kind of work, and its
elaborateness, being pretty sure indications of the
taste and purse of the woman who wears it.*

—From *The Modern Priscilla*, November 1905.
The Modern Priscilla was a sixteen-page monthly
magazine for women published from 1887 to 1930
that focused on needlework and housekeeping.

From *Harbor Hopes*

"I can't believe it, still," said Amy. She stood at
Caleb's grave, dressed in navy blue, the closest her
closet could come to black. "I can't believe he's gone."

"A funeral, instead of a wedding," said Carol,
putting her arm around Amy.

"The Coast Guard said probably something was
wrong with the blower; the fan. That it was a fuel
vapor explosion," said Joan. "That's hard to believe;
Caleb was so careful with his boat. And you said he

and your dad had checked the engine just the night before."

Amy nodded. "Everything was supposed to be fine. Working order. No problems. One of the guys down at the wharf said he probably didn't know what he was doing; that he'd forgotten to turn on the blower. But Caleb had been working with boats since he was eight. He knew how they operated. And I know he turned on the blower that morning because I heard it, before he started the engine and went out."

Ruth stopped me as I left the solarium. "I see Pete and Ethan have taken over our writers' room," she said. "What's happening?" She leaned on her walker. "I needed a break. I couldn't deal with Thomas and Marie anymore. And they're not telling me what's happening, when I suspect everyone else in this house knows."

Thomas and Marie hadn't told her? "The medical examiner ruled Marv's death 'suspicious,'" I explained, moving to the corner of the dining room so no one else would hear me. We weren't supposed to be talking about Marv's death. But, after all, Ruth hadn't even been at the lighthouse yesterday. She followed me, her walker rolling smoothly along the wide pine boards.

Needlepointed pictures of Haven Harbor were hung between Aurora's dining room windows. Gram had restored them for Skye over a year ago. Ironically, Ruth and I were now standing beneath the embroidered Haven Harbor Lighthouse.

"So Pete and Ethan are questioning everyone who was at the lighthouse yesterday when he fell," Ruth guessed.

"Exactly," I confirmed.

She shook her head. "That rules me out. I was here with Thomas and Marie arguing about the script, as usual." She frowned. "But unless someone pushed him, how could Marv's fall be anything other than accidental?"

"That seems to be the question," I agreed. "You've spent most of the past month here at Aurora."

"That's the truth," Ruth said. "More hours than I like to think about."

"And you've seen and talked with Hank and Marv; not just Thomas and Marie."

"True enough. They've interrupted our writing with ideas and requests almost every day. Thomas assured me it's common for the director and producer to do that. In fact, he's said it would happen even more often when serious rehearsals and filming started. So far the actors have just been going over lines."

"And working on blocking," I nodded. "I've seen a little of that, although Sarah and I have been spending most of our time working on the sets."

"I'm curious to see what you've come up with," Ruth put in. "Typical Maine rooms in the early nineteen sixties and then today? Seems to me you could have just moved over to my house."

"Something like that," I said, smiling. "But the Holly-wood version of a Maine home isn't necessarily the Haven Harbor version."

"I can imagine," she said drily.

"A question for you, though. Since you've seen Marv often, either because he was giving you script input . . ."

Ruth rolled her eyes.

"Or just because you were in the same house with him, would you say he's a heavy drinker?"

She looked at me in surprise. "I haven't thought about it. Everyone here seems to have a glass in their hand most of the time. But it's been so hot the past ten days, I didn't think much about it." She pointed to the glass in a holder attached to her walker. "I've been sipping lemonade myself. Some people are drinking water or iced tea. But, yes, the bar is always open. Every morning Ron Winfield checks it and replaces any empty bottles. It would be easy to add vodka or gin to lemonade and no one would be the wiser. At least not for a while."

"Ron Winfield. He's the chef, right?"

"Officially, that's what Skye calls him. But he not only cooks, he keeps the first floor clean, especially the kitchen, and he orders food and drinks."

"Sounds more like a housekeeper than a cook," I commented.

"I don't think he does anything with the upstairs," Ruth said thoughtfully. "I haven't paid much attention. But he's here early every morning and stays until after ten at night. I've only stayed that late one night, but he was still here, putting out trays of snacks for everyone gathered in the living room or heading for their bedrooms. I don't know if he stays downstairs that late every night. He's the one who would know how much alcohol is consumed by people here. But I can say Marv drank. Scotch, I'm pretty sure. I smelled it on him several times."

"Just at cocktail hour or in the evening?"

Ruth hesitated. "For sure, then. Almost everyone drinks then, except for Talia, who's on a diet, despite the fact that she looks as though a nor'easter would blow her to Canada. I've heard her refuse even lemonade, because there's sugar in it. But Marv almost always had a drink in his hand, no matter the time of day. And he wasn't holding a lemonade glass."

"Ruth? We're going to go over those first scenes again," Marie called across the room. "We decided the sun was too hot to work on the terrace, but Skye found a fan for the far corner of the living room."

"Coming," Ruth answered. She turned to me. "We were in the living room before, but Jon and Talia wanted to read lines, so we moved. I guess we've been moved again. Time to get to work."

"Have you noticed any changes in how people have thought about the script, since Marv's death?" I asked as she turned toward the living room.

"He wanted us to add a couple of scenes at the beginning. I guess that's what Thomas and Marie are ready to work on now." She turned her walker and headed for the living room. Then she turned back toward me. "Good luck. I hope this gets figured out soon."

She wasn't alone. And it sounded as though I should be talking with Ron Winfield, whether he was a chef, as Skye referred to him, or whether he doubled as a housekeeper. In either case, he'd spent a lot of time with Skye's guests. He might know more about Marv.

Chapter 21

Here in This Garden Here Below
Water Me That I May Grow
And When All Grace To Me Is Given
Then Transplant Me into Heaven."

—Elizabeth Marx of Reading, Pennsylvania,
stitched an elaborate sampler, including floral
crossbands, stars, flowering strawberry vines,
and roses, in 1802, when she was twelve
years old. When she was twenty-two she
married Christian Brobst.

Ron Winfield had finished removing the breakfast buffet
from the dining room and was filling the two dishwashers
in the kitchen and, I assumed, already planning lunch. I
stood in the doorway to the kitchen and watched him
for a few minutes. This would probably be a good time to
approach him. Filling dishwashers (one for glasses and
cups and the other for plates) shouldn't take too much
concentration.

He looked up at me and smiled. "May I help you?"

"Thank you," I said. I hadn't paid any attention to him
at breakfast. Ron was about my age (late twenties) with

short blond hair and eyes so blue I wondered if they were colored contacts. Where had Skye found someone whose eggs Benedict had been perfect, and who was willing to spend July and August cooking and cleaning up after a group of Hollywood types who probably ignored him when they weren't asking him to do something for them?

"Hi. I'm Angie Curtis. I live here in town," I started. "Breakfast was delicious."

"Thank you," he said, smiling while he put the last plates in the dishwasher and then stood. I'm five foot seven, and he was a good six inches taller than I was. Even taller than Patrick.

"I understand you're doing all the cooking at Aurora," I said. Glancing around I added, "And the cleaning up."

"True," he said. "I definitely prefer the cooking. But Ms. West wanted someone who would live in, and take care of everything. I don't do laundry or clean bedrooms, but everything connected with food is in my jurisdiction."

He didn't sound like a Mainer. "You're living in?"

"There's a small room on the third floor that was probably for a maid when this place was built. It's much smaller than the bedrooms the guests are using, but it's fine for me."

"I'll bet it's warm these days on the third floor," I said. Even my second-floor bedroom was hot on summer nights.

"I have a window fan," he answered, drying his hands on a dish towel and reaching out to shake mine. "I'm Ron Winfield. Are you one of the actresses?"

"Welcome to Maine, Ron," I answered. "And, no. I run a small local business. I'm working for Flannery Sullivan on the sets."

"Which are somewhere else, which is why I haven't seen you before."

"Probably. I was at the lobster bake the other night."

"I had that night off," he explained. "The caterers took care of everything."

"It must be interesting, working with all these movie people," I said.

He shrugged. "They eat, like other people."

"Where are you from?" I asked. I didn't want to hold Ron up too long, but he didn't seem concerned about getting back to work.

"New York City. Graduated from the Culinary Institute a few months ago. Ms. West called there and asked if they knew anyone who'd like to spend the summer in Maine and I decided it might be fun. And cooler than in the city, where most people I know are."

I wondered why Skye hadn't hired someone local to do the cooking, as she had other times. Although this time of year maybe everyone local already had jobs. "Have you gotten to see much of Maine?"

He laughed. "Not really. I've seen Haven Harbor, but that's about it. I'm pretty much on call from six in the morning, when I start making coffee, until most of the people staying here go to bed."

I looked over at the bar. "But the bar stays open all the time."

"It does. But I'm not a bartender. I make sure the beer is cold and there's plenty of iced tea and cold water and lemonade and coffee and that we don't run out of anything. There's a grocery store that delivers, so if I need anything from there, including liquor or wine or beer, I just order it and they bring it over. Sometimes Skye's son, Patrick, has picked things up for me. Believe me, keeping the bar set up is the simplest part of my job."

"What's the hardest?" I asked out of curiosity.

"Planning and cooking meals when I have no idea how many people will be here. Most days it's just the writers, and maybe a couple of other people here for lunch. But today"—he shook his head—"looks like half the town is planning to spend the day here."

I nodded. "I can see that."

"And everyone has their special diets. Vegan, no seafood, no eggs, no nuts, no lactose. Some days I think if I just served fruits and vegetables most people would be happy. Until, of course, someone is on the Atkins diet and asked for filet mignon with a foie gras sauce."

"Doesn't sound like fun to me," I said.

He shrugged. "It's part of being a personal chef. It's my first time doing it, so I learn something every day."

"Have you gotten to know the people staying here well?"

Ron's face went slightly blank. "I'm just the chef."

I pushed on. "Like, Marv Mason. The director, who died yesterday. Did you talk with him often?"

"He drank single malt scotch," Ron said. "And Thomas, the writer, drinks Irish. I had to order new bottles every day or two with those two staying here."

"So Marv drank a lot?"

"I wasn't counting shots. But, honestly, I don't think either of them were pouring shots. They were just filling glasses. All I know for sure is that the bottles emptied pretty fast. In this heat, most people have been drinking a lot of water, or other nonalcoholic drinks. Beer, too. I've ordered a lot of that. And maybe a glass or two of wine with dinner. But the scotch has disappeared on a regular basis." He paused. "Yesterday morning there wasn't even an empty bottle left on the bar."

"Someone took it to their room the night before?"

"That's what I guessed."

"Had Marv taken it?"

"I don't know who had it. I didn't see him with the bottle," said Ron. "Come to think of it, I don't remember seeing Marv yesterday morning. Maybe he skipped breakfast."

"Then who had the single malt?" I asked.

"As I said, I don't know. I was pretty busy at the time. Ms. West asked for breakfast to be early since a lot of guests were heading down to the lighthouse. I just served fruit and pastries. Nothing that required cooking." He looked at me. "Why so interested in what people are eating and drinking?"

He hadn't answered my question about who'd returned the bottle of single malt. But, then, he'd said he didn't know.

"Just curious," I said. "Since I haven't been here until today."

He looked at me as though he wasn't sure that was my real answer. "So you'll be here all day?"

"Probably. It depends on the police," I explained, gesturing toward the solarium in back of the kitchen where Pete and Ethan, I assumed, were still interviewing people.

"Then I hope you like crabmeat," he said. "I'm planning crabmeat sandwiches or salad for lunch. Along with the usual fruit and vegetable platters."

"Sounds delicious," I said. I was about to ask him about the scotch again when I felt Patrick's hand on my shoulder.

"Here you are. I've been looking for you. We've both been interviewed. How about a short walk?" he asked, ignoring Ron.

"I just came in to get a glass of lemonade," I said, moving toward the carafe on the bar. "Getting outside and away is a good idea. Nice to meet you, Ron. I'll look forward to that lunch. I love crabmeat."

Chapter 22

Simple sampler picturing Adam and Eve
and an apple tree above a mother and child,
and bordered by a simple pattern of vines.

—Acadian sampler inscribed "Marie Maguerite Ahiel,
agee de 11 ans, ce 16 jour du mois Daouet, 181(?)"

Aurora was set on a hill overlooking Haven Harbor.
The lawn was mowed in back of the house and beyond the
driveway that led to Patrick's carriage house. The harbor
could be seen from the floor-to-ceiling windows in his
first-floor studio.

On the other side of the large Victorian house were
several acres of woods. When Skye bought the property
last year the lawn had been an overgrown field, and the
woods full of dead trees, fallen branches, and overgrown
bushes. Nothing on the property could have been called
"landscaping."

Now the lawn was clear, most of the woods had been
cleaned out, and paths cleared. Skye had said next year
she planned to have gardens planted near the house and
the walkways leading from Aurora to the carriage house,

and in the center of the circular driveway, where once there had been a fountain.

Despite a schedule that normally allowed her to visit Maine only a few times a year, she kept in touch with the local businesses she hired to keep her home in order. And, of course, Patrick lived here full time, so he checked on the work being done, or not done.

"It should be cooler in the woods," I suggested. "And I haven't seen the work that's been done there."

"The woods it is, then," agreed Patrick. "I heard Marv talking to Talia a couple of days ago saying he loved the way the bushes had been cleared out so you could walk through the woods and still see the harbor. His only complaint was that there were no benches to sit on under the trees."

"He must have been walking during the day," I said. "In the evening I would imagine this area would be swarming with mosquitos. He wouldn't have wanted to sit and let them feast on him."

"Mom's got machines set up around the house that attract and kill mosquitos," Patrick said. "That way people can sit on the terrace or take a walk without being bothered by them. You weren't bitten by any at my birthday party, right?"

Of course. I knew there were machines that did that. I should have assumed Skye would have plenty of them, for the comfort of her guests. "At my house we used to have bats, in the barn and under the eaves of the attic. They took care of the mosquitos," I pointed out.

"The bats are gone?"

"White-nose syndrome is a horrible disease that's killed a lot of bats around here. It's sad. I always liked the bats. One year several babies lived between the storm window and the glass in one of our bedroom windows. They were so ugly and cute to watch! Once in a while one would come down the chimney and fly around the house. It was my job to throw a dish towel or pillowcase over it lightly and free it outside." I remembered those bats fondly. "I miss them. And now we have more mosquitos."

"Angie, you have skills I never thought of," said Patrick. "But, still, I'm not sure I'd appreciate bats flying around my house, even if they did eat mosquitos."

I shook my head. Patrick and I didn't always see things the same way. I suspected our differing feelings about bats were not critical to our relationship.

"I saw you talking to several people at the house. Did you learn anything that might help Pete and Ethan?"

"I don't think so. Although sometimes you learn something and don't know until later that it's important. Ron told me Marv drank single malt scotch, if that counts as critical information. I don't think it does."

Patrick shook his head as we continued walking into the woods.

The air smelled of pine, and crows cawed loudly above us, warning other birds that humans had invaded their territory. A murder of crows, I thought. I hoped they weren't trying to tell us something. "Ruth wondered whether they'd have to change the script again today. Marv had wanted changes made to the first scenes that she hadn't liked."

"Does that mean Ruth had a motive to kill Marv?" Patrick squeezed my hand.

"I suppose so," I said, smiling. "Except for the fact that she's eighty years old, and she wasn't anywhere near the lighthouse when he fell."

"Maybe she snuck out during the middle of the night and put kitchen grease on the rocks to make them slippery."

"I don't even think that's funny," I said. "I do wish I'd been able to find out something that would help clarify what really did happen."

"Someone could have drugged him."

"That's possible. I've been wondering how many pills the crime scene guys confiscated this morning. And who's going to start complaining when they don't have their prescriptions."

"I'm pretty sure they'll return any essential medications that have nothing to do with Marv's death," Patrick said. "And although the people staying here at Aurora would have had access to both scotch and their own medications, Pete and Ethan are also questioning the crew that was setting up the mic yesterday."

"I'm assuming that's to see who was where, and if anyone could have pushed Marv," I said. "Are they questioning Leo, too?" I hadn't seen him at the house.

"They are," said Patrick. "Dave brought him over about half an hour ago. He looked pale and scared."

"I'm not surprised. Being questioned by the police is not his favorite thing," I agreed. "If he and Dave are still there when we get back I'll try to talk with them."

Patrick glanced at his watch. "I know we haven't been out for long, but maybe we should go back. No one knows where we went, and if Mom wants something she'll be looking for me."

"No doubt," I agreed, thinking that Pete or Ethan might also be looking for me. "Is anyone going to be running lines today?"

"If so, it'll be informally," said Patrick. "Everyone's pretty uptight. The death of someone they all knew is understandably upsetting."

"Most of them saw it happen, too," I said, hoping no one had gotten a close look at the Marine Patrol recovering Marv's body.

"One good thing that's happened is Mom's being named the new director. Everyone seems relieved and pleased about that." He smiled down at me. "She's excited, but nervous, too. Although she's thought about directing before, this is a very sudden opportunity, under unfortunate circumstances."

"I suspect she'll do fine," I said. "It might even open a whole new career for her."

"You're right. And it will take some time before everyone is able to relax. Talia said she had nightmares last night," Patrick said. "I'm not surprised. And she wasn't one of Marv's biggest admirers."

"I thought she said he'd been her mentor when she first started acting," I said, choosing to ignore the fact that Talia and Patrick had been talking. After all, they had been friends.

"Oh, she's known him for a long time," said Patrick. "And he did help her get some roles early on. But I never had the feeling she liked him very much. And, after all, she's an actress. You can't always tell what she's really feeling."

Was that how he felt about his own mother? Skye was a much more famous actress than Talia. Or, maybe it was just what was true in the movie community.

"These pine trees are so tall and straight," Patrick said, pointing out a group of pines near the road. "Other than clearing out the underbrush, there wasn't any reason to add a path through there. Walking is easy."

"Those are white pines. The ones that were marked for masts for the King's Navy in colonial days," I said. "If a straight white pine was marked with red, it meant the King of England had claimed the tree, and it was illegal for anyone but a representative of the king to cut it."

"I'm assuming that was a while ago," said Patrick as we headed back across the lawn toward Aurora.

"Before the Revolution," I agreed. "And despite the

marks, not everyone paid attention. The king didn't get all the pines."

"So even royalty and money can't buy everything in Maine," said Patrick, putting his arm around me. "I'm learning that."

Chapter 23

*Very small sampler (four inches by six inches)
including one alphabet, several simple pine trees,
and five flowers on the bottom border.*

—Stitched by Abigail Minot Head, age eleven,
in Exeter, Rockingham County, New Hampshire.
Abigail lived from 1823 until 1914.

Patrick and I'd timed our walk well. Somehow Ron had managed to set lunch up by the time we'd gotten back to the house. Bowls of crabmeat salad, along with platters of bread and rolls, lettuce, and tomato were on the dining room buffet, supplemented by the usual selection of cut-up fruits, and a smaller platter of roast chicken for those who couldn't, or chose not to, eat seafood.

I made myself a generous crabmeat sandwich, added a few pieces of fruit to my plate, and took a glass of iced tea. I didn't have crabmeat often because it cost so much, and I intended to enjoy lunch.

"Pretty good restaurant," Dave Percy said in back of me.

"What are you doing here?" I asked in surprise. Then I

remembered. "Sorry! I was thinking about something else. Patrick told me you'd brought Leo here to be questioned."

"Right," he said a bit grimly as he served himself crab-meat and some of the potato chips I'd ignored.

I glanced around. "Where's Leo now?"

"Talking to Pete and Ethan," said Dave. "He was really nervous about being questioned. He kept saying he had nothing to do with Mr. Mason's death, so why would the police call him in?"

"I hope you told him to relax, and just answer their questions truthfully," I said. "In the meantime, why don't you join Patrick and me for lunch on the terrace?" Dave didn't know most of the people here. He'd been driving Leo back and forth to crew calls, and they'd both been at Patrick's birthday party, but he and I and Ruth were the only Mainely Needlepointers here now, and Ruth was no doubt with Thomas and Marie.

"Fine," Dave agreed. "I'd like to find out a little more about what's happening. Leo doesn't know, and I certainly don't."

"Follow me," I said. Patrick had already headed for the terrace.

An awning was shading part of the terrace, and, luckily, Patrick had chosen a table in that area. Dave and I joined him.

"Let me guess," said Patrick. "Leo's talking with the police?"

Dave nodded and took a sip of his lemonade. "Flannery called this morning to say that everyone who was at the lighthouse yesterday morning had to be questioned. Again. That included Leo."

"He was right in the middle of it all," I said. "He and two of the other guys on the crew were moving the boom when the wind caught it."

"That's what he told me," said Dave. "He was really upset. Not just about Marv's death, but about possibly being blamed for it. He kept saying they were trying to put the equipment where Marv wanted it, but the rocks were slippery, and then the wind came up."

I nodded. "I saw. He and the other young men were trying to follow directions, but it wasn't clear what they were supposed to do. And Marv wasn't the only other person there. Several of the actors, Cos and Linc and Talia, were also close by when the boom fell. It all happened so quickly. When I think about it, Leo and the two other crew members were lucky they weren't the ones who fell. The equipment looked very unsteady."

"They were trying to set up a boom on the ledges?" Patrick asked.

"They were," I confirmed. "I assumed they were trying to record the sound of the surf and the gulls."

Patrick shook his head. "That sounds crazy. They could buy background noises like that, and those rocks are treacherous. Once I was down at the lighthouse and saw someone trying to set up a tripod. He couldn't get it to stand; the ledges were too uneven. And a tripod's a lot smaller than a boom."

"Leo said they were just doing what they were told," said Dave, frowning.

"I believe that," I put in. "They were already having problems, but had everything pretty well set when Marv went down to talk to them. I couldn't hear what he was saying, but clearly he wasn't happy and was telling them to move everything. That's when it all went wrong."

"Talia said that, too," said Patrick. "She said she was next to Marv when he was hit by the equipment and fell."

"That's right. I guess she was," I said, trying to remember exactly who was where when it all happened. "I remember being surprised that she and Cos and Linc had followed

Marv down on the ledges. Cos and Linc know those rocks well; anyone who grew up in Haven Harbor would. But Talia and Marv and the crew didn't know how dangerous they were. Marv wasn't even wearing rubber-soled shoes."

"That's crazy," agreed Dave. "Luckily, all the crew members were wearing sneakers. Of course, if they're like Leo, they probably wear sneakers most of the time wherever they are."

I smiled. Dave taught biology at Haven Harbor High. He knew what young people wore.

"I wonder why Talia and our two local kids decided to get involved." I mused. "They weren't working with the equipment."

"Maybe they thought they could help in some way," Dave suggested.

"True," I agreed. "But I was surprised the actors were even at the lighthouse yesterday."

"Curiosity?" Patrick guessed. "I suspect they've gotten tired just going over lines, and except for Cos and Linc, they'd probably never even been to the lighthouse. Marv and Hank kept everyone pretty much contained and working, even though the actual filming hasn't started."

"That's certainly true of the writers," I agreed. "I know Ruth's tired. She and Thomas and Marie have been cooped up in the solarium until today." I glanced over at another table on the terrace, where the three writers were now eating lunch. "At least this morning they moved around a little, working in different places."

"I suspect they're just trying to stay out of the way," said Patrick. "Everyone's restless, not knowing how long this hiatus is going to last. And Marv's been telling them to change scenes and dialogue almost every day. I've heard Marie and Thomas complaining about it." He paused. "A couple of days ago Marie was saying this was the last time they'd work with Marv. That he was too demanding, and what he was demanding didn't always make sense."

"Well," Dave pointed out. "She was right. It will be the last time they work with Marv."

"I worry about Ruth," I said. "She doesn't seem worried about the contemporary part of the script, but she has some serious problems with the early part."

"That's understandable," Patrick pointed out. "The early part is based on one of her books. The sections with Mom and Talia are new."

Dave looked around, nervously. "Could Pete and Ethan still be questioning Leo? He's been in that room a while now."

"Are either of the young men who were working with him here?" I asked. I didn't know them, and there were a lot of people eating lunch, including a couple of people I thought were crime scene investigators. No wonder Ron said planning meals was a problem. When he'd ordered food for this lunch he'd probably assumed that the writers, and maybe a couple of other people, would be here. Instead, the terrace was crowded.

Dave looked around. "No. So maybe they decided to eat inside." He stood up. "I'm going to check. I'm sorry, but I'm worried about Leo. He's very nervous about police, and death, since his parents died. I can't see that he'd be in any trouble this time, but his nightmares last night were very real."

"Dave's right. Leo shouldn't be in any trouble," I agreed. "But I can understand his being uneasy about this whole situation."

"Of course," Patrick said. "I hope Pete and Ethan figure out what happened. Ideally, they'll decide Marv's death was an accident, so everyone can get back to work."

"I agree. I just want this investigation to be over. I'd think they'd be finished interviewing everyone by now."

"Unless they find something on someone's phone or laptop, or in one of the bedrooms that heads them in another direction, I wouldn't think there'd be a lot more for them to learn. They talked with everyone who was at the lighthouse yesterday, didn't they?"

"They did. But briefly," I agreed. "They were just trying to confirm what happened. They weren't looking for motives for murder."

"I wonder if they've found any motives today," Patrick said softly. "Marv wasn't the most popular guy around. But, murder? Being hit by equipment and falling into the ocean doesn't sound like homicide."

"Unless somehow it was planned," I thought out loud. "Pete and Ethan are probably looking at all possibilities."

Chapter 24

In emerald tufts, flowers purple, blue and white—
Like sapphire, pearl and rich embroidery,
Buckled below fair knighthood's bending knee—
Fairies use flowers for their charactery.

—From *The Merry Wives of Windsor*, written
by William Shakespeare (1564–1616)
between 1597 and 1601.

From *Harbor Hopes*

"It doesn't make sense," said Joan. "It was such a horrible accident."

"Unless it wasn't an accident," said Amy, more calmly than she felt. "Unless someone messed with the blower so it didn't ventilate the engine right. That could happen."

"But who would do that?" said Joan. "That would be like murdering whoever was on board."

"And who was working on Caleb's engine the night before he was killed?" Amy asked, looking *from one of her friends to the other. "And who didn't want me seeing Caleb?"*

"Your father may not have liked your being with Caleb," said Carol. "But he wouldn't have killed him!"

"I think he did," said Amy calmly. "I don't think it was an accident. I've thought about it, and I believe that. I know it can't be proved. There wasn't enough left of his boat to tell. But I can't live with my father anymore." She looked from one of her friends to the other. "I decided last night, and I packed."

"But where will you go?" asked Joan.

"I hoped I could stay with one of you. Just for a little while, until I figure out where I can find another place to stay. I want to be in Haven Harbor until I graduate."

Joan and Carol were both silent.

Then Carol said, "Part of our attic is wall-boarded off. My dad was going to make an extra bedroom up there, but never finished. Maybe you could stay with us until you figure out what you want to do. If you're sure you want to leave home."

"I'm sure," Amy said firmly. "As sure as I'll ever be. See if your family would let me stay with you. I'll pay for my room and board. I've been saving my money."

Saving for a wedding that would never happen.

My crabmeat salad was gone. Delicious, but now gone.

"I'm going to check with Mom and see if she needs anything done. Or if she has any clues as to how the afternoon's going to go," said Patrick.

I got up from the table, too. "I'll see if Dave found Leo." I headed for the living room, which was the direction Dave had taken. Certainly Pete and Ethan should have finished questioning Leo by now. I hoped he'd had some lunch, too.

Dave was pacing in the large hallway between the living room and dining room.

"Did you find Leo?" I asked.

"I did. But now he's back with Ethan and Pete. Seems the other two guys who were working crew with him told the police Leo was the one who'd messed up. That he was the one who dropped the boom."

"What?" I'd been there. I hadn't seen that.

"After all, he's the youngest. He's only sixteen. And it's his first time working with any of the equipment. The two guys he was working with are from Portland. They've known each other from other jobs, and they're twenty-two and twenty-three. Turns out they met in a theater class at college and have been freelancing at theaters in Portland."

"So given a choice, blame it on the new guy." And Leo was young. Enthusiastic, but young.

"Exactly. So now Pete and Ethan are questioning Leo again. He was close to tears when I talked to him. He's convinced that no matter what he does, he gets in trouble."

"He's lucky to have you," I reminded Dave. "He needs someone who has his back."

"I hope so. But I'm not sure how to solve this situation. I believe Leo. I certainly don't believe he was responsible."

"All three of them were together. Marv was there, too. Cos and Linc and Talia were pretty close, too. I can't see blaming Leo. It wasn't one person messing up. It was a combination of circumstances that resulted in Marv's slipping. Maybe he had on the wrong shoes. Maybe he had a morning cocktail. I don't know. But the equipment shifted, and then the wind took it down. It wasn't Leo's fault, or the fault of those other two crew members."

"I don't think Pete and Ethan are going to arrest the wind," Dave said drily. "I just hope they listen to everyone,

not just those other two guys. It's certainly possible that
Leo made a mistake. He'd never worked with that equipment before, and from what he told me, they were getting
conflicting directions from Marv and Flannery and maybe
even Hank, although I don't know why he would have been
getting involved. What would a producer have to do with
setting up sound equipment?"

I shook my head. "None of it makes sense. But at least
everything you've said points to Marv's death as accidental. No one on the crew, including Leo, had any reason to
want to hurt Marv."

Dave grimaced. "He'd been driving them all a bit crazy
with directions."

"He was the *director*, Dave. That was his job," I reminded him.

"True. And if Marv's death was an accident then no one
will be arrested."

"I certainly hope that's what happens," I agreed. "But I
still don't like the idea that Leo's being blamed, or blames
himself, for what happened. Let's hope Pete and Ethan
decide Marv's death wasn't a homicide."

"Dave, could we see you for a few minutes?" Pete had
joined us in the hallway.

Dave gave me a "what's happening now" look, and
followed Pete back toward the solarium.

Now I was restless. I glanced into the living room.
Hank was sitting with Ruth and the O'Days, no doubt
talking about the script. Linc and Cos were on the couch
near the fireplace with what I assumed were scripts in
their hands, but they looked a little too cozy to be reading
lines. Jon, who played opposite Talia, was by himself most
of the time. Right now he was looking through the books
in one of Skye's bookcases, maybe searching for something to read.

Skye and Patrick must have been somewhere else. I

walked back to the terrace, where the two young men who'd accused Leo of causing Marv's fall were eating bowls of fruit and drinking beers. Maybe the crabmeat was gone. Neither of them looked as though they were dieting.

What was happening in the solarium?

I sat down at the now-cleared table where Patrick and Dave and I had eaten lunch.

What if the police decided Marv's death wasn't accidental? Who would have wanted Marv dead?

With Marv dead the movie had lost its director. True, Skye would take his place. She certainly was the most experienced member of the cast, and Patrick had said she'd thought about directing in the past. But would she kill Marv to get a chance to do so? Not only did that sound ridiculous, but she hadn't been near Marv when he'd fallen. On the other hand, if alcohol and pills were to blame, then she'd had access to both.

What about the others? Jon hadn't been nearby, either, and I'd hardly ever seen him talking to Marv. I didn't know much about Jon, I realized. Maybe Patrick would know more.

Talia? She was close to Marv when he'd fallen. He'd been her mentor, and they'd worked together on several films, although not recently. She had pills, but so did almost everyone else on the set. Again, what would be her motivation to kill Marv? Now that he was dead she might miss out on some future film roles. The movie business was a business, after all. You wouldn't kill someone who could help you, even if you didn't particularly like that person.

Cos? Linc? I thought of them together because they were almost always together. They'd been on the rocks near Marv when he'd slipped. Why were they there? Why was Talia there? Why hadn't they stayed up at the lighthouse with the other actors?

I hadn't asked any of them why they'd moved down the ledges. Instead, we'd talked about how Marv had gotten a little too friendly with Cos, and had a reputation for being too cozy with young actresses. Cos hadn't seemed upset enough about his behavior to kill Marv. She was much more interested in getting ready for her freshman year at college.

Although, since Talia, Cos, and Linc were near the scene of what I was still hoping was an accident, they might have seen something I hadn't from my perch high above them.

I couldn't believe Leo or the other two crew members had done anything intentionally. Motivation? I couldn't think of one.

My mind was buzzing, and I was just about to go back to the living room and talk with Linc and Cos when Dave and Leo joined me on the terrace.

They looked seriously upset.

Chapter 25

My Mother's gone to dwell in heaven
And sing his praise who died for her,
And to her hand a harp is given
And she's a heavenly worshipper.

—Mary Louisa Van Saun, age eight, of Paterson,
New Jersey, stitched this verse as a memorial
to both her mother, Jane Louisa Van Saun,
who died in childbirth in 1841, and her infant
sister, Jan Eletta, who only lived eighteen days.
The verse and a gravestone under weeping
willows are surrounded by a vine of ivy.

"Those two guys from Portland? They told Pete and
Ethan it was my fault," Leo blurted out. "They said I
didn't know what I was doing, and I was looking at them,
not paying attention, so I threw the boom off balance. That
it's all my fault Mr. Mason fell."

"Seems two other people thought it was Leo's fault,
too," Dave said, looking at me. His fists were clenched,
and I didn't remember ever seeing him as angry. "Flannery
Sullivan and Jon someone, one of the actors."

"Jon Whyte," I filled in.

"Whatever. They both put the blame on Leo."

"But Flannery and Jon weren't even near the accident," I said. "They were up by the lighthouse. How could they have seen what happened that clearly?"

"They both said they knew it was me," said Leo, who looked on the verge of tears. "They knew it was me because I was the only one wearing a red shirt."

He *had* been wearing a red shirt yesterday, I remembered. "But, still, they weren't close enough to see what happened. What about Linc, and Cos? What did they say? They were close by."

"I don't know. The police didn't mention them."

"Well, I'm going to talk to them," I said.

"Maybe it was my fault," said Leo. "I didn't do anything intentionally. But I didn't know as much about the equipment as the other guys did. Maybe I *am* the one who messed everything up and killed Mr. Mason."

"No one said anything about killing, Leo," Dave said, turning Leo to face him. "The police said it was probably an accident. They were just asking what happened. Marv could have fallen because he asked you to move the boom. Or because one of the three of you holding it slipped a bit on the rocks and the boom went off balance. Or the wind caught it. Everyone agrees that a gust of wind came up at the wrong time."

Leo nodded slowly. "But four people blamed me! They said it was my fault."

"That doesn't make it true," said Dave. "Sounds to me as though Marv fell because of a combination of circumstances."

"Then why did Sergeant Lambert call me in a second time to talk to me? And why did he say I needed to keep in touch?"

"Because that's what police do," I said. "Don't worry,

Leo. Somehow we'll figure out what happened. I agree with everyone who's said Marv's death was probably an accident. And accidents are seldom the fault of one person. Especially this accident." I turned to Dave. "Do you and Leo have to stay here at Aurora? Or are you free to go home?"

"We can go home, as long as we let Pete know where we are."

"Then that's what you should do. The two of you, get out of here. Relax. I don't know—eat ice cream!" I could suggest that Dave have a beer, but that wouldn't be what Leo should do. "I'm going to stay here. I'll talk to people and see what I can find out. If I hear something you should know about I'll call you, or text."

"We'll do that," said Dave. "If I stay here I might say or do something I'd regret. Com'on, Leo. Let's get out of here. Pete and Ethan have my number if they have any more questions." He started for the front door and then turned. "You have my number, too, Angie. Thanks for helping."

I nodded and watched the two of them leave. Dave was about five feet ten inches tall. At sixteen, Leo was already several inches taller than that, and probably still growing. He and Dave were lucky to have found each other.

And it was clear I had to talk with Cos and Linc. Ideally, I should talk with them separately, in case they had different versions of what had happened in the past couple of days.

I still had that photograph that had been on June Mason's phone in my head. I hadn't heard anyone mention it except me. Pete and Ethan hadn't seemed to think it was important, although they had said they'd have to be in touch with her. Could the photograph of Marv and Cos have anything to do with Marv's death? I had no idea.

Right now I had no idea about a lot of things. Mainly, about whether Marv's death had been an accident or a murder.

Most likely, an accident. But, still, it was a mystery that needed to be solved.

First, though, I wanted to talk to Cos and Linc about yesterday morning.

Chapter 26

Useful and ornamental needlework, knitting, and
netting are capable of being made, not only sources
of personal gratification, but of high moral benefit,
and the means of developing in surpassing
loveliness and grace, some of the highest and
noblest feelings of the soul.

—(anonymous) From *The Ladies'*
Work-Table Book, 1845

Cos and Linc were where I'd last seen them: sitting close
together on a couch in the living room, scripts on the
coffee table in front of them.

I stood in the doorway of the living room for a few
moments and watched as Cos started giggling at something Linc said. They looked so happy, despite all that
had been happening around them. Had I been that happy
at their ages?

I knew I hadn't. I was just beginning to believe in that
kind of happiness now, as Patrick and I spent more time
together. And I was ten years older than Cos, and Patrick
at least a dozen years older than Linc. For a moment I felt

a twinge of jealousy. I hoped the happiness they'd found now would last.

As I was watching them, Cos looked up, saw me, and waved me over.

"What's happening now?" she asked. "We decided to stay clear of everyone. Pete and Ethan talked with both of us this morning, and they didn't have many questions. Have they decided whether Marv's death was an accident or not?"

Linc reached over and squeezed her hand. "We can't imagine why anyone would kill him, but the police must have some ideas, or at least guesses, or they wouldn't be keeping all of us here."

"You've helped solve mysteries in Haven Harbor before," Cos pointed out. "Do you have any ideas?"

"Not really," I said, sitting on an ocean-blue armchair next to the couch. I wanted to talk to each of them alone, but how could I do that without dismissing one of them? I plunged ahead. "Pete asked me to find out what I can about what happened yesterday, and about Marv. You've both been working with him, and with the others here, and those who were down at the lighthouse yesterday. Would you mind if I talked to each of you separately?"

Cos and Linc looked at each other. "I don't think that's necessary," said Linc. "We don't have any secrets from each other."

I wondered about that. Everyone had secrets.

Cos patted his hand. "It's all right, Linc. Angie interviewed me when there were problems a year ago. Police and detectives like to talk to people separately. Did you know Angie worked with a private detective in Arizona? Anyway, a few minutes ago you said you were restless and thought we should take a walk. Why don't you take that walk now, and I'll talk to Angie?"

Linc hesitated. "Are you sure?"

"I'm sure," Cos said, giving him a quick kiss on his cheek. "Then when you come back, I'll go for a walk and you can talk with Angie. It shouldn't take too long, should it, Angie?"

"Probably not," I agreed, impressed with how smoothly Cos had managed to separate the two of them. "And I'd really appreciate having a little time with each of you separately."

Linc didn't look happy, but he stood up. "I'll be back soon. I don't see what either Cos or I know that would help you, Angie, but we want this mystery solved as soon as possible. If the filming starts, then we'll know for sure we'll both be finished before our schools start. We've been worried Marv's death would hold up the whole production and mess up our schedules."

I nodded. "Skye is going to replace Marv. I assume you've heard that."

They both nodded.

"But I understand your concern. If I hear anything about the production schedule I'll let you know."

"Thanks," Linc said, and headed for the front door.

"So," said Cos. "What do you want to know?"

"Yesterday morning you were down at the lighthouse."

"Right. Skye had said any of us would be welcome to go down and watch, and Linc thought it would be fun. We were getting tired of going through the same lines most days, especially since, as soon as we'd memorized them, Marv or the writers would change them. We thought it would be fun to get away from the sets at the Anderson house and see what the crew was setting up. I have a scene at the lighthouse later in the movie, anyway. The scene where I go to mourn for my boyfriend, and decide to leave my father's house. So I wanted to see where they were going to film that."

"I was down at the lighthouse, too, on the other side of

the lighthouse from where you and the other actors were. I saw Marv head down toward the three young men setting up the boom."

"Right. He was upset. I think he'd been up pretty early. He smelled of scotch, and he was complaining about everything. He told Flannery that the crew didn't know what they were doing. Flannery said they were doing fine. Then Marv headed down the ledges to where the mic was being set up. He said he'd show them how it was done."

"What did you think?"

"I was glad he was leaving us to bother someone else. We wouldn't have to listen to his complaints anymore. Talia and Linc were watching him closer than I was. Linc said Marv didn't know the rocks, which of course he didn't, and that he was walking unsteadily. Linc said we should follow him and try to get him to go back to the lighthouse. We knew the ledges well, of course. We'd been climbing on them since we were toddlers! So we both took off." Cos hesitated. "Talia did, too. She said Marv was a pain, but he could get in a lot of trouble down on the rocks."

"So all three of you followed Marv?"

"Yeah. He probably didn't even notice. He was yelling at those kids on the crew. Leo Blackwell and the other two, who I didn't know. They were trying to pay attention to him, but a strong breeze came up, and they were fighting with the equipment. Linc yelled at Marv to stay away. That he was getting in the way, and distracting the crew. Talia got to Marv ahead of Linc, and she yelled at him, too. I'm not sure what she said, but everyone was angry at that point. Marv said something about 'stay out of something that's not your business.'"

"So Marv heard what Linc and Talia were saying."

"I don't know if he heard everything. It all happened so fast. We were just above where he and the crew were, and he was yelling at them. They hesitated. I'm not sure they understood what he wanted them to do. And while they were hesitating a strong gust of wind came up and pulled the boom out of one of the boys' hands and it knocked Marv down. You know what happened then. He fell off the rocks and into the water." Cos swallowed hard. "It was awful. All my life people have talked about how dangerous those ledges are. But I'd never seen anyone fall until then."

"The crew member who lost control of the boom. Was it Leo?"

"No, no. It was one of the others. The guy with the spider tattoo on his arm."

Chapter 27

Ye glittering toys of earth adieu
A nobler choice be mine
A real Prize attracts my view
A treasure all divine

—Sampler worked in silk on linen in 1834
by thirteen-year-old Mary Ann McCosh,
daughter of Samuel and Elisabeth McCosh,
in Washington County, Pennsylvania. Mary
Ann's work is bordered on three sides with large
flowers, and she's included a house, trees, and
birds on the bottom border, along with the name
of her teacher, Mary Tidball. Four years later
Mary Ann was also teaching embroidery.

Cos looked pale. "That's all. I don't know anything more
about Marv or about yesterday."

I saw Linc heading in our direction. "One more question, Cos. Did you ever see Marv taking medication of
any kind?"

She looked puzzled. "I think he had some allergy pills.

He said once there were too many wildflowers around here, and he blew his nose a lot. And I told you before I thought he had pills for high blood pressure. What does that have to do with anything?"

"I'm not sure. But I wanted to check," I answered. "Did he ever offer you any pills?"

"No. I don't have allergies," she said, looking glad that Linc was rejoining us. "Did you have a nice walk?"

"It's hot out there, but at least it isn't as stuffy as in the house," he said. "Are you finished talking?"

"We are," said Cos, and I nodded.

"Your turn, Linc. I'm going to get some lemonade and go and sit on the terrace," said Cos. "When you're finished, let me know."

Linc sat where Cos had been on the couch. Had I found out anything important from Cos? Marv drank scotch and took allergy pills. Cos thought the crew member with a spider tattoo was the one who'd dropped the boom. I'd let Pete know that. But still nothing that explained why Marv had fallen off the rocks other than he'd slipped.

Of course, the three crew members, including Leo, had been close to him, and so had Cos and Linc and Talia. Could any of them have pushed him? I hadn't seen that happen. But everything had happened so quickly, and they were all close to one another and to the equipment.

"So, what do you want to ask me?" Linc leaned back on the couch. "I can't think of anything I could say that would help."

I wasn't sure what he could say either. At least Cos hadn't said Leo caused Marv's accident. That might help Dave and Leo.

"Let's start with Marv. He hired you last spring to play the part of Caleb."

"Right. Actually, he hired Cos. He said she looked just right to be Amy. She suggested that I could be Caleb."

"No tryout? No reading the script?"

"Nothing. I don't think he really cared about me. He wanted Cos, and if she thought I'd do fine, that was okay with him. I agreed. The money was good, and spending time with Cos would be good. Plus, I'd probably never get another chance to be in a movie. It sounded like a fun way to spend the summer."

"He must have really been impressed by Cos."

"He was." Linc frowned. "Too impressed. I think he assumed she was naïve. A local girl who didn't know anything about the world."

"And was she?"

"No way. Her sister was in prison, so she'd lived through all of that, and her boss at the bookstore was always hassling her. If you ask me, the guy at the bookstore was a pervert. He was always making excuses for Cos to stay around, or work in corners where he was working and she couldn't move away from him. But Cos knew how to take care of herself."

"Why do you think she stayed working at the bookstore?"

"For the money, of course. He was paying more than other people in town. And Cos loves books, and history, especially Maine history. When it was quiet at the bookstore she could read a little. She'd rather be working there than washing dishes or waitressing someplace."

"So you both agreed to work on the movie."

"Right. When we signed those contracts last spring I don't think either of us had a clue Marv was the same kind of guy Cos had been coping with at the bookstore. But it was clear to both of us pretty fast. At least I was here. I hung around with Cos every chance I could. I suspect everyone thought we were teenagers in love." Linc's face reddened. "Maybe we are. But I was also trying to make sure Cos was protected. That she wasn't alone with Marv."

"You told me earlier that you took a lot of pictures this summer," I said.

"Right. It was pretty boring waiting around to read lines, or memorize lines and then have Marv or the writers change them. My uncle gave me a good digital camera when I graduated from high school. I really hadn't used it. But taking pictures gave me something to do. Hank yelled at me at first. I told you earlier: our contracts said no pictures. But I convinced him I was just learning, and I wouldn't show the pictures to anyone, or send them to anyone." Linc lowered his voice. "I did show a couple to Cos. They were of her, and I thought she'd like them. But I didn't send them, even to her, and I didn't post them."

"I know you said no one was allowed to take pictures. But I saw a lot of people clicking their cell phones at Patrick's party."

"Yeah," said Linc. "I noticed that, too. Maybe Hank was making an exception because the party wasn't part of the movie. I don't know. But I obeyed his rules. I took pictures, but I didn't show them to anyone, or send them, or post them." He grinned a bit. "Boy, have I got a lot of pictures!"

"Did you take any down at the lighthouse yesterday?" I suddenly thought. Maybe Linc had seen something that would help tell what had happened to Marv.

"Not yesterday. I'd been to the lighthouse thousands of times, so I left the camera in my car that morning," he answered. "So, no clues to exactly what happened are in my camera. But I saw as much as anyone else."

"You and Cos left the lighthouse and followed Marv down to where the sound equipment was being set up."

"We did. But we weren't really following Marv. We were following Talia."

"Talia? Why?"

Linc shook his head. "I'm really not sure. Cos has been pretty tight with her in the past week or so. And Marv was in a foul mood—sorry, but he was. Maybe he'd had too much to drink the night before, or he had a headache. I have no idea. But when everyone except the crew was up by the lighthouse, he kept cussing. I won't repeat what he said, but he was angry about everything. He didn't like where Flannery had told the crew to put the boom. He was angry because the script wasn't finished. He said no one cared about this film except for him, and no one was listening to him. That the actors should be practicing their lines and not sightseeing at the lighthouse. Skye tried to get him to calm down. She handed him a cup of coffee, but he knocked it out of her hand and it splattered all over the rocks. She jumped back. I think the coffee burned her hand."

As Linc talked, I realized I hadn't talked with Skye. She'd been busy with her guests and the police. Patrick had talked with her a few times, of course, but she and I had hardly spoken today, except when I'd congratulated her.

Linc continued, "Anyway, since Marv was in such a horrible mood, Cos and I stayed away from him. We went farther up, nearer to the lighthouse. After all, we'd seen those ledges and the lighthouse since we'd been kids. What we really were there to see was how they were going to set up the sound equipment. We knew how uneven the rocks were. We figured Flannery had been there before and found a place where they could balance the boom. But thinking back on what happened, I don't think he had. I don't think Flannery had a clue. He just told the three guys he'd brought with him to set up the equipment."

"And Marv was angry with him."

"Marv was angry with everyone. Some of what he was saying didn't even make sense."

"What do you mean?"

"I couldn't understand his words. They were—garbled,

I guess is what you'd call it. And then knocking the coffee out of Skye's hand. It just didn't make sense."

"Was Marv usually like that? When he was directing scenes?"

"Oh, he always yelled a bit. Mostly I figured because he wanted to make sure we all heard him. And listened to him. He was always saying no one listened to him. But yesterday morning he was on a tear. Wicked weird. That's why Cos and I stayed out of his way."

"But then you followed him down onto the ledges."

"We didn't plan to do that. But Talia tried to get Marv to calm down. She was the only one who was even near him when he took off toward the crew. Flannery was on the other side of the lighthouse, and Skye and Jon were back by the table where the coffee and doughnuts were."

"So Talia was talking to Marv."

"She kept telling him to relax. That he should sit down on one of the benches up by the lighthouse. That his blood pressure would go up."

"Did he listen to her?"

"No way. He called her a name he shouldn't have. Then he said no one was listening to him; that he'd have to do everything himself. And he headed down the rocks. Talia followed him, telling him to slow down, that the ledges were dangerous."

"And?"

"Of course, he didn't listen. He told her to shut up. That's when Cos said maybe we should follow them, too. She was afraid Marv or Talia would slip on the rocks and fall. Funny, because of course that's what happened."

"You were all close to the boom when it fell and hit Marv."

"Talia was closest. She and Leo even reached out to try to catch the boom before it hit Marv. But, you know, they didn't catch it. Marv moved to get out of the way, but he slipped. A lot of the rocks down there are covered with rockweed. Cos and I were careful not to step on it. We knew how slippery it was. I don't think the others were paying attention."

Linc shook his head. "All of yesterday morning was awful. Marv acting weird, and people shouting, and then Marv falling, and the police questioning everyone. I wondered if Hank or whoever would be in charge when Marv was gone would cancel the whole film. I'll tell you, Cos and I were ready to quit and go home. We'd thought being part of a movie would be fun. Yesterday was a nightmare."

Chapter 28

The star of Bethlehem
Brighter than the rising day
When the sun of glory shines.
Brighter than the diamond's ray
Sparkling in Golonda's mines
Beaming through the clouds of wo
Smiles in Mercy's diadem
On the guilty world below
The Star that rose in Bethlehem.

—Elizabeth Orme, aged nine, stitched
this sampler in Washington, DC.

Linc was the first person who'd said Marv was definitely
acting strangely yesterday morning at the lighthouse,
although several other people had said it wouldn't have
been unusual if he'd been drunk. Or, more likely, hungover.

Among those people was the medical examiner, who'd
also said he'd taken anti-anxiety pills. From what Linc had
described, it sounded as though he could have used some
of them yesterday morning.

Cos had said he took allergy pills. Could allergy pills

interact with alcohol? Maybe. But Pete had been pretty
clear that toxicology tests had shown the pills Marv had
taken were for anxiety, not allergies. Or what about pills
for high blood pressure? Talia and Cos had both suggested that.

It wouldn't have been unusual for someone his age to
take medication for high blood pressure. Especially someone in a high-pressure job.

No answers. Just more questions.

Cos and Linc were now talking with the writers. Maybe
they'd changed the script again, with or without Marv's
suggestions.

I wished I had my phone back. I wanted to talk to
Gram. And Sarah was probably wondering what was
happening.

I went back to the bar and poured myself a glass of iced
tea. The fans on the first floor of Aurora kept the air
moving, but even in an old house whose wooden walls
and high ceilings kept rooms cooler than ones built more
recently, a week of temperatures in the eighties, even on
the coast of Maine, meant the house wasn't comfortable.

Ron Winfield was soaking mussels in one of the sinks.
Lunch was over. He must have been starting dinner. And
something in one of the ovens smelled delicious. "Cake?"
I asked.

"Blueberry cake," he said, nodding. "And there'll be a
lemon sauce for it."

"Yum," I said. "I love blueberry season. So many different ways to prepare them, and all of them delicious."

"I agree. I've already served muffins, and they disappeared quickly. The only thing that wasn't as popular as I
assumed were my blueberry pancakes. I even gave people
a choice of blueberry syrup or maple syrup. But I heard
comments like 'too many carbs' and 'too many calories.'"

"Sorry I wasn't here that day. Those wouldn't have

been my concerns," I said. "My only complaint about blueberry pancakes, or blueberry anything, is when the cook skimps on the blueberries."

"A woman after my own heart. Or taste buds," he agreed. "So you're still here. I thought some of you who aren't staying at the house would be allowed to go home, or to wherever else you're staying, by now."

"A good thought. But Sergeant Lambert asked me to check on some things. You said Marv Mason's drink of choice was single malt, right?"

"Definitely. I had to order extra more than once."

"Are you sure you didn't see him drinking any yesterday morning, before most of the people staying here went down to the lighthouse?"

Ron frowned. "As I told you before, I don't remember seeing Mr. Mason at all yesterday morning. Maybe he'd left for the lighthouse early. But, who knows? Everyone was in a hurry to have coffee and something to eat, and then leave. Some mornings, like today, breakfast really turns into brunch. But yesterday the writers stayed here, but everyone else left early."

I was pretty sure Marv had been at the lighthouse when I'd gotten there. But, then, just about everybody else was there, too. I didn't know when they'd all arrived.

"Thanks, Ron. I've really loved your cooking. And mussels, cooked in wine and herbs, I'm guessing? With French bread for dunking?"

"Of course. And for those who don't want seafood, or are weary of it, I'll have chicken breasts in a wine sauce with rice as an alternative."

"And that blueberry cake with lemon sauce for dessert."

"And fruit, of course. This crowd is very big on fruit."

"Well, I hope I'm here for dinner," I said. "Have you seen Skye or Patrick recently?"

"Not in the past half hour. You could check the terrace. Or the solarium. I don't think the police are still interviewing people."

"Thanks. I'll do that," I said. I headed for the solarium first. Pete was there alone. I knocked on the door and he gestured that I should come in.

"Finished with the interviews?"

"Pretty much," he said. "How about you? Find out anything helpful?"

"Marv wasn't the most popular guy around," I said. "Especially with the young women. He spent a little too much time with them. He was also driving the writers crazy, changing the script almost every day. He drank single malt scotch. A lot of it. He took pills, but he told Cos they were for his allergies. Talia thought they might be for high blood pressure. And he was in a really bad mood yesterday morning." I hesitated. "Cos said if one guy knocked over the mic boom it wasn't Leo. It was one of the guys in the crew who had a spider tattoo."

Pete nodded. "A few details there I hadn't heard, but nothing conclusive, I'm afraid."

"I heard the two other guys on the crew were saying it was Leo's fault that Marv fell."

"They'd clearly gotten their stories together before I talked with them," Pete said. "But Ethan and I aren't convinced Leo did anything more or less than anyone who was near Marv when he fell. And, no motive. Ethan wondered if the two Portland guys came up with that story so no one would blame them. In any case, we told Dave to take Leo home."

"I'm glad he's not high on your suspect list," I said. "Have you been in touch with Marv's wife?"

"We found her. Or, she found us. She's right where we thought she was: at that hotel in Portland. I gave her my card when I saw her at the lighthouse, and she called to see when she could make arrangements to take Marv's body back to California. I told her she'd have to wait at least a few more days."

"Did you find out why she lied to me about when she arrived in Maine?"

"I didn't bother asking her. She knows we checked on her flight, and her hotel reservations. She said there was nowhere suitable for her to stay in or near Haven Harbor, so she decided to stay in Portland."

"Ninety minutes away," I said.

"Right. But she wasn't involved in the production. She's pretty much off our radar."

"Would you mind if I talked with her?" I said. "I did meet her yesterday morning, and I'd think she'd be lonely, by herself in a strange city, when her husband has just died."

Pete shrugged. "If you want to, sure. I don't think she'll be much help knowing what happened here in the past couple of days, but there's always the chance she knows something from the past that might help us."

I nodded. "And any chance I can get my phone back? I assure you I didn't call Marv, or text anyone about him. I'd like to be in touch with Gram."

Pete smiled. "We took everyone's phones and computers and tablets this morning, of course. But I figured we weren't going to find anything of value to us on yours, so I still have it."

The basket he'd been using when he collected phones that morning was in the corner of the solarium. It was now almost empty. Probably the crime scene folks had taken most of them.

He handed me mine. "Here. Now you can be connected to your grandmother. And, if you decide to go to Portland and you learn anything, let me know, too."

"Thanks, Pete. Anything else you need from me right now?"

"I don't think so."

"I'll check in with Gram, and then go to Portland. Which hotel is June Mason staying at again?"

"The Eastland."

"Of course," I said, smiling. The Eastland Park had been renovated and was officially called the Westin Portland Harborview now, but it was the most famous hotel in Portland. It had been built in 1927 and was still called the Eastland by locals. Many famous people had stayed there over the years, but the ones mentioned most often were Eleanor Roosevelt and the Roosevelts' dog, Fala, who stopped there on their way to the Roosevelts' summer home on Campobello Island. Although few hotels allowed dogs in those days, and officially, neither did the Eastland, Eleanor Roosevelt always called ahead and Fala was considered a special guest.

I suspected Mrs. Mason didn't know the history of the Eastland/Portland Harborview when she'd arrived, but she'd know it by now. That hotel was proud of its history.

"I haven't seen Skye or Patrick recently. If you see them, would you let them know I've left, and where I'm going?" I asked.

"No problem," said Pete. "Wish I could come up with some reason to leave, too. Between the heat and everyone asking when they can get their phones back, it hasn't exactly been a fun day."

"Any more details from Augusta?"

"Nothing from the medical examiner. The crime scene guys found a lot of medications this morning and are keeping a list of what they found, and how many doses, and so forth. They need to get anything necessary back to the owners this afternoon."

"Anti-depressants? Tranquilizers?"

"I don't have a list yet, but a number of people had medications in that general category. And our technical group is still going through all the phones and computers and tablets. If they find anything important, they'll let us know. So far there's been silence from that direction."

"Hope you get some more information soon," I said.

"So do I. Who knows? Maybe you'll come up with something in Portland. Do assure Mrs. Mason we're doing the best we can, and will be in touch as soon as we have any answers."

Chapter 29

*Light or fancy needlework often forms a portion of the
evening's recreation for the ladies of the household,
and this may be varied by an occasional game at chess
or backgammon. It has often been remarked, too, that
nothing is more delightful to the feminine members of a
family, than the reading aloud of some good standard
work or amusing publications.*

—"Of the Manner of Passing Evenings at Home,"
The Book of Household Management
by Isabella Beeton, 1861.

I slipped my phone into the pocket of my jeans and
headed for my car. With a houseful of people missing their
cell phones I didn't want anyone to notice I'd managed to
retrieve mine. I'd been planning to call Gram from my car,
but then realized someone walking around the property
might see me. I didn't want to seem paranoid, but I could
just as easily stop in to see Gram before I headed for
Portland. I'd already decided not to call June Mason before
I left. It would be too easy to say "don't come" on the telephone.

Gram was home, as I'd hoped, and happy to see me.

"So, fill me in. Have Pete and Ethan figured out exactly how Marv died? How is everyone taking this?"

"Everyone at Aurora except the writers was down at the lighthouse when Marv slipped and fell. The police got a warrant, so they've confiscated everyone's phone and laptop and any other electronic devices, and have been checking rooms for medications."

"Medications?" Gram asked. "Wait, before you answer. Lemonade or iced tea or water?"

"Iced tea would be wonderful," I agreed. "I love that you make yours with fresh lemons and mint."

"Mint's just outside in the garden," Gram answered, pouring me a glass. "And the rectory stays pretty cool. The minister before Tom had air conditioners installed for the downstairs, and we don't use the rooms upstairs often anyway, so we just close them off when we don't have company."

Gram's enormous yellow Maine coon cat, Juno, rubbed herself around my ankles. She probably was sending a message to Trixi that I'd been visiting another cat.

"You're lucky. The heat's been getting to me. Skye has a lot of fans at Aurora, but no air-conditioning," I said, sitting at the kitchen table. Gram poured herself a glass of lemonade with mint and joined me.

"I'm surprised. She spent so much fixing that house up last year," Gram noted. "Although she probably figured she was in Maine, so she wouldn't need air-conditioning here."

"True. No one in Maine had air-conditioning when I was growing up," I said. "A lot of the restaurants and motels have air-conditioning now."

"Have you seen that old motel out on Route One? It still has a big sign out front saying 'Stop here! We have heat!'"

"I noticed that! Either they're not up-to-date with the

times, or they think that's funny now." I took another drink. I should have been bloated today, I'd had so much to drink, but I was still hot and thirsty, even in Gram's cool kitchen.

"So, why are the police checking medications?"

"The medical examiner ruled Marv's death 'suspicious.' His blood alcohol level was very high, and he'd also ingested a lot of anti-anxiety medication. If he hadn't slipped on the rocks when the boom hit him, he could have died from what was in his system."

"So, assuming he wasn't trying to kill himself, did he accidentally take all that alcohol and drugs, or did someone else give them to him?"

"Exactly, Gram. He was definitely known as a drinker. Expensive drinker, too. Single malt scotch, which he sometimes even had to start his day."

Gram raised her eyebrows. "Interesting."

"And tranquilizers, or anti-anxiety pills, or sedatives—seems pretty much everyone at Aurora had some of those. Film productions must be very stressful places."

"So no answers yet," said Gram. "By the way, is Ruth over there?"

I nodded. "The writers are still writing. Or at least talking about writing. Marv wanted some of the scenes changed, and I guess they're doing that, despite everything. I talked with her briefly this morning. She's with Marie and Thomas all the time."

"I keep thinking about what she said the other night at her house," Gram said. "And I'll admit I've made a couple of phone calls."

"Phone calls?"

"Well, we know Ruth often bases her books on events here in Haven Harbor, right?"

I nodded.

"And the book they're basing this movie on was one of

her first, so the real incident she was thinking of took place in the late fifties or early sixties. As it happens, I remember people talking about a sad story in town. Two teenagers were in love. The girl's father didn't approve because the boy wanted to be a lobsterman, and he wanted better for his daughter. Her mother had died, and her father was known to be very possessive; he really didn't want her to leave home, and certainly not when she was young."

"And?" That certainly sounded like the script for *Harbor Heartbreak*.

"And one day the boy was out lobstering and his boat blew up. No one knew exactly what happened, but the girl was convinced her father was responsible; that he'd done something to the boat's motor."

"That sounds like the story Ruth was telling us the other night."

"Exactly. And, as Ruth said, the girl here in the harbor never spoke with her father again. She moved out; lived with the family of one of her girlfriends. A couple of years later she married someone else. Her husband joined the army and was sent to Vietnam and came home injured. . . ."

"The girl was Ruth, then!" I said. "She once told me. Not about the young lobsterman or her father, but about marrying Ben. That was when she started writing her erotica. He'd lost his leg in Vietnam and was in an army hospital in Texas, and she joined him down there until he was well enough to come home. But he was never able to work. I don't know if it was his physical injury, or what we now call PTSD, but for years she took care of him and supported them both by her writing. They bought that little house where she lives now."

"All correct," said Gram. "That's what really happened, as Ruth lived it. But when I started asking around town about it, I heard another version of the story."

"Another version?"

"Not everyone believed her father had sabotaged that boat that blew up. Ruth was convinced he had, because he'd felt so strongly about her not marrying the young lobsterman. That's the character Linc plays in the movie, right?"

"Right," I agreed. "Cos plays Amy, the Ruth character. Linc plays Caleb."

"Well, anyway, turns out some people in town had other ideas about what might have happened to that boat. People were pretty sure someone had tampered with the engine so it would blow up, but they didn't all think Ruth's father had anything to do with it, and he always denied it."

"Who did they think did it?" I asked.

"Ben," said Gram. "The man she married. Turns out he'd had a crush on her for years, and he didn't want her to marry the young lobsterman, either. Ruth didn't know anything about that, but when people began asking questions, Ben married Ruth and joined the army."

"He got out of town."

"Exactly. That was before the draft. He didn't have to go. By the time he got back the story was ancient history, and Ben was disabled. If Ruth ever heard the rumors, she didn't admit them. Her father had died by then, too."

"So she never spoke to her father again?"

"That's the story," Gram confirmed.

"But the real story is that she might have married the man who killed her first love."

"The real story, yes. But there's no proof. It's just a story."

"And one Ruth would certainly not want in the film."

"Although it would make for a more interesting plot," Gram pointed out. "I wonder if anyone else working on the film has heard that version of the story. You said Marv was trying to get the writers to change the early section of the script."

"I don't know exactly what he wanted them to do. I did hear he wanted stronger scenes between Amy and her father. But I don't even think there's a 'Ben' character in the script. Although in one scene Sarah and I heard them rehearsing Amy did say she was going to see the fireworks on the Fourth of July with several friends, and not all the names she mentioned were girls."

"Was Ruth down at the lighthouse when Marv died?" Gram asked.

"No. None of the writers were," I said. "And certainly Ruth couldn't take her walker down on the ledges and push Marv off!"

"Of course not. But she could mix a drink for someone," said Gram. "Or someone else could have done it for her if they'd heard her story and decided the film should tell the truth."

Chapter 30

Chester Goodale, born Sept. 1764,
married Asenath Cook Aug. 10, 1790,
who was born October 11, 1770.
The births of their children are as follows . . .

—A genealogical sampler stitched in 1809 by
sixteen-year-old Laura Goodale, daughter of
Chester and Asenath, with a strawberry vine
border. Asenath took the sampler as proof of her
marriage when she submitted her application
for a Revolutionary War Veteran's Pension.

The drive to Portland took about ninety minutes, as usual,
although the road was crowded with summer traffic. I was
thankful I'd splurged and paid extra so my car included air-
conditioning. Not everyone in Maine had it, and this July
was one of the times it made life much more comfortable.

Next time the heat was driving me crazy at my house I
should just go for a drive.

The Westin Portland Harborview was a few blocks off
the highway, close to Congress Street, and across the
street from the Portland Museum of Art. Portland wasn't

an enormous city, and you could walk to most commercial areas like the Old Port and the Arts District from the hotel without much trouble, although when the temperature was this high, or in the winter, when cold winds were blowing in across the Gulf of Maine, driving was the preferred option.

I pulled into the parking garage next to the hotel, hoping June Mason was in her room this hot afternoon and hadn't decided to visit any of the museums or shopping areas, or even move to another hotel down in the Old Port, the area by the water where boutiques and restaurants and their patrons filled the streets.

The clerk at the front desk wouldn't tell me June Mason's room number (privacy and safety, he reminded me) but did agree to connect me to her room. I picked up the lobby phone he pointed to and hoped she'd answer, and be willing to see me.

"Hello?" Her voice sounded tentative.

"Hello, Mrs. Mason," I said. "This is Angie Curtis. We met at the lighthouse in Haven Harbor yesterday and talked a little?"

"I remember you," she replied. "Have you heard anything new about the investigation?"

"Not a lot," I admitted. "The police are still questioning people. But I was coming to Portland"—a bit of an untruth—"and thought you might like some company."

She didn't respond.

I glanced at a nearby poster advertising the Top of the East, the hotel's rooftop lounge. "Maybe I could buy you a drink at the hotel's lounge? It has a beautiful view of the city and harbor."

Silence, again.

"Or we could go for a walk through the Arts District?

There are a number of galleries nearby, and the Portland Museum of Art."

"It's too hot outside. I thought Maine was supposed to be cool. I walked a couple of blocks this morning, but I wasn't comfortable. Art's not really my thing anyway. And I was afraid I'd miss a telephone call from the police if they called the hotel. They said they'd let me know when I could arrange to take Marv back home to California."

"Then the lounge? Or I could come to your room and we could order some tea or wine from room service."

She hesitated again. "Did the police send you to question me?"

"No!" I said, although Pete did know I was headed to Portland. "I've just been thinking about you, and thought you might like some company."

"All right." June's voice sounded as though she didn't want to argue or question anymore. "I'm in room 486."

"I'll be there in a few minutes," I said.

I ignored the DO NOT DISTURB sign June had hung on her door and knocked. As usual, I was wearing jeans and a T-shirt. She wore tan slacks and a brown sweater set I suspected was cashmere. No wonder she'd been hot outside this morning.

"What a beautiful room," I said. Room 486 was a small, sophisticated suite furnished with a desk and couch and extra easy chairs as well as a king-sized bed. The walls were white, and the bedspread, pillows, and pictures were all shades of navy and red. A bit of a maritime theme, but not cutesy, the way some Maine hotels and restaurants were decorated. It could have used a needlepointed cushion, though.

The floor-to-ceiling windows overlooked Portland and Casco Bay. The view from the rooftop lounge might show a bit more of the area, but room 486 was certainly more than acceptable. "What a wonderful view!" I said.

June hadn't said anything. Then she sighed. "I suppose I should thank you for coming. You're right. I've had a difficult couple of days here. It probably would be good to talk to someone." She gestured to the couch. I sat there as she sat in one of the chairs. "Shall I order something for us? I'll admit, I haven't been eating much."

A bottle of single malt scotch was on the desk in the corner. It was almost empty. Maybe June and her husband shared that preference? A bottle of Pellegrino was also on the bedside table nearest to the window.

"It's early for dinner. Maybe they have a fruit and cheese platter? Or tea sandwiches?" she asked. "And would you like a glass of wine or some other drink?"

"Water would be fine. I'm driving."

"Of course," she said. "Why don't I order those tea sandwiches, and some sparkling water, then."

She called room service while I thought through what I should say. But she spoke first.

"So, how did you know I was staying here?" she asked. "And why are you here? We talked for a few minutes yesterday. There was no reason for you to follow me to Portland."

"I didn't follow you here. I had a delivery for my business to drop off," I lied.

"Your business?"

"I run Mainely Needlepoint. We do custom needlepoint for decorators and customers, as well as needlepointed pictures and pillows for high-end gift shops. We also identify and repair antique needlepoint, when that's possible."

"Interesting," she said. "So how are you connected to *Harbor Heartbreak*?"

"I'm working on the sets." I didn't know how well June knew Skye, but I decided to be blunt. "I'm also dating

Skye West's son, Patrick. One of the screenwriters is also a Mainely Needlepointer."

"I see," she said. "Small town, everyone connected."

"Something like that," I agreed. "I grew up in Haven Harbor."

"And how did you know I was here?"

"Sergeant Lambert told me," I admitted. "I've been worried about you. It must have been a shock to see your husband die. You hadn't come back to Haven Harbor as far as I knew, and you weren't at Skye's house, where your husband had been staying and where most of the major people involved with the film were. So I asked Sergeant Lambert if he knew where you were, and he told me."

"I see."

"I'll admit, I was also curious. You told me you'd flown in from Los Angeles the night before I met you. You showed me a picture taken that night here in Maine. But Sergeant Lambert said you'd been in Maine for two days before that."

"He told you that?"

"Of course, whoever sent you that picture would have sent it to you the night before Marv's accident. But why did you tell me you'd just gotten to Maine when you'd been here for at least forty-eight hours?"

"You seem like a smart young woman. I suppose it might have occurred to you that I'd gotten similar pictures before the one I showed you. And that I might have wanted to talk with my husband about them."

"But you didn't go to Skye's house, where he was staying."

"No. He didn't want me involved with his business. I called him, and he came here."

Maybe that explained the bottle of scotch.

"Was he here the night before he died?"

"He was. We were both here. We had a lot to talk about.

He left early that morning to get back to Skye's house, change, and then get to the set. He'd told me about Haven Harbor and the lighthouse, and I decided I'd like to see it all. I didn't tell him I was going to go there. I had a rental car. It wasn't a problem."

"Until you saw what happened when you got there."

"Exactly."

"Has Sergeant Lambert told you your husband's death has been ruled suspicious?"

"Suspicious?"

A knock on the door meant our sandwiches had arrived. June signed for the food the uniformed hotel employee put on the coffee table between the couch and the chairs.

"Suspicious? I was there. I saw him slip and fall. It was an accident."

"He did slip and fall," I agreed. "But his blood alcohol level was very high, and he'd also taken a number of anti-anxiety pills. It's surprising he hadn't fallen before the boom hit him. He was very unsteady when he was on the ledges. You might have noticed that yourself."

"The police said this?"

I nodded. "They're interviewing everyone who was at the lighthouse that morning. I assume they've talked with you."

"Briefly," she admitted. "What you've just told me explains why they asked what medications Marv was taking."

"And he'd been drinking quite a bit in the days before the accident," I said. "Or so some of his fellow guests at Aurora, Skye's home, have said."

June shrugged. "Marv drinks. That isn't a secret."

"Who sent you those pictures?" I asked.

"I told you. I don't know," June said.

I reached over and took one of the small sandwiches. Tuna and cucumber. "But he'd had other relationships with young women on the sets of movies he'd directed, right? At least that's what I've heard."

"There's always gossip around movie sets," said June. "Marv and I've talked about that before. The young woman in this movie? She was nothing new."

"Then why did you fly all the way from California to Maine?"

June sat back in her chair, sipped her scotch, and smiled at me. "I'd never visited Maine before. I'd heard it was a beautiful place."

I finished my sandwich. It was delicious, but I was still full of crabmeat from lunch.

Suddenly June stood. "I think maybe you'd better go. If the police want to talk with me, they know where I am. I just want to take Marv's body back home. I don't see that talking with you is helping me. In fact, I suspect you're doing your own investigation. I don't need that, and neither does Marv. He's dead. It was an accident. Now you should go."

I nodded. "Maybe you're right." I got up and walked to the door.

Chapter 31

Remember now thy Creator in the days
Of thy youth while the evil days come not
Nor the years draw nigh when thou shalt
Say I have no pleasure in them.

—Susan Salter, age ten, stitched this sampler
in Elizabethtown, New Jersey, in 1826.
She married George Wallace in 1843.

Driving home I realized I'd been a bit heavy-handed, and I hadn't found out anything helpful, except that Marv Mason hadn't spent the night before he died at Aurora. June had seemed very cool about everything. But she might still be in shock.

She'd flown to Maine, her husband had died, and now she was waiting to fly home to California.

Had she really decided to come to Maine to see the state? I suspected not. But if her husband had a history of relationships with young actresses, and she'd received pictures of him with Cos, then it made sense that she might have decided to check the situation out herself.

What had she and Marv talked about that night before

his death? That bottle of single malt in his wife's room was almost empty.

Had he brought the scotch, or had she?

Although that wasn't important. Room service certainly could have delivered one or more bottles, and probably had. I hoped June ate the rest of the sandwiches we'd ordered. Sitting alone in a hotel room and drinking scotch without eating didn't sound like a good idea.

But, then, I didn't know how much she normally drank.

I glanced at the clock in my car. I should have eaten more sandwiches. I'd be getting back to Haven Harbor too late to check out Ron Winfield's mussels. They'd sounded tempting. I should buy some myself and check a recipe book. My cooking skills were better than they'd been a year ago, but I still felt more relaxed ordering at restaurants than depending on my own expertise.

Luckily, Patrick was a good cook.

I drove north on Route 295, enjoying the air-conditioning in my car, but still puzzled by Marv's "suspicious death."

It hadn't been a problem to establish that he drank heavily. Not only had no one denied that, most people had known he drank single malt scotch. Expensive single malt scotch, I added to myself. But, after all, he was a famous Hollywood film director. He could probably afford to drink whatever he preferred.

He'd probably been drinking with his wife in Portland the night before he died. He'd stayed the night in Portland. He would have had to get up early to drive the ninety minutes back to Haven Harbor. His wife had said he'd gone to Skye's house to change, which made sense, although no one I'd talked to at Aurora had seen him at the house that morning.

Had he arrived, showered, and then left for the lighthouse that early? Why would he need to get to the lighthouse before anyone else?

I'd left Patrick's carriage house what I considered early. The sun was just rising. I'd cleaned up at my home, changed clothes, fed Trixi, and then gone to the lighthouse, getting there at about eight, as I remembered. I'd thought I'd be there early, but everyone from Aurora was already there. Ron had said he'd just served a basic breakfast that morning because people were so anxious to get to the lighthouse.

How early had everyone arrived? I made a mental note to ask Patrick. He'd said he'd driven a group of them. Not everyone had rented cars, and there wasn't room for much parking there in any case.

Ron also said there was no single malt on the bar that morning. He hadn't known who'd taken it, but I hadn't heard of anyone but Marv drinking scotch. Could Marv have taken a bottle from Skye's bar after Patrick's party? That would explain the bottle in his wife's Portland hotel room.

That was probably the easiest explanation. Wife in town, probably some serious talking going to take place, and Marv had fortified himself with a bottle no one else was going to be drinking.

Which left the pills. Okay; a lot of people had anti-anxiety pills. Marv probably did, although no one had confirmed that, and I'd seen his wife taking some.

Could she have drugged his scotch in Portland?

She could have. She had scotch and pills.

But if she'd drugged him late at night he might not have woken up, and he'd definitely driven from Portland to Haven Harbor early the next morning. The drugs would have acted sooner than that.

On the other hand, would he have poured himself a generous glass of scotch (from a bottle that wasn't on the bar) at dawn the next day, taken a handful of pills, and then driven to the lighthouse?

Wouldn't that combination of drugs and alcohol slow him down? Instead, those I'd talked to said he was "in a bad mood," yelling at everyone. Although I'd seen him just before he'd fallen, and he definitely wasn't steady on his feet. That could be a sign the drugs and alcohol were starting to affect him.

I sighed.

I'd go home, find something to eat (I definitely should have eaten more of those tea sandwiches, despite my crabmeat lunch), and then make a couple of phone calls. Pete would want to know if I'd found out anything in Portland, and I wanted to check yesterday morning's timeline with Patrick.

I felt close to figuring out what had happened, but I wasn't there yet. Close, but no solution.

Chapter 32

With ink and pen.
These marks will give.
The lives of men.
To all that live.

—M. Mary Cook (1806–1869) worked
this sampler in black silk in August of 1818.
She included three alphabets. Mary was
born in Skaneateles, New York, but
stitched her sampler in Marcellus.

The Mainely Needlepoint Web site had sent me three new
orders: two eider duck cushions and one schooner, and
I had a telephone message that a gift shop in Brunswick
could use another dozen balsam Christmas tree decorations. Luckily, I had two of the three cushions in stock
and enough of the balsam decorations to fill the order.
Thank goodness for winters when people had time to do
needlepoint.

I packaged up the orders after Trixi inspected the boxes
I was using to ensure they were sturdy enough. In the
meantime I heated water and cooked enough for a small
plate of linguine for my supper. I'd had a hearty breakfast

and lunch, so I wasn't really hungry, but if I didn't eat something now I'd be back in the kitchen by nine tonight. I cheated with the linguine and used canned clams and clam sauce, only adding fresh scallions and grated parmesan.

My dinner wouldn't be considered acceptable at Aurora, but it was fine for me at home.

Plus, I had cinnamon rolls for dessert.

Packages ready to mail, kitchen cleaned up, and Trixi fed (the most important task on my list, of course), I sat in the living room and started making calls.

Patrick answered immediately. "Hey! I thought you'd probably come back for dinner tonight," he said. "You missed some fantastic mussels. And the lemon sauce for the blueberry cake was to die for."

"Glad to hear you're still alive, then," I said. "Try to get Ron's recipe for the blueberry cake and sauce, will you? Sounds like we should try it."

"Not sure I'll be successful. Chefs have their secrets. But I'll try," he answered. "So, how did your trip to Portland go? Did you see Marv's wife?"

"I did. I didn't stay long, but I did find out Marv spent the night before he died in Portland with June. He left there very early yesterday morning. Told June he was going to Aurora, shower and change, and then go to the lighthouse."

"That makes sense."

"I'm a bit confused about the timeline for yesterday morning, though. No one I talked to at Aurora said they'd seen Marv yesterday morning until they got to the lighthouse. You took a carload of people over there, right?"

"Sure. Mom told everyone to eat quickly, and we got out of here by seven fifteen or so. She'd made sure there were doughnuts and coffee at the lighthouse, so no one starved."

"And was Marv at the lighthouse when you dropped people off?"

"I don't know. You'd have to ask one of them. I drove Talia, Jon, and Hank. Mom left about the same time we did, but she drove herself. I think Flannery went with her. I don't remember seeing Marv at the house, either. That's interesting. I hadn't realized he was on his own. But he did have a rental car."

"Why would he want to get to the lighthouse so much earlier than anyone else?"

"I have no idea. But my crew got there about seven thirty. I just dropped them off and came back to the house. Where, I might add, I had a decent breakfast with the writers. Ron whisked us up a couple of omelets. We were all relieved that the house was quiet."

"That I understand! Today was crazy over there."

"So did you find out why Marv's wife came to Maine earlier than she'd told people?"

"Not really. But she had gotten pictures of Marv and Cos before the one she'd shown me. She said she knew Marv got involved with young actresses, and she wanted to cut that off."

"Makes sense."

"And there was a bottle of scotch in her room. She must drink single malt, too."

"The couple that drinks together. Interesting. But it doesn't help the police much."

"No. It doesn't. I'm going to call Pete now. He asked me to let him know what, if anything, I found out in Portland."

"Then you go ahead and do that. After you left someone from Augusta came and gave everyone back their medications and cell phones and computers, so there was great relief at Aurora. But if the crime scene or technical people found anything of value in the investigation they didn't share it with anyone. Everyone's expecting to go back to work tomorrow, and Mom's working with the writers tonight to finalize at least one scene to rehearse then."

"So Ruth is still at Aurora? The poor woman."

"She was there when I left, about half an hour ago. I'm at my place now. Want to come over and join me?"

"Tempting, but no. This was a long day, and I still have to talk with Pete. I don't even know what I should do tomorrow. Maybe I'll check with Sarah and see if she's heard anything."

"Sounds like a plan. Talk to you in the morning, then! Sleep well."

"And you."

I put the phone down. Everyone had their phones back? Had the technical folks been able to see the photos June had received? They should be on someone's phone.

A question to ask Pete.

Chapter 33

Women have a permanent advantage over men.
Not only does timidity in them naturally find more
graceful expression, but they can generally find
something legitimate to do with their hands—
some little occupation with the needle, the shuttle,
or the fan—to mitigate the pains of embarrassment,
from which men's hands have no safer refuge
other than the pocket . . .

—"On Awkwardness," March 1862,
Godey's Lady's Book Magazine.

I called Pete and told him what I'd learned from June, which wasn't much. "Patrick told me you'd returned phones, laptops, and meds to those staying at Aurora. Did the forensic people in Augusta find anything important?"

"Not really. You were right when you said most people in that house had prescriptions for anti-anxiety. Certainly Marv did. And, yes, texts showed that not everyone working on the film was happy with Marv. The general consensus was that he'd been a pain. He hadn't been happy with the script, or the sets. He'd been spending too much time with Cos Curran, and several people were concerned about her. He'd yelled at almost everyone."

"So you have a lot of suspects."

"In some ways, yes. But none of those complaints about Marv sound serious enough to be motives for murder."

"Did your tech folks find out who'd sent Marv's wife the pictures of him with Cos?"

"No. But several people reminded us that no one involved in the production was supposed to take pictures. With the exception of Linc, who had special permission, if anyone took pictures, they'd deleted them."

"So no easy answers. What about Talia's phone? She was taking pictures down at the lighthouse right before Marv fell."

"Whatever she took she deleted. If Hank had let people take pictures it would have made our investigation easier. Nowadays it seems there are always pictures of a crime scene, or nearby. But in this case, nothing."

"Are you ready to declare Marv's death accidental?"

"Not yet. But we were tempted today. It certainly would make our work a lot easier."

"Is the film going back into production tomorrow?"

Pete sighed. "I guess that's up to Skye, since she's the new director. By the way, she was looking for you this afternoon. Wanted to talk with you about something. I told her you'd gone to Portland to talk with Marv's wife, and she didn't question that. I did ask her if she knew June well."

"And?"

"She said she'd met June a few times over the years, but they weren't close friends. She also said Talia knew June. Both Skye and Talia had worked with Marv before, as had Hank, of course. But my impression was that those relationships were all professional, not personal."

"Marv had a reputation for being a bit too aggressive with women in his movies. Especially young women."

"True. And verified. One of the techies in Augusta did Internet searches on him, and it appears his involvement with young actresses is pretty widely known, at least in the Hollywood community."

"In the past couple of years there's been a lot of publicity about powerful men working in films using their power and influence with young actresses," I pointed out. I wasn't a fan, so I didn't know much about it, but the national news had been covering that as part of the Me Too movement. I couldn't imagine anyone's not knowing about it, at least in general. "Had Marv been officially accused of inappropriate behavior?"

"Not officially. But lots of rumors and inuendoes."

"I don't know about Skye, but Cos and Talia could tell you more about that."

"They have," Pete agreed. "But neither of them accused him of rape, although they agreed on the word 'misconduct,' and both said working with Marv made them feel uncomfortable. Have to say, I wondered why Talia agreed to be in this film, knowing that going in, as she did. Cos, of course, would have had no idea."

"Talia filled her in once they were both here."

"Linc and Talia made sure Cos wasn't alone with Marv. And she seemed pretty confident about taking care of herself, although she also seemed relieved that now she wouldn't have to watch him all the time."

"If everyone goes back to work tomorrow," I wondered, "What are you and Ethan going to do?"

"We're taking tonight off. Tomorrow we'll read through our notes and see if any more questions need to be answered before we reach a conclusion. Now that everyone has their phones and is back on social media, I suspect we'll have to deal with the press, too. I already have a stack of call backs from media people here in Maine and throughout the country."

"What are you telling them?"

"Most I'm just ignoring. The people I know, I'm giving the basic 'ongoing investigation' line," Pete said. "What more is there to say right now?"

Chapter 34

Elizabeth Holland is my Name
English is my Nation
Boston is my Dwelling Place
And Christ is my salvation.
When I am Dead and Gone
And all my bones are Roten
I leave this Sampler Behind
I May not be Forgotten.

—Elizabeth embroidered this sampler when she was thirteen. In 1743, on her eighteenth birthday, she married Edward Gyles in Boston. They had two sons.

Despite my exhaustion I didn't sleep well that night. My mind kept running through all the people who knew Marv Mason. Some of them, like Talia, Cos, and Linc, owed their acting careers to him, although Cos and Linc didn't value the opportunity as Talia had. What about Skye, who'd worked with him over the years? Hank, who'd agreed to finance *Harbor Heartbreak*? June, his wife, who'd stood by him for years while he seduced younger women?

He hadn't been easy to work with; he'd yelled and changed his mind about what he wanted from the writers, the actors, and the crews. He'd had a problem with alcohol.

He'd had access to both his alcohol of choice and his anti-anxiety medications. Distracted by the production he wasn't happy about, had he combined the drugs with alcohol and unintentionally poisoned himself? Had someone else mixed a potent cocktail for him? And, in either case, when? According to his wife he'd been in Portland until early in the morning, and then headed back to Aurora. No one I'd talked to had mentioned seeing him at Skye's house that morning.

I could understand Marv's taking an anti-anxiety pill that morning. Maybe, depending on what his body was used to, more than one. But, if so, they hadn't worked. Everyone agreed he'd been yelling at practically everyone down at the lighthouse. And would he have drunk enough scotch that morning to have raised his alcohol levels to the degree the medical examiner had said? He had been drinking scotch the night before, in Portland, and I hadn't asked June how late they'd stayed up that night. Maybe he'd only had an hour or two of sleep.

I thumped my pillow and tucked part of it under my neck, trying to get comfortable. Trixi peered down at me from her perch on my second pillow, as though asking why I was still awake, and why I didn't relax, stop moving around, and let her sleep, too.

I wasn't worried about Trixi. She'd sleep most of the next day. Cats slept an amazing number of hours every day.

But I wasn't a cat. I'd have to get up and figure out what had happened to Marv. He might very well have slipped on the wet rocks and rockweed, especially when the boom headed toward him.

I hadn't heard anyone say they'd pushed him, or that they'd seen anyone else push him.

If his blood levels hadn't shown the alcohol and drugs in his system, Pete and Ethan would have called Marv's death an accident. Accidents happened. The question was whether he'd been more likely to slip and fall because of the drugs and alcohol in his system.

Probably, yes.

I pounded on my pillow, which was now wet with my perspiration and frustration. My bedroom window fan wasn't helping.

Sometime after midnight I finally fell into a troubled sleep full of nightmares.

When I woke the temperature had dropped and a strong breeze had come up. I stumbled out of bed, still sticky from perspiration, and went to stand in front of one of the windows.

The sky was dark with clouds. I hadn't paid attention to weather forecasts in the past few days, but it looked as though a storm was coming in.

I turned off the window fan. If it rained heavily, the fan would blow the rain into my bedroom. Trixi looked up at me, her mind clearly on breakfast.

"I'm going to take a shower first," I explained to her. "And then drink lots of coffee. I need to get over last night."

She didn't look as though she understood, but she was patient. She followed me into the bathroom, and sat outside the shower, watching me, and waiting for me to get on with her day.

Which I did. Clean jeans and T-shirt; sandals (I wasn't going to climb any rocks today) and a clip to hold my wet hair back from my face.

While beans for my coffee were grinding, I cleaned and refilled Trixi's dishes and she went to work emptying them. I soft-boiled two eggs and then toasted two pieces of bread, buttered them, and sprinkled them with sugar and cinnamon.

My breakfast might not be as elegant as Ron Winfield's at Aurora, but it was my sort of comfort food. I ate slowly, enjoying the flavors, and deciding when I'd contact Skye. Pete had said she wanted to talk with me.

After all, yesterday I'd talked with almost everyone else.

I texted her, and she replied immediately. *Meet me at Patrick's before the day really starts.*

Why would Skye want to meet me at Patrick's carriage house?

I didn't know, but I answered that I would.

Where were Ethan and Pete this morning? Pete had said today they'd assess what was happening with their investigation and decide what to do next. I hoped they had more constructive ideas than I had.

Right now all I knew was that I'd wash up my breakfast dishes and go to talk with Skye.

She'd replaced Marv as the director. Maybe she had some ideas about the film. Or about what had happened to Marv.

Chapter 35

My God I never long'd to see my
Fate With Curious Eyes
What Gloomy Lines are writ for me
Or what bright scenes
Shall Rise in thy fair book of Life and Grace
May I but find my name recorded
in some humble place
Beneath my Lord the Lamb.

—Ruth Lemmon worked her sampler in 1760,
when she was thirteen years old, in Marblehead,
Massachusetts. She married John Prentice in
1770 in Marblehead, and they had one daughter,
also born in 1770. Later they moved to
Londonderry, New Hampshire.

The security people guarding the gates to Aurora and
Patrick's carriage house were being kept busy today.
Pete had guessed giving Skye's guests back their access to
the media, social and otherwise, would mean everyone
would be in touch. Publicity was a critical part of show
business, and every time Marv's death was mentioned, so

was *Harbor Heartbreak*. Fans would hear about the film before cameras had recorded even one scene.

The guards recognized me and waved me through the gates. I drove past Aurora and down the drive to Patrick's carriage house. Heavy rain had started to fall. No one would be eating breakfast on the terrace this morning.

Had Flannery planned to re-create the scene at the lighthouse today? If so, the weather was definitely not cooperating.

I parked right outside the door to the carriage house. It wasn't Aurora's original carriage house; that one had burned down during renovations to the big house early last summer. Skye and Patrick had both been living in the smaller building then, and Patrick had been burned in the fire. His hands and arms were badly scarred. But during his recuperation, most of it in a hospital in Boston, he'd designed another carriage house, including a studio, where he could live and paint after he returned to Haven Harbor. The exterior of the newly designed carriage house had Victorian touches, to fit with Aurora. But the inside was modern, and Patrick's first-floor studio had three glass walls, allowing light in during most of the day. He was painting again, but more slowly than he had before.

Although I'd seen people who didn't know him staring at his hands, I was now used to them. Patrick never mentioned his scars anymore, although I'd sometimes seen him struggle to hold brushes or kitchen tools. He'd managed to open and eat his lobster at his birthday party without any problem.

This morning he opened his door as soon as I'd pulled in. I raced through the downpour into his house, and his arms, and then stepped back. Skye was sitting on his couch, waiting for me.

"Thank you for getting here so quickly, Angie," she said. "The weather has turned dreadful, but at least the rain should cool everything down a bit. Come and sit with me." She patted the space next to her on the couch.

"Coffee?" Patrick asked.

"No, thanks. I just had a cup at home," I answered.

What was Skye so anxious to talk with me about?

"Congratulations, again, on being the director to replace Marv," I said. "Everyone I talked to yesterday seemed very pleased that you'd be taking over."

"Thank you," she said, nodding. "I'm excited about that, although, certainly, it isn't under the best of circumstances. I very much want the questions about Marv's death resolved so we can get on with the production and not be distracted by police or questions."

I nodded. "That makes sense. Have you heard from Pete or Ethan this morning?"

"No. I thought you might have."

"I talked to Pete last night, after I got back from talking to June Mason in Portland. I hadn't learned a lot."

"I know the police were questioning everyone yesterday," said Skye. "And they'd asked you to talk to some of my guests, too. I didn't realize you'd talked with June. You're very skilled at finding out secrets, Angie. I've seen that happen before when you worked with the police."

"Thank you." What was Skye getting at? Was it good or bad to uncover secrets?

"I asked you to come here because I didn't want anyone you talked with yesterday to see you talking with me. I wanted to catch up with what was happening. And I thought you should know a few things people might not have told you yesterday."

"Oh?" I asked.

"I know you were asking about Marv's drinking. And he definitely drank too much. I'm sure you heard that from more than one person."

I nodded.

"But Ron Winfield told me you'd asked who drank single malt scotch, and he told you only Marv did."

"That's right. Although his wife, June, may also drink it. She had a partial bottle in her hotel room."

Skye hesitated. "I don't think June drinks scotch. That bottle may have been there for Marv. And June wasn't at Aurora in the past week. What you might not know is that several bottles of that scotch disappeared during the past week. Marv drank single malt, but he didn't drink *that* much scotch."

"Someone else was drinking it."

Skye nodded. "I assume so. If you need to focus on who was drinking what, you need to investigate further."

"I understand."

"And I've already left messages for Pete and Ethan this morning. Now I'm telling you. Come up with the name of someone who killed Marv, or drop this whole investigation. Leaving everyone wondering what's going to happen is encouraging the media to speculate, and is making everyone working on *Harbor Heartbreak* nervous. We need to get this resolved quickly. Today, if at all possible. Now that I'm the director, I'm being held responsible for everything connected to the production that's happening or not happening. I don't want to lose control, or, almost worse, have people think I've lost control."

Skye took a rain slicker off the pegs next to Patrick's front door. "I'm going back to Aurora now. I've inherited Marv's problems as well as his title, and right now I have to talk with the writers. And with Talia. Seems she has her own ideas about what the script should be, and was trying to get Marv to agree with her. Last night she took me aside and tried to convince me she was right. That Marv hadn't understood how important the changes she wanted were. She was sure I'd be on her side."

"I didn't realize there were sides when it came to the

script," I said. "Although Ruth's a friend of mine, and I know she's been concerned about all the revisions she and Thomas and Marie have been asked to make."

Skye nodded. "This morning I'm going to meet with all three of them, and with Talia, and see if we can make sense of what's happened, and finalize the basic story. Maybe if we get everyone together in one room we can pull it together. Otherwise, we can't start filming. And we've already lost a crucial couple of days."

"I understand. I'm sure the writers will appreciate your being involved." I hesitated. "But what has Talia got to do with changes to the script?"

"Talia always wanted to be a screenwriter. She's wanted that for years, hasn't she, Patrick?"

"That's true. She's always talked about writing. Marv encouraged her. He promised years ago that if she cooperated with him, he'd read any screenplays she wrote." He grimaced. "I don't know if he did. But I know he never directed any."

Skye shook her head. "I don't know what Marv might have told Talia. All I know is what he told me: that she'd written several scripts that were disasters. I've never read one, so I can't tell you whether he was right or not. But I do know she thinks she can do a better job with the script for this film than's been done so far, and she was driving Marv and Thomas crazy with her ideas. I want to sit down and hear the whole story. I'm the director now, so I'll be the one to approve any changes."

She pulled up the hood of her slicker and stepped out into the rain.

Chapter 36

In the sightless air I dwell
On the sloping sunbeams pley
Delve the cavern's inmost cell
Where never yet did daylight stray.

—On her sampler Mary Bishop included three
large and two small floral arrangements and the
initials of members of her family who had died.
Her words are from a poem ("Song of a Spirit")
by Ann Ward Radcliffe (1764–1823), a popular
English writer. Mary did not date her sampler.

Patrick and I looked at each other. "Wow," I said. "Your
mom is taking control."

"Sounds like it," he agreed. "What about this investigation? Can it be wrapped up today? Ideally, I'm sure Mom
would like it dropped. I don't think anyone at Aurora
thinks Marv was killed. He died in an accident. A horrible
one, but, nevertheless, an accident."

"What about the levels of alcohol and drugs in his
system?"

Patrick shook his head. "Maybe he took that stuff himself?"

"It's interesting that your mom made a point of saying several bottles of single malt disappeared from her bar in the past week, but didn't say who took them."

Patrick shrugged. "Who knows? I assume she didn't know. Maybe Marv did. Maybe Ron Winfield has a friend who really likes single malt, and he took them. If anyone at Aurora had taken them and they, full or empty, were in one of the bedrooms there, the police would have found them when they searched the house. Unless they were found and Pete hasn't mentioned that to you, no one at Aurora took them."

"Marv himself could have taken one bottle when he went to Portland to talk with his wife," I pointed out. "I saw a bottle there. Same brand as in the bar at Aurora."

"That accounts for one bottle," Patrick said. "Mom said 'several bottles.'"

I shook my head. "I have no clue."

"Okay. Changing the topic a bit, do you know anything about what Talia's been bothering the writers about? You had dinner with Ruth the other night."

"I did. Ruth's upset about being asked to make a lot of changes in the script. She assumed it would be based on what she wrote in her book *Harbor Hopes*. You know a lot of her stories were about events that really happened here in Haven Harbor. Gram told me *Harbor Hopes* was based on Ruth's own life. She was Amy."

"Wow," Patrick said. "That explains why she'd be sensitive about any changes. They're about her."

"That's what I assumed. But Gram talked to some people in town who remembered, and they said what Ruth wrote in the book might not be the real story of what happened, although after Caleb was killed 'Amy' didn't live with her father again and, in fact, may never have spoken with him after that."

"Why not?"

"She believed he'd sabotaged the lobster boat and killed the young man she loved. But there were rumors in town that her father wasn't responsible. That the engine and blower on Caleb's boat had been tampered with, but it wasn't her father who'd done it. The man Ruth married a couple of years later had."

"So she might have married the man who killed Caleb?"

I nodded. "That's what some people thought. But Ruth didn't say that, and didn't write that, and maybe she never knew. Or she knew, but didn't want to admit it."

"Or it wasn't the truth. Maybe her father was the guilty party after all," said Patrick. "That's all interesting, for sure. And it explains why Ruth is upset she's been asked to change the script. But what does it have to do with Talia? Why would she want the script changed? And, assuming her changes have something to do with how Caleb died, then how did she find out the rumors around town?"

"I don't know. And even if she somehow heard them, and wanted the script modified, how would that have anything to do with Marv's death?" I said. "None of it makes sense." I looked out the windows. Torrents of rain were still coming down, flooding the driveway.

"What are you going to do today?" Patrick asked. "It definitely doesn't look like a beach day. Or a lighthouse day."

"Very funny," I answered. "I still have unanswered questions. But someone must have the answers. Maybe if Pete and Ethan pull everyone together who knows something the truth will come out."

Patrick shook his head. "You think someone's going to stand up and say, 'Look at me! I drugged and killed Marv Mason!'"

"Maybe not," I admitted. "But I'll bet Pete and Ethan have a few ideas of what might have happened. And I do, too."

"You think you know who killed Marv? Who?" Patrick asked.

"I don't know for sure, so I'm not going to say anything. Not even to you," I said. *Especially not to you,* I thought. "But I am going to talk to Pete and Ethan. Maybe we can come up with some answers." I looked out the window again. "Do you have an umbrella I could borrow?"

Chapter 37

The Lose of a Father is much
But the loze of a Mother is Moor
But the Lose of Christ is such
As none can restore.

—Stitched in 1815 by nine-year-old Margaret
Arndt in Pennsylvania. Margaret married Henry
DeHuff in 1833 and they had six children.

Fifteen minutes later I was wet, but not drenched, and at
the Haven Harbor Police Station. "Could I speak with
Sergeant Pete Lambert, please?" I asked, closing the golf
umbrella Patrick had loaned me. "Or Detective Ethan
Trask, if he's in?"

"You're Angie Curtis, right?" checked the clerk as she
picked up the phone. "Angie Curtis is here to see you,
Pete. Shall I send her back?" She nodded at me. "He said
they'd see you. He's in the interrogation room with Detective Trask."

"Thanks," I said. The Haven Harbor Police Department
was a small one, and when Ethan was in town investigating
a murder he often used their one interrogation room as a

temporary office. I'd been there before. I walked down the narrow hallway that led to the few offices in the building.

Pete and Ethan both stood as I knocked on the door and then walked in. "Good morning," said Pete. "Let me guess. Skye West laid down the law. We have to find a murderer today or get out of her life, and that of the movie production crew."

"Bingo," I agreed. "Have you come up with anything new since we talked last night?"

"Not really," said Ethan. "We do think some of those people staying at Aurora have previous relationships and know more about each other than they're admitting to, but nothing's been hinted that would explain why anyone would murder Marv Mason. Dislike him, for sure. He was a powerful Hollywood figure and a pain. But kill him? We can't see anyone who would benefit from that."

"Except, of course, his wife, who would inherit their estate. And Skye, who is now directing the film. But we haven't any evidence that would point to either of them," said Pete. "What about you?"

"I have an idea, too," I said. "But, like you two, no proof. But, also like you, I believe there are secrets in that house. I'm wondering what would happen if we used the classic Agatha Christie method."

"What?" asked Pete.

"If we got everyone who's involved in one room and asked key questions. It would embarrass some people, no doubt, but it also could lead to more information coming out, and our being able to identify the murderer."

"So you do believe Marv Mason was murdered?"

"Yes. And, no, I don't think he was pushed off the rocks. I think someone doctored a glass of his favorite scotch and made sure he drank it that morning, before anyone went down to the lighthouse."

"Then is his wife on your suspect list?" Ethan asked. "Because he was with her early that morning."

"But after he left Portland he drove all the way to Haven Harbor. Wouldn't the drugs and alcohol have kicked in before he got back to Aurora?"

Pete and Ethan looked at each other, and Ethan nodded.

"On the other hand, his wife says she doesn't know anyone he worked with well. I'm not sure that's true. She's also now a wealthy widow who knew her husband had been having relationships with young actresses for years. She must have found that embarrassing, at minimum, especially since what he was doing seemed to be common knowledge. And the only reason she's given us for coming to Maine was because someone who knew her well enough to have her personal e-mail address sent her photographs of her husband with Cos Curran."

"I believe she said she'd come here to see what a beautiful state it was," said Pete, smiling.

"Right." Ethan drummed his fingers on the worn oak table. "I assume you're suggesting June Mason be a part of this gathering."

I nodded. "Definitely."

"What about the crew? The young men who lost control of the boom mic down at the lighthouse? Are they on your list?"

"If you think they should be. But I think they just happened to be there. If Marv hadn't had alcohol and drugs in his system he might not have fallen."

"He should have been wearing more appropriate shoes," said Pete, shaking his head. "Do we know who suggested he wear those leather-soled shoes he had on that morning?"

"Clearly his death at that moment was the result of a perfect storm," I said. "The wrong shoes; the boom falling; and the wind that came up at the wrong moment. But from what you've told me the medical examiner said, even without all those factors, he probably would have died from the drugs and alcohol. The combination of everything else just meant his death looked more like an accident."

"That's all true," said Pete. "But what if we get everyone together and no one talks? What if we end up with no more information than we have right now?"

"Then, we're no worse off," I said. "And those people are used to being interviewed, on television and by other media. I think they'll talk. Especially if they think they might ultimately get some publicity from it."

"Not necessarily good publicity," Ethan pointed out.

"But isn't all publicity good publicity?" I asked. "Seems to me I've heard that somewhere."

Chapter 38

*She watched and taught the girls that sang
at their embroidery frames while the great
silk flowers grew from their needles.*

—From *The Feast of Lanterns* by Louise Jordan
Miln (1864–1933), New York: A. L. Burt, 1920.

Pete and Ethan and I did a little more planning, and then I left. We'd decided on four o'clock that afternoon for our gathering, Ethan had convinced June Mason to join us at Aurora, and I went home. I wanted to think through the next few hours, and maybe even take a nap.

I'd just walked in when Patrick called. "What have you and your police pals dreamed up this time?" he asked. "I just talked to Mom, and she's furious. You're calling everyone together this afternoon to discuss Marv's murder?"

"Pete and Ethan are calling everyone together," I corrected. "But, yes, I'll be there. Your mother said she wanted all this settled today, right?"

"Sure, she said that. But she didn't think you were going to pull everyone together the way they do in old movies, and expect people to tell their secrets or confess to murder. Mom still thinks Marv's death was accidental."

"I wish it were," I said. "If his blood levels had been normal, the police would have thought so, too."

"He drank too much. Maybe he took a couple too many pills," said Patrick. "It happens. That doesn't mean someone killed him!"

I didn't say anything.

"And I notice I haven't been invited to this momentous gathering," he continued.

"Consider yourself not a suspect, then," I said. "Between your mom and me I'm sure we'll let you know everything that happens."

"Is Ruth going to be there?"

I hesitated. "I think they included the writers."

"You think Ruth might have killed Marv?"

"I don't think anything," I said, lying to him. "But the police wanted to include anyone who might have information that would lead to their finding out who killed Marv. That's all. If they're successful, they'll leave everyone else alone, just as your mother wanted."

"I think the whole idea is crazy. So does she."

"But she agreed?"

"Yes, she agreed. I take it she wasn't given much choice."

"Then we'll just have to wait and see what happens," I said. "In the meantime, I think I'll take a nap."

I put the phone down. I really didn't want to upset Patrick or Skye. But she'd been pushing to get the mystery of Marv's death solved, and if it all worked the way I hoped it would, that would happen this afternoon.

Then I could repair any rifts between Patrick and me.

I hoped.

Chapter 39

From low Pursuits exalt my mind
From every vice of every kind
And never let my Conduct tend
To wound the feelings of a friend.

—Pennsylvania sampler stitched by ten-year-old
Margaret Jane Arbuckle at the Mary Tidball
School in Allegheny County, 1847. Margaret
surrounded her words with dramatic flowers,
birds, and a large strawberry plant.

A normal July afternoon in Maine was still light. Perhaps
there'd be a few clouds, or even showers, but four hours
before sunset there'd be no need for artificial light.

This afternoon was the exception. It had been "raining
buckets," as Gram would put it, since early morning, the
sky was dark, and the wind was increasing. I'd listened to
the radio news on my way to Aurora, wondering if thun-
derstorms were on their way, but the Portland weather
report was focused on rush hour traffic and flooded roads,
and hadn't mentioned thunder or lightning.

Just as well. With the amount of rain we'd had, the
ground would be wet, and with the winds picking up that

could mean trees down. Lightning would just increase the risk of downed branches and resulting power outages.

I had enough on my mind this afternoon. I didn't want to worry about the logistics of driving around closed roads now, or whenever the meeting was over.

I was approved by Skye's hired security people, and pulled my car in back of Pete's police cruiser. Several rental cars were parked in the drive as well, which didn't surprise me. Maybe one of them was June's? How hard had it been for Pete and Ethan to convince her to drive ninety minutes north from Portland in this wicked weather?

Skye herself opened her front door. "Thank you," I said as I shook the rain from Patrick's umbrella and hung it in her wide front hall.

She didn't reply. She just pointed to the living room.

Aurora was quiet. I heard a little murmuring coming from the living room, but the only other noise was what sounded like a blender or food processor in the kitchen. Ron Winfield had not been invited to this meeting and was getting on with his next task: cooking and serving supper. What did he think of all that was happening?

I was the last to arrive. The living room was full. June Mason was sitting next to Talia on the couch. Ruth was sitting in the highest armchair, which was also the easiest to get in and out of. Her pink walker was by her side.

I didn't take a complete inventory, but it looked as though, as planned, everyone staying at Aurora was present. Pete nodded at me. He and Ethan were standing by the fireplace.

"I think everyone we expected is now here," Ethan said. "As you've all figured out, we're here to talk about Marv Mason's death. You all know he fell from the rocks near the Haven Harbor Lighthouse two days ago, and most of us, police included, assumed his death was an accident. But as some of you may know, and some of you not,

Maine's medical examiner determined that one of the major reasons he fell was that he had a dangerously high blood alcohol level, and he'd ingested much more than the usual dose of a common anti-anxiety medication."

I had assumed that most people in the room had known those facts, but, glancing around, I saw several people squirming. Those who had prescriptions for anti-anxiety drugs? No way of knowing.

"All of you knew Marv drank heavily. When Pete and I talked with you yesterday, most of you mentioned that he 'smelled of scotch' most days, and not just most evenings. It seems clear he had a problem with alcohol. Ron Winfield, Skye's chef, restocked the bar here regularly, so he noticed who was drinking what. Several of you said Marv was the only one drinking single malt scotch. But that wasn't true." Ethan turned to where Talia and June were sitting. "Talia, you drink single malt scotch," he said.

"I don't drink," said Talia, staring at Ethan. "I don't know who told you that, but they're lying."

Ethan nodded. "That's what you tell people. And I understand your agent got you into AA for a while. But you've had some problems over the past few years, when you haven't been working, and alcohol was one of them. Isn't that true?"

Skye hesitated, but then spoke up. "When Talia called Marv and begged to be in this film, I hesitated about recommending her. I knew she had a problem. But I'd also heard she was trying to manage it, so I decided that if he hired her she'd have to stay at Aurora, not be alone at a bed and breakfast or inn." Skye looked straight at Talia. "I told you I didn't want any problems at my home or during the filming. But when Ron told me bottles of single malt were disappearing, I checked. You had one full bottle and two empties in the closet of your room."

"The crime scene guys didn't find any liquor in Talia's

room. Are you sure?" Ethan looked concerned. "I can't believe they would have missed something like that."

"Absolutely sure," said Skye. "Because I'd already removed them myself."

"When did you do that?"

"The afternoon of the day Marv died. Understand, I didn't think they had anything to do with his death. I just knew Talia was upset about Marv's death, and I didn't want her drinking."

Talia looked down. June reached over and touched her hand.

So Skye hadn't invited Talia to stay with her so she'd be close to Patrick. She was watching Talia's drinking. Had Patrick known Talia had a drinking problem? Had she had that problem when they were a couple?

"You thought no one would notice if you just drank at night. But I was watching you. And I knew you well enough, from the years you were acting in Marv's movies, and the years you were dating my son, so I knew what triggered your drinking. Unfortunately, I didn't think through all of that when I agreed Marv could hire you, and you could stay here."

"What do you mean by 'triggered,' Ms. West?" asked Pete, who'd left the fireplace and was now standing by the door to the front hall.

"Talia, shall I tell people about your problems with Marv? Or would you rather do that?" asked Skye.

Talia looked up defiantly. "He was a sexual predator. He ruined lives. He ruined mine. He 'discovered' me, and then used me in several films when I was still a teenager. I'd planned to go to college. I wanted to be a screenwriter, and he promised to help me. I believed him. I gave up my dreams of college and acted in those films. And then he dropped me." She turned to June. "You know what he was like! I wasn't the first girl he'd done that to, and I probably wasn't the last. I wasn't strong enough to resist him."

June nodded. How much had she known, and for how long?

Cos, who was sitting with Linc by one of the windows overlooking the terrace, spoke up. "Talia, I don't know about your drinking. But I do know you helped me a lot this summer. You told me what Marv was like, and you warned me not to get involved with him. You were wonderful. If it hadn't been for what you told me, I might have fallen for his lies."

"I'm glad I helped," Talia said, turning to look at Cos. "I looked at you and I saw the girl I'd been when I first met Marv. And I was jealous, too. You're going to college. You'll be able to determine your own future. You even have a wonderful guy to support you."

"I am lucky," said Cos. "But one of the reasons I'm lucky is that you're stronger than you think you are. It couldn't have been easy for you to tell me what you did. But you did. And it made a major difference."

Skye looked at the two of them. "I'm surprised, Talia, given what you've just told us, that you begged Marv for this job. Why do that if you weren't comfortable working with him? If he'd ruined your life, as you just said?"

"I'm not a young actress anymore. Marv wouldn't be interested in me that way now. And I hadn't worked in several years. I needed this job. June was the one who suggested I do it."

"June!" Skye said, looking at Marv's wife. "You suggested that Talia work with your husband? Did you know their history?"

"I knew," said June. "And Talia's right. She's almost twenty-five. Marv preferred younger women."

"But how did you two even know each other?" Skye asked.

Talia and June looked at each other. Then June said, "We met in AA."

AA membership was private. Secret. Talia and June had just admitted they were members. When I thought people in this room had secrets, that was one I hadn't imagined. I hadn't even known June and Talia were friends.

The room was silent. I suspected everyone was digesting what they'd heard.

Talia continued. "Cos, you helped me, too. Another reason I wanted to work with Marv—besides the money, of course!—was that I hoped I could convince him that I might not be a great actress, but that I could write. I've always loved history. You and I talked about that."

Cos nodded. "We've talked about Maine history, especially."

"Exactly. And, although of course I knew Ruth had written the book *Harbor Heartbreak* was based on, you told me about her other books. And about how people here in Haven Harbor thought her book wasn't just based on a real story. It was a real story. Only, she'd changed what really happened."

Ruth looked at Cos. "You didn't tell her those old rumors."

"She did, actually," said Talia. "And I thought those 'old rumors,' as you just called them, were a lot more interesting than the script we were working on. I thought maybe if I told the real story to Marv, then maybe he'd understand that I knew what made a great story. That I could write a screenplay he'd want to direct. Then, when he wouldn't listen, I talked to Thomas, and told him."

"But I wasn't interested either," said Thomas. "Your job was to act in this film, not rewrite it. And not change what

Ruth wanted the world to know about her, and about Haven Harbor."

"Is that why you started drinking again, Talia?" asked Pete. "You'd made a friend in Cos, but Marv wasn't happy with your acting, and he wouldn't listen to your ideas for the script. Is that why you sent pictures of Cos and Marv to your friend June? You wanted her to see that what she'd predicted would happen was happening. And you wanted to get back at Marv for not helping you or listening to you."

"Sending pictures to a friend isn't the same as killing someone!" said Talia.

Chapter 40

To take grease spots out of silken or woolen cloth, dip a piece of clean flannel into spirits of turpentine, and rub the spots until they disappear, which will not be long. To take ink out of linen, take a piece of candle, melt it, and dip the spotted part of the linen into the melted tallow. It may then be washed and the spots will disappear without injuring the linen.

—*The New England Economical Housekeeper and Family Receipt Book* by Mrs. E. A. Howland. S. A. Howland: Worcester, 1844.

"True enough," agreed Ethan. "But you were the person who sent those pictures to June."

"I did. She and I'd talked before I came to Maine. Marv promised her he'd reformed. He wasn't seducing young actresses anymore, and he was staying here at Skye's, so he wouldn't have had the privacy even if he'd been tempted. But June wasn't convinced. I promised her I'd watch Marv and let her know if he started falling into old familiar patterns. So when I saw him paying special attention to Cos, I made sure June knew, too."

Pete turned to June. "So that's why you came to Maine. You came to check up on your husband."

"I loved the man, but even a loving wife can only be understanding for so many years," said June. "I didn't know how far the situation had gone. But I trusted Talia to let me know what was happening. Talia had observed Marv all too closely over the years. She knew what to watch for."

"And when did you tell your husband that you were here?" Pete asked.

"I called him when I got to Portland. He told me I should stay in Portland. That he didn't need the distraction of a confused and angry wife showing up in Haven Harbor."

"But you came to Haven Harbor anyway. You were at the lighthouse when Marv fell."

"I'd insisted we talk. He'd driven to Portland after the birthday party here at Aurora the night before. And, yes, you were right. He brought a bottle of scotch with him, and drank most of it. He told me Talia was wrong. He wasn't having an affair with Cos Curran. He was behaving himself."

Cos gasped. "He was telling the truth! I wasn't sleeping with him. Honest!"

"He also said Talia was being a pain. She was following him around, and trying to get him to agree to change the script. She wanted more lines, and she wanted the whole film to be more dramatic. Marv knew Talia and I'd become friends. He suspected she had something to do with my coming to Maine, which, of course, was true."

"Did you tell him about the pictures I'd sent you?" asked Talia. "Because if he'd known I did that, it would be grounds to break my contract. We weren't supposed to take any pictures or post anything about the film on social media."

"I knew that. And I didn't want you to get in trouble.

I didn't tell him about the pictures, Talia. But I did say I'd heard rumors about his behavior, and I was tired of that happening every time he directed a new film. That I'd had enough."

"How long did he stay in Portland?" asked Ethan. "And how much did he drink?"

"He drank about two thirds of the bottle he'd brought," said June. "We talked—'argued' is probably the better word—until maybe two in the morning. Then he announced he was going back to Haven Harbor, but I stopped him. I told him he'd had too much to drink. He needed to sleep. He wasn't happy, but he lay down. I think he passed out at that point."

"So when did he leave Portland?"

"Maybe around five? He said he had to get cleaned up and go to the lighthouse. He was still upset about our conversation, but he was also convinced that none of the people involved with setting up the shots at the lighthouse knew what they were doing, and he had to be there."

June paused. "Okay. What happened was probably my fault. He was still so angry, so upset, that I suggested he take a couple of anti-anxiety pills to help him calm down. I told him he'd alienate everyone on the set if he didn't pull himself together. So I handed him four pills, and he picked up the glass of scotch he'd been drinking the night before and took them. I just wanted him to relax a little!"

I noticed Pete and Ethan looking at each other. Were they going to arrest June? She'd just confessed to killing her husband.

"Why did you drive to the Haven Harbor Lighthouse?" asked Pete.

June shrugged. "I was curious. I slept a little more after Marv left the hotel, but then I woke up and was restless. I'd never seen a lighthouse up close. So I decided, 'Why not?' I had a cup of tea and got in my car and headed north. It took longer than I'd thought to get to Haven Harbor, and I remember thinking, 'No wonder Marv left so early.' I got to the lighthouse by, maybe eight thirty? I don't remember exactly."

"And you saw Marv fall."

"First I heard him yelling at the people near him: the crew by the boom, and Talia, and the others. I didn't know most of them. I thought, 'Maybe I should have given him more of those pills. He certainly hasn't calmed down.' But then he fell, and, of course, all I could think about was that the man I loved was dead." She looked around the room. "I know Marv wasn't perfect, but he was my husband, and, despite everything, we loved each other." Her eyes had filled with tears, and Talia gave her a hug.

"So Marv left Portland and drove back here, to Aurora," said Ethan. "He'd been drinking heavily the night before, in a short time period, so although he'd had a couple of hours of sleep, there was still alcohol in his system when June gave him four pills to help him relax, and he drank a little more scotch. Not much, but enough to affect him. And then he got in his rental car and drove ninety minutes." Ethan shook his head. "He was lucky not to get in an accident along the way, but that time of day the traffic isn't too heavy. He made it back to Haven Harbor, although I suspect he wasn't feeling at his best then. So. Who saw him when he got here?"

The room was silent as Pete and Ethan looked from one person to another. Finally, Thomas spoke up. "I saw him. I couldn't sleep that morning, so I'd come down to the living room before anyone else was up, and I was reading. It was about six. The only one around was Ron. He was in the kitchen, starting breakfast, and he saw me. When the coffee was brewed he brought me a cup, which was much appreciated. I was sipping the coffee when I heard a knock on the front door. I couldn't imagine who would be there at that time of the morning. I thought maybe one of the security guys had a question, so I opened the door. Marv came in. He looked pretty much out of it—hair uncombed and clothes askew."

"Did he say anything?" Pete asked.

"I asked him, you'll pardon the language, 'Where the hell have you been? You look a mess.' He didn't answer. He stared at me as though he didn't know who I was, and he stumbled up the stairs. I knew his room was on the second floor, so I watched until I was sure he'd gotten that far." Thomas looked a bit embarrassed. "I knew Marv's reputation. I figured he'd found someone to spend the night with." He turned to Cos. "I didn't think it was you, Cos, despite how attentive he'd been to you, because I knew you lived at home with your parents. But I figured he'd found someone else. I didn't think anything more about it. I went back to my book and my coffee."

"We know Marv was the first person to get to the lighthouse that morning. The security guards there confirmed that," said Pete. "But he arrived closer to seven than six thirty. He probably showered and shaved and changed his clothes here, as he'd planned. But, although Thomas just told us he'd stumbled up the steps, when the medical examiner had his blood checked, Marv had a lot more in his system when he died than the four anti-anxiety pills June told us she gave him."

"That's all I gave him. I swear!" said June. "Maybe if he was still upset and felt out of control he took more pills here? He had some of his own. The ones I'd given him were mine."

"No. I gave him more." Talia stood. "I went downstairs to the kitchen in my bathrobe to get a cup of coffee before I got dressed. Ron may remember; I spoke to him briefly. He was busy putting out some pastries and fruit for breakfast, but I didn't see anyone else downstairs." She looked over at Thomas. "You could have been in the living room, Thomas. I didn't look in there. I just wanted my coffee. I was taking it to my room when I ran into Marv."

"He was in the hallway?" asked Pete. "Or did you go to his room?"

"He was in my room," Talia said, blushing. "One night I'd given him a glass of the scotch I'd hidden in my room, and he remembered it was there. I'd left my door open when I went downstairs." She turned to June. "He was totally dressed and all. He'd poured himself a drink from the bottle in my closet."

"Did he say anything?" asked Ethan.

"He said he didn't feel well, and he thought the scotch would help. I asked him why he didn't go down to the kitchen and get a drink from the bar, but he said, no, he didn't want anyone else to know he was drinking that early, but"—Talia swallowed deeply—"he figured I'd understand. He was shaking a little, and I suggested he sit down on my bed. Then I told him I had some pills that might help. I gave him"—Talia looked around, as though she was prepared for someone to attack her any minute—"I gave him about a dozen pills. He didn't even ask what they were. He just said he could use all the help he could get, and he swallowed them."

"With the scotch he was drinking?" asked Pete.

"Yes. Then he left my room and went downstairs. I listened and heard the front door close a few minutes later, so I figured he'd left for the lighthouse."

"And, somehow, he managed to get there," said Ethan grimly.

Talia looked down at June. "I didn't know you'd already given him medication. I didn't want him to die. I just wanted him to calm down and stop yelling at everyone."

The room was silent. Then Ethan said, "Talia Lincoln, you're under arrest for the murder of Marv Mason." He handcuffed her, and then hesitated. "And Mrs. Mason, I'd like you to come with me to answer some more questions." Ethan and Pete led the two women to the door.

"Call the best lawyers you know," Skye called out as they left.

June looked back at her and nodded. "Understood. Neither of us killed Marv."

Chapter 41

The fireside hours of winter may be made a source of profit as well as interest. In this connection should be mentioned the high prices often commanded for elegant embroideries and knitting and crochet work in fine woolen of rich colors. Shawls, clouds, hoods, and afghans, wrought after tasteful patterns, may occupy the fingers while the eye is running down the pages of a book, or the mind engaged in pleasant conversation. Such occupation is not work, and, when directed by an eye well educated in the effects of colors, may produce articles of great beauty and value.

—The Philosophy of Housekeeping: A Scientific and Practical Manual by Joseph Barwell Lyman and Laura E. Lyman. Hartford, Connecticut: S. M. Betts & Company, 1869.

"It was Talia?" Patrick sat back on his couch, still in shock from what I'd just told him. "I would never have suspected Talia. And Pete and Ethan took June with them, too?"

"Well, if Talia is guilty of murder, she didn't do it alone. Marv was already drunk and June had given him pills to relax him while he was still in Portland." I hesitated. "I'd like to read the medical examiner's report. Marv was obviously in bad shape when he walked down over those rocks at the lighthouse. It's amazing he got that far. Then he slipped. If he'd collapsed and died at the top of the hill, by the lighthouse, or in his car on the way there, then Talia and June, or maybe just Talia, would be responsible. But if Marv was still alive, drugged and drunk, but alive, when he hit the water, did they really kill him? Or did he hit his head on the rocks when the tide pulled him in? Did he drown?"

"If he drowned, then technically it was an accident, right?"

"Right. Maybe neither Talia nor June was responsible for his death. Marv could have been perfectly sober and in control and then slipped, fell, hit his head or drowned. It's happened before down at the lighthouse. But because he wasn't in full control of himself . . ."

"Attempted murder?" Patrick guessed.

"Perhaps so. But I suspect they both will get very good lawyers, who'll argue they were both trying to help Marv, and didn't intend to kill him."

"I'd believe that," said Patrick. "Talia was angry at him, and from what you've said, so was June. But to kill him?"

"Before they got out the door your mom advised them to call a good lawyer."

"June certainly has the money to pay for one, and I'll guess she'll help Talia, too. Circumstantial evidence."

"And in the meantime, your mom will come up with

someone else to take Talia's part in the movie, and the show will go on."

"And I think you and I will have a drink," agreed Patrick. "Red or white wine?"

"Anything but single malt," I agreed. "I don't even want to think about scotch."

Chapter 42

These violets scent the distant gale;
They grew in lowly bed,
So real worth new merit gains,
By diffidence o'erspread:
But as the fragrant myrtle wreath,
With all the rest survive,
So shall the mental graces still
Through endless ages live.

—Jane Winter Price filled her sampler with
a large vase of brightly colored flowers,
and stitched a verse from an English reader
published in 1816. Jane was born in 1818
in Charles County, Maryland. In 1849 she
married Josiah Woods McHenry and they
moved to Shelby, Alabama.

From *Entertainment News*

Yesterday the recent death of director Marvin Mason on
the Maine set of his movie *Harbor Heartbreak* was ruled
an accidental drowning. Actress Talia Lincoln, who had

been questioned in the case, was released, and will resume her role in the film, which is now being directed by celebrated actress Skye West. "It's a sad time," Ms. West said. "We all will miss Marv's brilliant creative direction, but filming is continuing, and should be complete by Labor Day. We're dedicating *Harbor Heartbreak* to his memory."

RECIPES

Ron Winfield's
Blueberry Cake with Lemon Sauce

Blueberry Cake ingredients:
   1¾ cups flour
   1¼ cups wild Maine blueberries (cleaned, if fresh;
      drained, if frozen)
   ⅓ cup butter, softened
   1 cup sugar
   2 eggs, beaten, room temperature
   ½ cup milk
   ½ teaspoon salt
   ½ teaspoon vanilla
   2 teaspoons baking powder

Preheat oven to 375 degrees. Butter rectangular sheet cake pan.

Mix ¾ cup flour with blueberries and put aside.

Cream butter and sugar together until light. Stir in beaten eggs.

Add dry ingredients and wet ingredients, alternately. Beat well. Then add blueberries and mix gently. Pour into pan and bake 20–30 minutes, until flour mixture does not stick to cake tester.

Lemon Sauce ingredients:
   1 cup butter
   2 cups sugar
   ⅔ cup water
   2 eggs, beaten
   Juice of 2 lemons (6 Tablespoons)
   Grated rind of 2 lemons

Mix together all ingredients in saucepan, cook over medium heat, stirring until mixture comes to boil. Makes 3 cups of sauce.

Serve warm lemon sauce on top of blueberry cake.

Cake may be warm or room temperature.

Serves about 8.

Maine Wild Blueberry Pancakes

Ingredients:
   1 egg
   1 cup milk
   1 Tablespoon lemon juice
   1 Tablespoon maple syrup
   3 Tablespoons melted butter
   1 cup flour
   2 Tablespoons sugar
   2 teaspoons baking powder
   ½ teaspoon salt
   1½ cups wild blueberries (cleaned, if fresh; drained, if frozen)

Separate egg yolk and white. Beat egg white until it is stiff.

Mix egg yolk, milk, lemon juice, maple syrup, and melted butter.

Blend flour, sugar, baking powder, and salt.

Mix dry ingredients and liquids.

Stir until all the flour is moist. (The batter will be slightly lumpy. That's okay.)

Stir in the blueberries.

Finally, stir in the egg white.

Lightly oil griddle or frying pan. (If using a nonstick pan, oil is not necessary.)

Heat until drops of water sizzle when dropped onto cooking surface.

Drop batter onto griddle using large spoon.

Turn pancakes when they are puffed and full of bubbles.

Brown on both sides.

Serve with butter and warm maple syrup.

Makes 14–16 four-inch pancakes.

Books by Lea Wait

Mainely Needlepoint Series
Twisted Threads
Threads of Evidence
Thread and Gone
Dangling by a Thread
Tightening the Threads
Thread the Halls
Thread Herrings
Thread on Arrival
Thread and Buried

Shadows Antique Print Mystery Series
Shadows at the Fair
Shadows on the Coast of Maine
Shadows on the Ivy
Shadows at the Spring Show
Shadows of a Down East Summer
Shadows on a Cape Cod Wedding
Shadows on a Maine Christmas
Shadows on a Morning in Maine

Mainely Murder Series
(under the name Cornelia Kidd)
Death and a Pot of Chowder

Justice & Mercy: A Post–Civil War Mystery

For Ages 8 and Up

Stopping to Home
Seaward Born
Wintering Well
Finest Kind
Uncertain Glory
Pizza to Die For
Contrary Winds
For Freedom Alone

Nonfiction

Living and Writing on the Coast of Maine

About the Author

LEA WAIT lives on the coast of Maine in a home built in 1774. She graduated from Chatham University and has an MA and DWD from New York University. When she was in her thirties she was an adoption advocate and adopted four daughters as a single parent. Now she's the grandmother of eight and writes mysteries and historical novels about people searching for love, acceptance, and a place to call home. A fourth-generation antique dealer, she loves history and includes tidbits about the past even in her contemporary books. Lea blogs with other mystery writers from Maine at www.mainecrimewriters.com and can also be found on Facebook, Goodreads, and on her Web site, www.leawait.com.

Connect with  Us

Visit us online at
KensingtonBooks.com
to read more from your favorite authors, see books
by series, view reading group guides, and more.

 Join us on social media

for sneak peeks, chances to win books and prize packs,
and to share your thoughts with other readers.

**facebook.com/kensingtonpublishing
twitter.com/kensingtonbooks**

Tell us what you think!

To share your thoughts, submit a review,
or sign up for our eNewsletters, please visit:
KensingtonBooks.com/TellUs.

Grab These Cozy Mysteries
from
Kensington Books

Follow P.I. Savannah Reid
with
G.A. McKevett

Available Wherever Books Are Sold!

All available as e-books, too!

Visit our website at **www.kensingtonbooks.com**